# 13

# TREASURES

# 13

## TREASURES

### Michelle Harrison

SCHOLASTIC INC.
New York Toronto London Auckland
Sydney Mexico City New Delhi Hong Kong

First published in Great Britain in 2009 by Simon & Schuster Children's

ISBN 978-0-545-39210-5

12 11 10 9 8 7 6 5 4 3 2 1                11 12 13 14 15 16/0

Printed in the U.S.A.           40

First Scholastic printing, September 2011

For Mum,
and for my niece,
Tanya

1

She was aware of their presence in the room before she even awoke.

An ominous twitching had begun in Tanya's eyelids, a sure sign that trouble was on its way. Her eyes opened groggily. As usual, she had reverted to her childhood habit of sleeping with her head under the covers. She was uncomfortable, yet reluctant to shift position. If she did it would alert them to the fact that she was awake.

Beneath the stifling covers, Tanya longed to kick the sheets back and allow the soft summer breeze drifting in through the window to wash over her. She tried to tell herself she had dreamed it; maybe they were not really there after all. Still she lay unmoving—for deep down she knew they *were* there, as surely as she knew she was the only one who could see them.

Through the covers she could sense them, could feel the air in the room charged with a strange energy. She could even smell the earthy dampness of leaves, fungi, and ripened berries. It was *their* smell.

A quiet voice cut through the darkness.

"She sleeps. Should I rouse her?"

Tanya stiffened beneath her sanctuary of sheets. She still had the bruises from the last time. They had pinched her black and blue. A sharp prod in the ribs made her gasp.

"She is not asleep." The second voice was cold, controlled. "She is pretending. No matter. I do so enjoy these little . . . *games*."

The last traces of drowsiness left her then. There was no mistaking the underlying threat in those words. Tanya prepared to throw back the sheets— but they were strangely heavy all of a sudden, weighing down on her—and they were growing steadily heavier.

"What's happening . . . what are you doing?"

She clawed at the sheets, frantically trying to push them away. They seemed to be wrapping themselves around her like a cocoon. For one terrifying moment she struggled for breath before managing to free her head and suck in a lungful of cool night air. It was several seconds before she noticed that the glass star lantern covering the bedroom lightbulb was directly in front of her face.

Suddenly, Tanya realized why the bedclothes

were so heavy. She was floating in midair, five feet above her bed—supporting the full weight of them.

"Put me *down!*"

Slowly, through no control of her own, she began turning sideways in the air. The bedclothes promptly slid off and fell to the carpet, leaving Tanya hovering facedown above her bed in her pajamas. Without the shelter of the covers she felt horribly vulnerable. She pulled her hair back from her face and scanned the room. The only living thing she saw in the darkness was the cat: a ridiculous fluffy gray Persian curled in a ball on the windowsill. It got up, giving her a haughty look before turning its back to her and settling down once more.

"Where are you?" she said, her voice shaking. "Show yourselves!"

An unpleasant laugh sounded from somewhere near the bed. Tanya felt herself being propelled forward, and before she knew what was happening she had turned a full somersault in the air, followed by another... and another.

"Just stop it!"

She heard the desperation in her voice and hated it.

The somersaulting stopped and, finally, she landed on her feet—upside down on the ceiling. The curtains billowed weirdly in the breeze. She averted her eyes, trying to steady herself. It was as if gravity had reversed for her only. The blood was not rushing to her head, her pajamas were not falling upward, and her hair was now tumbling down her back.

She sat down on the ceiling, defeated. This was the reason they came in the middle of the night. She had figured that much out a long time ago. At night she was completely at their mercy, whereas in the day, if she happened to be caught in any strange situation, she had a far better chance of passing it off as a game or trick of some kind. Just one of many "games" and "tricks" over the years.

She couldn't remember the first time she had seen them, exactly. They had always been there. She had grown up chattering away to herself as her parents looked on at first in amusement, then later, with concern.

As the years passed she had learned to lie convincingly. Talk of fairies did not wash well with adults once you were past a certain age. There were no more of the knowing looks and fond smiles that came with infancy. Tanya did not take it too personally. People didn't believe in what they couldn't see.

The incidents had become more vindictive of late. It was one thing having to cut out a few tangles after an encounter with an enchanted hairbrush, or finding that the answers to homework had been mysteriously tampered with overnight. But this was serious. For months now, Tanya had harbored a nagging worry that eventually something bad was going to happen, something she couldn't explain her way out of. Her worst fear was that her increasingly weird behavior would land her on the couch of a psychiatrist.

Floating around in the air was not a good predicament. If her mother awoke to find her walking about on the ceiling, it wouldn't be a doctor she called—it would be a vicar.

She was in trouble of the worst kind.

There was a waft of cool air on her face, and Tanya felt the brush of feathered wings skim her cheek. A large, black bird swooped at her shoulder, its glittering eyes blinking once before the bird morphed as quickly as a shadow would vanish in the sun. Silken black hair and the pinkish tips of two pointed ears replaced the cruel, curved beak, as a woman not much larger than the bird shifted into its place. She wore a gown of black feathers; it was stark against her ivory skin.

"Raven," Tanya whispered. She watched as a feather fell from the fairy's dress and floated lightly to the carpet. "Why are you here?"

Raven did not answer. She alighted at the foot of the bed, next to two small figures, one plump and ruddy-nosed, the other dark-skinned, wiry, and skittish looking. Both were watching her intently. The smaller of the two was the first to speak.

"You've been writing about us again."

Tanya felt her face burn. "I haven't, Gredin...I didn't."

Gredin's yellow eyes glittered, shockingly bright in contrast to his nut-brown face. "But that's what you said last time. And the time before."

Outside, a dark, rectangular object was drifting toward the open window as though carried on the breeze. It soared gracefully through the curtains and into the room, and halted before Tanya's dismayed face. It was a journal, fairly new and in good condition—but covered in soil. She had buried it beneath the apple tree in the garden that afternoon. How foolish she had been.

"Yours, I believe?" said Gredin.

"I've never seen it before."

The plump little fellow next to Gredin snorted.

"Oh...come now," he said. "You wouldn't want to be up there all night, would you?" He reached up and gave the peacock feather in his cap a light stroke, then twisted his ratty moustache around his forefinger. The feather shimmered at his touch, rich with enchantment. The fat little man removed the quill from his cap and gave it a deft flick.

The diary opened, releasing a clod of earth that fell to the floor and broke over one of Tanya's slippers. A muffled sneeze came from inside the slipper, and then a fourth and final fairy emerged from inside it, hoglike and ugly. The creature beat its ragged brown wings with some effort and landed in a clumsy heap on the bed. After regaining its balance it began scratching vigorously, showering the bedclothes with molting fur and fleas, then gave a cavernous yawn, rubbing its snout with tiny brown paws.

Once, when she was smaller, and before her parents' divorce, Tanya had been sulking ungraciously after a telling-off. After a few minutes her mother had snapped, "Don't be such a little Mizhog."

"What's a Mizhog?" Tanya asked, curious despite herself.

"It's a horrible hoggy creature that's always miserable," her mother had replied. "And with that face you're pulling, you look just like one."

This was something Tanya remembered every time she saw the flea-bitten brown fairy. Its hangdog expression fit the description of her mother's invented creature so perfectly that, in her own mind, Tanya would forever think of it as a Mizhog. As the creature, unlike the other fairies, had never put forth a name for itself, the name Tanya had selected stuck.

Aside from its fleas and the smell, which reminded her of a wet dog, the Mizhog was fairly unobtrusive. It never spoke—at least, not in any language Tanya could understand—was always hungry, and had a habit of scratching its belly. Other than that, it seemed happy to observe its surroundings with its soulful brown eyes—the only one of its features that could be described as beautiful. It stared up at her now, wide-eyed and unblinking, making strange little snuffling noises in its throat.

The diary bobbed in front of Tanya's face. Hastily, she returned her attention to it.

"Read it," said Gredin.

"I can't," said Tanya. "It's too dark."

Gredin's eyes were as hard as flint. The pages of the diary began turning frenziedly, this way and that, as if trying to decide on an entry to settle upon. Eventually they rested on a particularly rushed-looking passage toward the end.

Tanya recognized the date immediately—it was less than two weeks ago. The writing was barely legible; her eyes had been so blurred with tears she had hardly been able to see her own hand. Then the hairs on the back of her neck stood on end as her own voice echoed softly from the pages, not quite loud enough to wake anyone, but certainly loud enough for her to hear. It sounded distant, as though its journey through time had weakened it.

"They came again tonight. Why me? I hate them. HATE them..."

The excruciating passage went on and on, and Tanya could only listen in horror as her voice spilled from the diary, recounting one page after another, angry, frustrated, and hopeless.

The fairies watched her all the while—Raven subdued, Feathercap and Gredin stony-faced, and the Mizhog scratching its flea-infested belly, disinterested.

"Enough," said Gredin, after what seemed like an age.

Tanya's voice broke off immediately, leaving only the sound of the pages flicking back and forth, as if by some invisible hand. Before her eyes, every word she had written slowly faded and vanished like ink drawn into blotting paper.

The diary fell to the bed, disintegrating on impact.

"There is nothing to be gained from this," said Raven, gesturing to what was left of it. "You will bring only misery to yourself."

"Not if someone had read it one day," Tanya said bitterly. "And believed me."

"The rules are simple," said Feathercap. "You speak of us to no one. If you continue to try then we will continue to punish you."

The remnants of the diary stirred on the bed, lifting from the covers like fine sand, before flying through the open window out into the night.

"Gone. As if it never was," said Gredin. "To a place where rosemary grows by a stream that flows uphill. The domain of the piskies."

"I don't believe in any stream that flows uphill," said Tanya, still smarting from having her innermost thoughts broadcast for all to hear.

"Heathen creatures, piskies," Gredin continued. "Unpredictable. Dangerous, some say. Whatever they touch becomes twisted and warped. And the rosemary—otherwise renowned for its aid to memory—grows tainted. The properties are reversed."

He paused for effect. Tanya, wisely sensing this, did not interrupt again.

"Now, there are some folk, known to the fairies as the cunning folk, who are familiar with the qualities of herbs and plants such as rosemary. For even piskie-tainted rosemary has its uses. In the correct quantities it has the power to extract a memory from a mortal head forever, such as the memory of an old sweetheart. Very helpful in some circumstances.

"But the fairies—much as it pains them to have dealings of any kind with the filthy little piskies—also have their own uses for this magical herb. It comes in particularly useful when humans stumble upon the fairy realm unexpectedly, and witness things they have no business seeing. Usually, a small dose sets the situation right and the human is none the worse for it, seemingly waking from a pleasant dream— albeit with no recollection of what the dream was about. However, it has been known to be administered in the wrong quantities. Entire memories have been wiped, just like that." Gredin snapped his fingers, and Tanya flinched.

"Of course, this is mostly accidental and rare, but sometimes...just sometimes, it is used as a last resort to silence those who otherwise refuse to be silenced. A highly unpleasant fate, most would agree. The poor souls can't even remember their own names afterward. Unfortunate, but necessary. After all... one cannot speak of what one cannot remember."

Tanya suddenly tasted fear in her mouth.

"I won't write about you again."

"Good," said Feathercap. "For you would be a fool to attempt it."

"Just answer me one thing," said Tanya, as brazenly as she dared. "I can't be the only one. I *know* I'm not the only one—"

Gredin silenced her with a look.

Her descent was sudden and unexpected. Feeling herself begin to fall, Tanya instinctively grabbed the only thing at hand—the star lantern covering the lightbulb. There was a terrible cracking noise as the wire strained under her weight, and the plaster of the ceiling around the fixture came down in plate-sized chunks, cracking further as it hit the floor. Then the lantern came away in Tanya's hands. The lightbulb smashed as she fell to the floor and the lantern went flying out of her grasp and hit the wardrobe, shattering.

As Tanya lay winded, she heard the landing creaking with anxious footsteps. She did not need to look up to know that the fairies would be gone, vanishing as they always did like a scattering of leaves on the breeze. Then her mother was in the room, pulling her up by the shoulder, causing her to cry out. Tanya caught her exclamation of disgust as she surveyed the mess.

"Mum..." she croaked. "I—it was a nightmare....I'm sorry...."

Even in the moonlight Tanya could see the resigned expression on her mother's face. She released her grip on Tanya's arm and slowly sank down on the bed, her hands clenched into balls that she pressed into her eye sockets.

"Mum?" Tanya whispered. She reached over and touched her mother's arm.

"I don't know what to do anymore," her mother said quietly. "I can't cope with this...this *attention* seeking of yours. I can't cope with *you*."

"Don't say that. I'll be better; I promise I'll try."

Her mother gave a weary smile. "That's what you always say. And I want to believe you...to help you, but I can't. Not if you won't talk to me—or to a doctor—"

"I don't need a doctor. And you wouldn't understand!"

"No. You're right, love, I don't. The only thing I do understand is that I'm at the end of my tether." She paused to look around at the mess. "Well, you're going to clean it all up in the morning. Every last bit of it. And the damage comes out of your pocket money, however long it might take. I'm not having this anymore."

Tanya stared at the floor. A shard of glass glinted in her mother's bare foot. She knelt down and gently pulled it out, watching as a dark bead of blood formed in its place. Her mother did not react. Instead she got up and shuffled to the door, her shoulders drooping, her feet crunching over the fragments of glass, uncaring.

"Mum?"

The bedroom door closed, leaving her in darkness. Tanya lay back on her bed, too shocked even to cry. The look on her mother's face had said it all. How many times had she been warned, how many times had she been told about the so-called last straw? Because now, as she listened to the muffled sobbing from the room across the landing, she knew that tonight really had been the last straw for her mother.

The car moved slowly along the winding lane. On either side of the road lay acres of nothing but golden fields and green trees, the latter forming a dense canopy of leaves and branches overhead that the July sunshine could barely penetrate. Occasionally, a farmhouse or paddock of animals would come into view in the distance, but apart from this there was little else to see, for it was the heart of the Essex countryside. The built-up views of London were long gone.

In the backseat of the car Tanya sat staring stonily at the back of her mother's head. "I still don't see why I have to stay with *her*. There must be somewhere else I can go."

"There isn't anywhere else you can go," said her mother, her face pale with lack of sleep and devoid of her usual makeup. "We've been through this a hundred times already."

"Why can't I just go to Dad's?" said Tanya.

"You already know the answer to that. He told us weeks ago that he'd be working away a lot over the next few months. You can't stay in an empty house."

"I can't believe this. A week, a lousy *week* into summer holidays, and now I have to spend a huge chunk of it with *her*," said Tanya. "I wouldn't have minded going to Nana Ivy's."

"Well, Nana Ivy isn't here anymore. She died three years ago, and it wouldn't hurt you to make more of an effort to get along with the grandmother you've still got."

"Yeah, because she really goes to a lot of trouble for me, doesn't she? It's bad enough being stuck in that horrible cobwebby house for a couple of days at a time, and even then, it's only because you insist on it!"

"That's not true."

"Yes, it is! She doesn't want me there any more than I want to be there, and we both know it! Name one time, just once, that she's ever invited me of her own accord," Tanya challenged.

Her mother stayed silent.

Tanya pursed her lips. "No? Didn't think so."

"That's enough! You brought this upon yourself with your behavior last night—not to mention the last few months." Her mother's tone softened. "I need a break. I think we both do. Just for a couple of weeks, that's all. I'm being as fair as I can—I'm even letting you take Oberon with you. And then, when you come back, we're going to have a serious talk."

Tanya said nothing, trying to will away the awful lump in her throat. After a few wordless moments her mother turned on the radio. It was a pointed end to the discussion.

A low whine came from the throat of the slightly overweight brown Doberman whose bottom was wedged between Tanya and a large carryall containing her belongings. She rested a hand on the back of his head, scratching behind his silky ears to comfort him, and gazed out of the window miserably. Her protestations had not made the slightest difference. The outcome was the same. She would be staying with her grandmother until further notice.

The journey continued. In the front of the car, her mother stared straight ahead at the road. In the back, Tanya continued to scowl at her mother's head with all her might.

❧❧

"Here we are."

Tanya looked in the direction her mother had pointed to but could see nothing, only rows of dense trees and bushes.

"It's a bit more overgrown than usual."

"It's always overgrown," Tanya snapped. "If it was any worse we'd have missed it completely."

There were so many trees lining the lane that it was impossible to see where it ended. Branches and twigs scraped along the side of the car, and numerous fairies were flying out of the trees, disgruntled at the interruption. One settled on the window next to Tanya and stared at her inquisitively. It remained there for about a minute, a grubby finger rummaging in its nostril all the while. To her relief it soon became bored of sizing her up and flew back into the trees.

She sighed, knowing to expect more of the same. Somehow, the fairies always knew she could see them, and it seemed to draw them to her like a magnet, even when she did her utmost to feign ignorance of their existence.

The lane continued, twisting and turning as though it were part of a labyrinth they would never find their way out of. Eventually, the trees grew sparser and the road lighter, and after a final turn to the left the car drew to a halt before a huge set of padlocked gates. Worked into the wrought-iron framework were two words: ELVESDEN MANOR. On a stone pillar on either side of the gate a gargoyle bared its teeth. Her mother blasted the car horn a couple of times and glared at the clock on the dashboard.

"Why haven't they opened the gates yet? We told them to expect us around ten o'clock." She tooted again in annoyance.

Several minutes passed with no sign of anyone coming. Tanya averted her eyes from the gargoyles' unwelcoming expressions. Over the top of the high wall, she could just make out the roof of the house.

"We might as well get out and stretch our legs," said her mother, opening the door and clambering out. Tanya followed, glad to escape from the hot, cramped car. Oberon bounded over to the trees, first sniffing, then marking his new territory.

"All this fresh country air will do you a world of good."

Tanya shot her mother a venomous look and stared around at the land outside the gates. In the distance she could hear bells ringing out, and recalled a little church nearby. Apart from this the house stood alone, and although the journey had taken little more than a couple of hours it felt as if they were in the middle of nowhere, completely isolated from the rest of the world. Tanya shielded her eyes from the sun and gazed into the distance. A dark figure was walking briskly toward them.

"It's Warwick," said her mother, sounding relieved.

Tanya lowered her gaze and kicked at a pebble. She was not particularly fond of the manor's grounds-keeper. Years ago, when her mother had been there as a child, the job had belonged to Warwick's father, Amos. When Amos had retired the job had been passed along to his son. The two of them lived in the house along with Tanya's grandmother, Florence, and Warwick's son, Fabian, who was, in her mother's words, "a nuisance." Although this did have a slight ring of truth to it, Tanya could not help feeling some sympathy for Fabian, whose mother had died when he was five. Judging by what little guidance he'd had from his father, it was no surprise he had turned out to be difficult.

Warwick drew closer. He was wearing a long overcoat that looked far too warm for the weather, and dirty moleskin trousers that were tucked into equally dirty boots. His straggly dark hair was peppered with gray and tied back loosely; and his skin was brown and leathery, evidence that he spent much of his time outdoors. His only greeting was a sullen nod.

He strode past them, unlocking the gates, and then motioned for them to get back into their car. Tanya noticed with distaste that he had an air rifle strapped to his back. The gates creaked as he swung them open, and then he stepped to one side to allow the car to pass.

As always, Tanya's eyes widened as she drank in the sight of the house. There was no question that it would have been an impressive view when it was first built in the late eighteenth century. It had close to twenty bedrooms—not including the old servants' quarters—and almost as many parlors and sitting rooms, once decorated lavishly. Had it been properly maintained, it would probably still be beautiful.

Instead, thick ivy climbed the cracked walls, growing wilder with each year, even snaking over the windows like leafy shrouds. Most rooms were now either locked or in various states of dilapidation, and the vast, once splendid grounds spanning the house ran wild and unkempt. The forecourt at the front of the house was a frothing sea of weeds; the only things that graced the gardens were a few trees and a disused water fountain. It had not worked for as long as Tanya could remember.

After parking they waited at the door for Warwick. He strolled heavily across the gravel in the forecourt and up the steps to the grand front door, ushering them inside. Oberon remained outside, panting in the shade of the house.

The smell of the hallway was always the same, damp and musty, with an underlying hint of Florence's perfume. Tanya grimaced at the sight of the peeling, faded wallpaper in disapproval, wondering for the hundredth time why her grandmother continued to live in such an enormous house when it was clearly too big for her to look after.

On both sides of the gloomy corridor were doors that Tanya knew from experience would be locked. Few rooms in the house were in use these days. Farther along, the hallway opened out into a lobby, where there were several more doors and the main set of stairs, which led up to a small landing and then branched off in two different directions to the first floor.

The second floor, which had served as the old servants' quarters, was pretty much out of bounds to everyone except Amos. Tanya could remember having been up there only once for a dare, and had raced back down shrieking after Fabian pretended to have seen a ghost.

"This way," said Warwick, speaking at last in his usual brusque manner.

On the first landing stood an old grandfather clock that never worked properly, despite being mended several times. Tanya had a pretty good insight into why: it had been full of fairies for years. This was another reason she hated the place—it was absolutely crawling with fairies. She followed Warwick up the stairs, leaving her mother below. The moment her back was turned a snide voice sounded from the depths of the clock.

"Look out for the little one. She's tricketty."

Tanya ignored it and climbed the final few stairs. At the top she froze. A trail of richly colored feathers led to a rickety dresser, on which sat a fat ginger cat with one eye and a mouthful of feathers.

"It's stuffed," said Warwick, sounding bored.

Tanya spotted a stuffed pheasant on the floor with its head and half its feathers missing, and felt a mixture of relief and revulsion.

"Spitfire! Go on, get out of it!" Warwick ordered.

Spitfire stared back with his unblinking eye and continued to chew insolently. Warwick stepped past him in exasperation and paused by the first door on the left.

"Your room."

Tanya gave a mute nod. The room he had shown

her to was the same one she always stayed in, so being escorted to it seemed rather pointless. She could think of only two reasons why Warwick would want to do this, either to make himself appear courteous, or because he did not trust her not to go snooping in other rooms. Going by what she knew of his general demeanor, she concluded that it was more likely to be the second reason.

Like most of the rooms in the house, Tanya's was spacious but sparsely furnished. The carpet was threadbare, and the walls were covered in lavender paper that was peeling off in some places. In the corner there stood a small table and chair, and in the center a bed had been freshly made up, the crisp white pillowcases still retaining their creases from being pressed. A thin scarlet blanket lay folded at the foot.

On the wall opposite the bed was a cast-iron fireplace, next to which was a door to a small bathroom for her personal use. Unfortunately it also happened to be inhabited by a slimy, amphibian-like fairy with a penchant for all things shiny. Tanya had lost many a watch and several items of jewelry to the thieving creature, and, more than once, witnessed a bewildered Warwick retrieving all manner of glittering objects out of the sink pipe in the bathroom.

Above the fireplace hung a painting of Narcissus and Echo, the handsome youth gazing at his reflection in a woodland pool while the maiden looked on, unnoticed. Tanya had never quite decided whether she liked it or not.

She deposited her bag on the bed and emptied it. Unsurprisingly, after she had put everything away the room still looked as empty as ever. Tanya placed her slippers at the foot of the bed, vaguely recalling a time when Spitfire had left a rat's tail in one of them. She concluded now that the chances of a repeat were unlikely. At sixteen, Spitfire was practically an antique in cat years. Apart from attacking the stuffed game in the corridors, the most he was capable of catching these days was a spider or two, or perhaps a housefly if he was lucky.

She walked over to the windowsill and trailed her finger along it, leaving a thin line in the ever-present layer of grime. The view from the window looked out over the gardens at the side of the house, in which she saw a few wild rosebushes and a couple of trees. Beyond the walls sat the church with its tiny graveyard, and in the distance, a vast expanse of woodland known as Hangman's Wood.

She watched as her mother clambered into the car in the courtyard, ready to leave, and was glad she had chosen to avoid saying good-bye. At best it would have been upsetting, and at worst caused another argument.

Tanya walked back to the bed and slowly sank down on it. In the cracked mirror of the dressing table her reflection was split into two. Twin faces with brown eyes and dark hair stared back from an olive-skinned face. Tanya averted her eyes. She had never felt more alone.

3

Deep in the heart of Hangman's Wood an old caravan stood alone, half hidden by the thick foliage and cool shade of the towering trees. It was painted a bright, daffodil yellow, yet despite its vibrant color the caravan largely went unnoticed, as this was a part of the woods where people seldom ventured.

Most would have found these surroundings unnerving; but for the old gypsy woman who inhabited the caravan, the forest gave her the solitude she craved. Here she spent her days living a simple life, evading the townsfolk and their stares: some curious, some hostile, and some afraid.

It had long been said that the gypsy woman possessed powers of witchery. Her extensive knowledge of the plants and herbs growing wildly in the forest meant that she was able to remedy many an ailment. For the most part she kept to herself, sharing her remedies only when invited—and then only for a price.

But there was something else the old gypsy woman had that was of interest to a number of the townsfolk, and it was something that could not be attributed to her plants, herbs, or anything else. It was her ability to see into the past, and into the future. Those who were not afraid enough to stay away came to ask her to tell them these things, and so she did, accepting their money for her trouble.

Sometimes, however—and more frequently these days—the power evaded her and she was unable to tell them anything. On other occasions she saw things that they would not want to know, and so kept her silence. She had no name for this power other than the second sight, as her mother and her grandmother before her had called it. In younger years it had come to her freely, often in dreams. Lately it lurked at the edge of her awareness, needing to be invoked.

She did not like to summon it unless she had to.

At this time the old woman was listening to the wild birdsong through the open window. Her coarse gray hair was plaited into a simple braid, away from a weathered and craggy face. Her eyes, despite her age, were a bright cornflower blue, alert and birdlike, and held a certain kindness.

The woman raised her gnarled hand to her

temple, feeling a familiar ache that was gradually becoming stronger. She got up and shuffled into the kitchen area, her gaze wandering briefly to the shallow pool collecting in the sink thanks to a leaky tap. Murky, distorted shapes were beginning to swirl in the water.

She closed the window and pulled the drapes, leaving the caravan in near-darkness. In a small cupboard, she reached past numerous jars and bottles and removed a wooden bowl and several candles. After filling the bowl with water, she placed it on the table and lit the candlewicks with a trembling hand.

The old woman took a seat at the table and leaned in close, the lines etched in her face accentuated by the dancing light of the flames. The throbbing in her temple was escalating, sending jolts of pain through her skull. Quickly, she muttered an incantation and the pain ebbed away, leaving her still and quiet in her chair.

The temperature in the caravan dropped, and the flames of the candles glowed blue. Shivering, the old woman clasped her shawl more tightly about her frail shoulders and gazed into the wooden bowl. The water clouded and then cleared. Shapes loomed. Dark colors merged and then separated. Her fingers twitched unavoidably as tiny electric shocks prickled at her skin. Then came a series of hazy images, playing out like a soundless film.

A clock struck midnight. Through the window

of a nursery, the moon illuminated a child sleeping in its crib and then vanished behind a single cloud. When the moon reappeared the crib was empty, holding nothing but a small bear with a tuft of stuffing protruding from a slash on its middle, and the pristine white bedclothes were now covered in tiny, muddy footprints. The old woman frowned, trying to make sense of what she was seeing. Too soon the water cleared, and for a moment she thought the vision was over, but then a new image appeared.

The water depicted a girl of twelve or thirteen with chestnut-colored hair and dark, expressive eyes. The girl in the water looked sad. Sad that nobody understood and that nobody listened. But the water told that she was not alone. The water showed what was all around her. For the girl in the water could see things that others could not. The girl had a second sight—of this there was no question—but not as the old woman knew it.

❖❖

The old woman was still rubbing warmth back into her hands long after it had returned to the caravan. The cold got into her bones too easily these days. As the afternoon sun streamed into the caravan with its reassuring glow she sat motionless in her chair, continuing to stare into the bowl before her, where the watery images had long since gone. All she was left with now were questions.

The woman finally arose from the table and absentmindedly began to put away the bowl and the candles, her aged hands trembling as she did so. She knew enough to realize that fate would ensure that the girl's path and her own would cross—and soon.

It was with a heavy heart that Tanya trudged down-stairs for lunch that afternoon. Her mother had left two hours ago, and the thought of being trapped at the manor with all of its cobwebs and locked doors for the next couple of weeks was too horrible for words.

Her grandmother had arrived back in her old Volvo station wagon laden with groceries. After a brief, stony welcome, Tanya helped fetch the bags from the car. Almost immediately she noticed the dead fairy on the windshield. Initially, she thought it was an oversized fly or bug, but a closer inspection confirmed that it was definitely a fairy, like none she had ever seen before.

It was tiny, the smallest she had ever come across, smaller even than her little finger. Its minute hands were pressed flat against the glass, and only one of its wings was intact. The other was smeared across the windshield.

Tanya gagged and turned away. She had never seen anything dead before, aside from a cat that had also been hit by a car, and other smaller creatures that Spitfire had killed. A fairy was different somehow.

Consequently, her appetite was ruined. Tanya stirred her soup, nauseated, unable to stop thinking about the broken, lifeless body on the car outside. Much as she detested fairies, she could not find it in herself to just leave it there like a squashed insect. She decided then and there to give it a decent burial as soon as she got the chance.

Lunch was served at the oak table in the kitchen, which had not been neglected like most of the other rooms. Its activity and warmth had attracted a cantankerous old brownie, more often than not asleep in the tea caddy, and a shy little hearthfay who busied herself keeping plates warm and ensuring that pots did not boil over. Tanya had never managed to get a proper look at her, for she moved like lightning, darting from one darkened corner to the next. All Tanya had ever glimpsed were long, spindly fingers, a dishcloth dress, and a curtain of red-brown hair that she hid behind.

During the autumn and winter when the fire was lit, she was most commonly found warming herself on the hearth behind the coal bin. In warmer months when there was no fire, the hearthfay sought out any other source of heat in the kitchen, with the exception of the microwave, which seemed to scare her.

One feature of the kitchen Tanya particularly liked was a set of stairs in an alcove next to the fireplace that spiraled upward and around to the first and second floors. It was now blocked off at the point where it disappeared around the corner, having not been used for some time. Years ago it had been used by servants to take trays of food and other such items back and forth quickly from the kitchen, and Tanya thought it a shame that it had been filled in, for she had always longed to explore it.

A small window nestled in the brickwork of the alcove, and the steps currently served as shelves to store items of kitchenware. On winter evenings when the fiery embers glowed in the grate, the alcove was filled with an almost ghostly light. But now, not even the mysterious staircase could lift her spirits.

"Not hungry?"

Tanya looked up and saw that her grandmother was watching her intently. Her thin face was accentuated by white hair that was scraped into a severe knot at her nape.

"I'm a bit tired," Tanya lied, glimpsing spindly fingers warming themselves against the recently boiled kettle. "Where's Fabian?"

"He's around somewhere. His school holidays started last week, so at least you'll be company for each other."

Tanya's heart sank to new depths. Having Fabian for company was a hideous thought—he tended to latch onto her whenever she visited, following her about incessantly. He seemed to be a bit of a loner, never bringing friends home, and he had little regard for other people's privacy. Most of the time she could tolerate him in small doses—but two weeks was different. She slumped down in her chair and pushed her bowl away. Things were going from bad to worse.

After lunch Tanya helped tidy up, using the opportunity to pilfer a few items in order to bury the fairy. When her grandmother's back was turned she tore a piece of cardboard off a cereal box and slipped it into her pocket, then emptied a box of matches into the trash can and pocketed the box.

Her grandmother's car was parked at the side of the house, overlooked by a number of windows, the majority of which were in empty rooms; so the chances of being seen were slim. The only threat was Warwick. He had a tiny den at the side of the house that he was forever popping into and out of to fetch tools and gardening equipment. At the moment he was nowhere to be seen, so Tanya decided to take her chances.

Using the cardboard, she scraped the fairy away from the glass and eased it into the matchbox, trying, not very successfully, to avoid looking at the dried blood trailing from the creature's nose, nor the sickening angle at which its head was lolling. She attempted to get the wing that had been ripped away into the matchbox, but this proved more difficult than she had anticipated, and so she abandoned the task. It would simply have to be buried with one wing.

The back garden was an overgrown mass of bushes and brambles that had not been tended to in a long time. After trampling through and sustaining several cuts to her arms from the thorns, she found a plant with tiny yellow flowers at the base of a horse chestnut tree, and began to dig. Oberon, who had followed her outside, observed with delight before joining in enthusiastically. He dug several holes nearby at remarkable speed, showering Tanya with dirt, then sat patiently beside her, his wet nose coated with a layer of dark brown earth.

When her own hole was deep enough, she plucked a single flower from the plant and laid it in the matchbox with the fairy, before placing the box in the earth and filling the hole back in. Afterward her fingernails were caked with dirt, but she did feel a little better. She wandered back around to the side of the house and stood in the shade of a towering oak tree, rinsing her hands under an outdoor tap. As she turned to go back inside, a figure leapt out of the tree and landed about two feet away from her.

"Hello," said Fabian. "What are you doing?"

"Me?" Tanya said indignantly, as her thumping heart returned to its normal pace. "What are you doing hiding in trees and jumping out at people? You scared me half to death!"

"Sorry," said Fabian, grinning in a way that infuriated her.

Tanya glared at him and wiped her hands on her jeans. At twelve, Fabian was a few months younger than she was, but in the year since she had last seen him he had shot up by several inches and now towered over her. Apart from this his appearance remained largely unchanged. He was a spindly-looking boy whose head seemed too large in proportion to the rest of his body. His sandy hair was thick and wavy, and as well as flopping unmanageably in all directions, was in need of a good trim. Unlike his father, Fabian was pale and pasty, reflecting a life spent indoors with his nose crammed in one scientific book after another. Propped on his thin, straight nose, thick spectacles magnified a pair of intelligent blue eyes.

Tanya's mother didn't like Fabian much. She found him insolent, and it annoyed her that he tended to call adults by their first names, including his father and Amos, which Tanya had to admit even she found odd.

When she had seen him last, the previous summer, Fabian had been roasting insects by deflecting sunlight through a magnifying glass and recording the time they took to burn in a brown leather-bound book that he carried everywhere with him. When questioned, his distracted reply was, "research."

His odd appearance now suggested more of the same. He was dressed entirely in green except for brown boots and a hat. He had attached a number of sprigs of twigs and leaves to the hat and the top he was wearing in some sort of camouflage attempt, and clipped to his glasses was a handmade device consisting of two magnifying glass lenses held together by wire and tape.

"So what *are* you doing?" Tanya asked, her curiosity getting the better of her. "Capturing more helpless creatures to torture and kill?"

Fabian shrugged. "Actually, it's more of an... observational project."

"What are you observing?"

He grinned aggravatingly. "What were you burying in the garden?"

"A dead mouse," she said, half expecting him to ask her to dig it up so he could experiment on it.

For a few seconds he simply stared at her.

"Sad," he said eventually. "You could've given it to Spitfire to munch on."

They stood glaring at each other until their eyes watered, neither wanting to be the first to blink or break their gaze. Fortunately Tanya was good at it, having had plenty of practice with the kids at school. Fabian was the first to look away. She felt mildly smug over her small victory as she marched back into the house, leaving Fabian glowering as he clambered back up into the tree.

❦❦

Back inside, Tanya headed for her room. She was almost upon the first stair when she noticed that the door to a room on the right that was usually locked was ajar, allowing a chink of light into the darkened hallway. She drew back from the stairs and crept toward the room. There was no sound from inside. Tanya pushed the door open gingerly and stepped into the room, then met with a wonderful sight.

Books by the hundreds lined the walls from floor to ceiling, covering almost every subject imaginable. A huge writing desk sat in the corner by the window, thickly coated in a layer of dust. Stacked on top of it were even more books.

She pulled several out from the shelves. Clouds of dust flew up as she flicked through them; it was obvious that they had remained untouched for many years. As her finger trailed the spines she saw that some of them were extremely old, dating back to the late eighteenth century. She opened the first, curiously titled *Myth and Magic Through the Ages,* and searched through the index until she found what she was looking for.

"Faeries," she whispered aloud. "MYTHICAL BEINGS OF LEGEND AND FOLKLORE, ALSO KNOWN AS FAIRIES, FAYRE, FEY, OR THE LITTLE FOLK. THE WORD 'FAERIE' COMES FROM THE FRENCH, AND FIRST CAME INTO USE IN ENGLAND FROM THE TUDOR PERIOD, WITH REFERENCES FEATURING IN LITERATURE THROUGH THE AGES.

"IT WAS WIDELY BELIEVED THAT IF A FEY CHILD WAS BORN UGLY, SICK, OR DEFORMED, THE FAERIES WOULD STEAL A HEALTHY MORTAL CHILD AND LEAVE THE FAERIE CHILD IN ITS PLACE. THESE STOLEN CHILDREN WERE KNOWN AS CHANGELINGS.

"IN PAST TIMES IT WAS COMMONPLACE TO LEAVE

GIFTS FOR THE FAERIES. PEOPLE BELIEVED THAT IF THEY LEFT FOOD OUT FOR THE LITTLE FOLK, THEIR KINDNESS WOULD BE REPAID WITH GOOD LUCK.

"PROTECTION FROM BOTHERSOME FAERIES INCLUDED VARIOUS SIMPLE METHODS AND DEVICES SUCH AS CARRYING SALT, WEARING THE COLOR RED, OR TURNING CLOTHING INSIDE OUT, KEEPING AN IRON NAIL IN THE POCKET, OR BEING NEAR RUNNING WATER."

"Faeries," Tanya whispered, running her finger lightly over the old-fashioned spelling on the page. It seemed to suit them somehow, these strange creatures that hounded her.

She fumbled in the top drawer of the desk, finding nothing but some old papers and a few curled-up insects. She slammed it shut. The second drawer of the desk was either locked or jammed, but in the third she found a scrap of paper, a pen, and an antiquated silver charm bracelet. Intrigued, she lifted the strange piece of jewelry from the drawer.

It was heavy and cold to the touch; and though it was tarnished, the fine workmanship was clear to see. Each charm had been beautifully and lovingly crafted. She set it on the table, wondering how long it had lain in the drawer, undisturbed, and who the last person to wear it had been.

She turned back to the scrap of paper and began to write, then hesitated. If the fairies found it there was no telling what they might do this time. She did not doubt for a second that Gredin was capable of turning her into a gibbering wreck with no memory.

*But I didn't write it,* she told herself. *I'm just copying it. He didn't say anything about that.*

She scribbled down the passage from the book word for word, then folded the paper carefully and put it in her pocket, before casting her eyes hungrily down the rest of the page. "*See also Faerie Glamour, The Thirteen Treasures, Faerie Courts: Seelie and Unseelie.* All right…let's see," she murmured, turning the pages once more.

FAERIE GLAMOUR: A MAGICAL ILLUSION SO POWERFUL IT CAN FOOL ONLOOKERS INTO BELIEVING WHAT THEY SEE IS REAL; A MASK OF DECEPTION WHICH CAN MAKE THAT WHICH IS HIDEOUS A THING OF BEAUTY. GLAMOUR ALLOWS FOR CHANGE OF SHAPE, SIZE, OR FORM; THE ABILITY TO MASQUERADE AS AN ANIMAL—COMMONLY BIRDS OR CREATURES OF THE AIR—OR EVEN HUMANS.

FOR A FAERIE TO SUCCESSFULLY POSE AS A MORTAL REQUIRES A CONSIDERABLE AMOUNT OF POWER, YET OFTEN IT IS THEIR BEHAVIOR THAT MAY ALERT THE MORE WARY HUMAN TO THE DECEPTION. SPEECH MAY BE STILTED, OLD-FASHIONED, OR RHYMING. SIMILARLY, CLOTHING MAY BE OUT-OF-DATE OR INAPPROPRIATE. NATURAL FORMS— ACORNS OR PEBBLES ENCHANTED WITH A GLAMOUR OF THEIR OWN TO APPEAR AS COINS, FOR EXAMPLE—MAY ALSO BE USED IN PAYMENT FOR GOODS, ONLY TO RETURN TO THEIR ORIGINAL STATE HOURS OR DAYS LATER.

Tanya snapped the book shut, breathless with

the excitement of the discovery. She gathered into her arms the remaining books she'd selected, ready to leave, when a small book propped on the desk caught her eye. It was *A Midsummer Night's Dream* by Shakespeare, lavishly illustrated. Curious, she set her books down and reached for it.

As she leafed through the pages a loose sheet of paper floated to the floor. She knelt and saw that it was a clipping from a local gazette, dated June 22nd, just over fifty years old. It was faded and yellow with age. **MISSING GIRL**, read the headline, in bold letters.

A HUNT WAS LAUNCHED YESTERDAY FOR THE DAUGHTER OF A LOCAL REVEREND WHO FAILED TO RETURN HOME LAST NIGHT. POLICE ARE BAFFLED BY THE DISAPPEARANCE OF MORWENNA BLOOM, AGE FOURTEEN, WHO VANISHED AFTER WALKING IN HANGMAN'S WOOD YESTERDAY EVENING, SEEMINGLY WITHOUT A TRACE.

A POLICE SPOKESMAN REVEALED THAT THERE ARE MAJOR CONCERNS FOR THE SAFETY OF THE GIRL, LAST SEEN BY A SIXTEEN-YEAR-OLD LOCAL BOY NEAR THE NOTORIOUS HANGMAN'S CATACOMBS, WHICH HAVE CLAIMED SEVERAL LIVES OVER THE YEARS AND ARE A WELL KNOWN SUICIDE SPOT. POLICE QUESTIONED THE BOY, WHO WAS LATER RELEASED WITHOUT CHARGE. ONCE AGAIN, LOCAL

RESIDENTS ARE APPEALING FOR THE HOLES TO
BE FENCED OFF IN THE INTEREST OF SAFETY.

Tanya slipped the clipping back into the pages.

The Hangman's Catacombs lay deep in the forest behind the manor, plunging down into the earth and winding into underground tunnels that went on for miles. It was believed that the holes were natural caves, though there was some speculation that they were old chalk mines. Only in recent years had railings been constructed around each entrance to prevent people from falling into them, but still, Warwick repeatedly forbade Fabian and Tanya to go any farther than the brook that ran along the edge of the woods. Tanya had never felt any inclination to venture into the forest anyway. The teeming population of fairies sure to dwell there was deterrent enough.

Someone cleared their throat behind her.

She jumped and spun around. Her grandmother stood in the doorway.

"What are you doing in here?"

Tanya gulped noisily, knowing guilt must be written all over her face.

"I was just...the door was open, and I just wanted to look at your books."

Florence walked into the room and pulled a book from one of the shelves.

"Some of these are very old," she said, tracing a line in the dusty cover. "Some have been here since the house was built, just over two hundred years ago."

Tanya fidgeted. She had been expecting to get told off.

"I found this," she said, taking the newspaper clipping out of the book again. "It's about a girl who disappeared fifty years ago."

A strange look crossed her grandmother's face, something almost like fear. But then too quickly it was gone, replaced by her usual impassive expression.

"She was my age...we went to the same school. Her father was the reverend of the little church nearby."

"Were you friends with her?"

"Yes," said Florence. "For a time, when we were younger." She stopped abruptly, looking troubled. "We...drifted apart."

"Was she found?" Tanya asked.

"No," said Florence. "She was never seen again." She placed the clipping on the table and blew at a cobweb. "This room could do with a good clearing out. Warwick promised me he would do it weeks ago, but he still hasn't got around to it."

"Perhaps I could help," Tanya offered, thinking of the opportunities it would create to search for more information.

Florence eyed her, her expression unreadable.

"Thank you. I'm sure Warwick would appreciate your help."

Her slate-gray eyes lingered on the charm bracelet.

"I wondered where this had disappeared to,"

she said, lifting the bracelet up to the light. The tarnished charms sparkled faintly in the sun.

"Does it belong to you?" Tanya asked.

"Yes," said Florence. "It's an old heirloom. It's been in the family for years."

Tanya looked at the bracelet properly, counting the silver charms. There were thirteen of the curious little things. Each was ornate and exquisite, the more striking among them a key, a jeweled goblet, and a tiny candelabrum.

"It's beautiful," she said.

"It's a heavy, awkward thing," said her grandmother. "I haven't worn it in a very long time." A faraway look came into her eyes. "In past times, people treasured charms such as these. They wore them to ward off evil—like talismans for luck and protection." Unexpectedly, she handed the bracelet to Tanya. "Perhaps you might like to have it? There's some silver cleaner under the sink that'll make it like new."

"Oh," said Tanya, taken aback. "Thank you." She fastened the bracelet onto her skinny wrist, confused by her grandmother's uncharacteristic generosity.

With a stiff nod Florence left the room, leaving the door open behind her. Reluctantly, Tanya followed. There was no sign of her grandmother. She hesitated, then quickly reentered the room and grabbed the *Myth and Magic Through the Ages* book, closing the library door softly behind her. Up on the first-floor landing a faint scuttling could be heard from inside the grandfather clock, and as she drew nearer she thought she could hear the lodgers quarreling. She paused to try and listen to what they were saying, but the voices stopped immediately, so she crept onward, past the staircase and into the kitchen.

Having barely eaten at lunch, Tanya was ravenous. After making herself a sandwich she filled a tall glass with orange juice, then sat down and ate in silence until a strange sound caught her attention. A muffled snoring was coming from the direction of the tea caddy, and she suddenly remembered the brownie living there. It was a foul-tempered little creature, breaking crocks and souring milk when it was displeased, which was often.

When she had finished her food and drained the pulpy remnants of her juice, she washed and dried her plate, careful not to make too much noise for fear of waking the brownie, then tiptoed out of the kitchen. The hallway was empty, although it seemed Fabian had been along at some point, as a number of leaves and twigs were strewn across the floor.

She climbed the staircase up to the first floor, then went into her room, checking that the corridor was clear before locking the door behind her. Normally, she did not bother to lock herself in, but on this occasion it was necessary, as she did not want anyone to see what she was about to do.

Carefully, she knelt before the fireplace and rolled back the carpet, exposing the rough, unpolished wood beneath. Using her fingernails, she pried up the loose floorboard that no one else knew about and heaved it aside to reveal a space below that was large enough to hold a shoebox—a space she had discovered when she was seven years old. It had been her secret hiding place ever since.

She checked for spiders, then lifted out the box and removed the lid. Inside were a couple of stories she had written, a few family photographs, and a bulging old diary. She clenched her jaw. The fairies evidently had yet to discover this one.

She pulled the notes out of her pocket and read through them again, before placing them at the bottom of the box. After fixing the floorboard back in position, she unfurled the carpet and tucked the book from downstairs beneath the blanket at the foot of her bed, her head full of the potential wealth of information awaiting her in the library downstairs.

It was only later, when she got up and went over to the dressing table, that she noticed the black feather on the floor, like one that would belong to a bird from the crow family. A raven, perhaps.

5

Tickey End was a small market town, the kind of place where people took their dogs to the grooming parlor and washed their cars dutifully every Sunday morning, and neighbors vied to see who could build up the most extensive collection of garden gnomes. It was also the kind of town where everybody knew everybody, and if you were a stranger curtains would twitch as you walked past.

It did, however, have a marvelous main street in which there were so many interesting and unusual shops it would take an entire day to look around properly. On Tuesdays, Wednesdays, and Saturdays there was a market in the square, where traders shouted to sell their wares and customers haggled to get a good deal. Rich colors were always in abundance, from the glistening silver scales of freshly caught fish to the vibrant hues of ripe fruit, and at the right time in the morning the scent of freshly baked meat pies and apple tarts wafted deliciously through the air.

Numerous antique and curiosity shops stood in the back streets, away from the hustle and bustle of the main street. It was these kinds of shops that Tanya could quite happily spend hours in.

Tuesday morning, she woke early and walked half a mile to the dilapidated bus shelter, eager to escape the gloom of the manor, if only for a few hours. Unfortunately there was a catch. Her grandmother had allowed her to go only on the condition that Fabian accompanied her.

The journey to Tickey End took around fifteen minutes, and was a pleasant, scenic route, although the air always reeked of manure from the nearby fields. After leaving the bus they headed for the square, where the market was already teeming with a jostling crowd.

Soon after arriving, Tanya spotted a stall that was selling fabrics, silks, and ribbons in every color of the rainbow. Her fingers lingered on a tray of silk scarves, the sort girls had been tying in their hair since the beginning of summer in an ever-growing trend. The pretty Asian girl on the stall was wearing a turquoise scarf of the same design. Never one for trends or fashion, Tanya was just about to move away when she spotted one in red. Remembering the passage in the book she had found, she passed the scarf to the girl and delved into her pocket.

Fabian sniggered. "I always had you down as more of a tomboy," he said.

Tanya ignored him. When the girl handed her the brown paper bag and her change, she immediately put the scarf on, eager to determine whether there had been any truth in the old book. They moved on through the market, Fabian pausing to admire some science fiction comics, and Tanya spending the last of her change on a huge marrow bone for Oberon to gnaw upon her return. It clunked uncomfortably against her leg in the carrier bag as she walked.

"What time is it?" she asked Fabian, after looking at her wrist automatically yet again before remembering her watch was gone. True to form, the drain-dweller had stolen it that morning from the side of the bathtub.

"Quarter to twelve," Fabian replied. "We've got half an hour before the next bus."

Tanya nodded, flexing her sore feet. After she'd walked around Tickey End for two hours, Tanya's feet were raw in the new summer sandals her mother had bought her. She did not want to walk around for much longer. However, she was eager to get back to the manor for another reason—she had arranged to help Warwick clear out the library that afternoon.

They headed into Wishbone Walk, Tanya's favorite street in Tickey End. All the buildings were old and uneven, and it was crammed with the quaint little shops that she so loved. There were also numerous little pubs and inns dotted along the way, which would be filled with raucous laughter later in the day.

Fabian mopped his brow, humming a little tune that he would break from every so often to share a snippet of local gossip. Despite herself, Tanya was enjoying listening to him, though she would never admit to it. Fabian was a mine of information, and had a gift for storytelling, something Tanya had noticed a long time ago. When he was relating an incident that was of interest to him, Fabian's eyes lit up and he became animated, reminding Tanya of an overly enthusiastic schoolteacher or an actor onstage. He suddenly pointed to a pub called the Spiral Staircase.

"The garden of that pub caved in last winter. All the rain must have weakened the earth…it was the catacombs underneath, see. Lucky it didn't happen in the summer, when people would have been sitting out there. Now a lot of the residents have had to take out a special insurance in case it happens to them. And this little inn here is really old—did I ever tell you about the secret passage that runs from underneath it all the way to the manor?"

"Only about a million times," Tanya said with a groan. "I can't believe you still believe in those secret passages. It's such rubbish—"

"It's not rubbish!" Fabian protested. "It's true… there was a tunnel leading to the manor—it's in the local history books. But it's been blocked off, or caved in—none of the books agree on which. It was common with big old buildings; they had secret tunnels to escape through, in case of invasions. There was meant to be another one as well, leading to the church."

"All those times you had me on wild goose chases, trying to find your secret passages." Tanya snorted. "We never found a thing. Someone probably just made the whole thing up to try to make Tickey End seem interesting."

"Well, it was fun looking for them," said Fabian. "Even if we never found anything."

"I suppose it passed a few rainy afternoons," Tanya said ungraciously. "Anyway, my grandmother and your father have always said that there aren't any tunnels—that it's all rumors."

"They would say that," Fabian said darkly. "They don't want us snooping around looking for them. And if anyone knows the secrets of the house, it's Warwick."

"Why do you call him and Amos by their first names?" Tanya asked. "Why don't you call Warwick 'Dad'?"

Fabian shrugged. "I used to, when I was little."

"So why not now?"

"I don't know. I just...don't."

"But it's odd," Tanya persisted. "And you know it annoys him."

The ghost of a smile that crossed Fabian's lips told her that this was exactly the desired effect. It vanished as he smoothly changed the subject.

"Now there's a place that gives me the creeps," he continued, as they walked farther along the lane. "The old children's home."

Tanya followed his eyes to a ramshackle building set back from the road. It was obviously derelict, its windows either broken or boarded up and its brickwork crumbling. The barbed wire fence that surrounded it made it look cold and cruel and desolate. She wondered how she had never noticed it before.

"It just looks sad to me," she said. "But buildings like that usually are. Children's homes aren't exactly the happiest of places."

Fabian shook his head. "I didn't mean because it was a children's home—I meant because of what went on there...the disappearances."

"Disappearances?"

"Some kids vanished from there just over a year ago, babies and toddlers mainly. Never older than about two or three. There was a huge investigation and it got closed down."

A chill wrapped itself around Tanya's heart as she remembered the newspaper clipping about the missing girl she had found in the library. It seemed that Tickey End had a history of its children vanishing into thin air.

They lapsed into silence, continuing along the lane. Tanya peered into shop windows here and there, trying to take her mind off the children's home. On the corner of the street a tiny shop was set back from the rest. Tanya recognized it as a shabby, nameless little place with blanked-out windows and peeling paintwork that had stood empty for the past year. Now, however, it was evidently under new management, for not only had it been given a fresh coat of paint but it also had a name: Pandora's Box. Instantly intrigued, Tanya called to Fabian, who was kneeling down and sketching something in his notebook.

"I'm just going in here."

Fabian stopped sketching and looked up. "We don't really have time—we should start making our way to the bus stop."

"You go on ahead," said Tanya. "I'll meet you there."

Fabian rolled his eyes. "I'll wait here. Just be quick."

A bell jangled above her head as Tanya pushed the door open. Inside, the shop smelled of incense. A plump woman with rosy cheeks and a kindly face was sitting behind the counter flicking through a magazine. Tanya maneuvered herself carefully around shelves crammed full of all manner of curiosities.

There were a number of jars and bottles containing dried herbs, plants, and powders. She found herself staring at one labeled DRAGON'S BLOOD, before moving onward past figurines of witches, wizards, and goblin-type creatures, crystal balls and trays of semiprecious stones. Then she spied a bookshelf at the rear and began to make her way toward it. Once there, she scanned the contents—a vast range of tarot, astrology, and the like—hoping to find further information on fairies. Much to her disappointment there appeared to be nothing that would be of much use to her.

Just then, the bell on the door rang as someone else entered the shop. Tanya craned her neck to see who it was, annoyed in case Fabian had come to drag her away. But it was not Fabian. Out of the corner of her eye Tanya noticed an old woman, laden with heavy shopping bags, shuffling about slowly.

Through the window she saw that Fabian had finished sketching and was now looking impatient, and decided to leave. However, as she turned to go around a display of highly stacked boxes she collided with the old woman, who was coming the opposite way. Her shopping bags crashed to the floor, sending peaches and apples rolling in every direction.

"Sorry," Tanya mumbled, embarrassed. She knelt to help the woman. "Are you all right?"

The old woman stared back at her but did not reply. Tanya saw that her hands were trembling very slightly. Her skin was paper thin, lined deeply, her hair worn long and braided. The clothes she wore were old-fashioned. In several places there were holes that had been sewn up time and again. An odd expression flickered over the old lady's face. Tanya swallowed nervously, her mouth suddenly dry. Something about the woman's face was haunting, and she did not like the way she was staring at her.

"I really am sorry," she said again, averting her eyes as she handed back a bag of the bruised fruit.

The woman rose slowly, and stretched a closed hand toward Tanya.

"I think this is for you."

Not wanting to seem rude, Tanya held out her hand. She felt a sharp tingle as the gnarled fingers brushed against her own, like a mild electric shock. The woman placed something cold, smooth, and heavy in her palm. Tanya looked down.

It was a tarnished brass compass, circular in shape with a long neck chain. Most of the letters were absent, probably worn away over the years. She stared at it in confusion. Did the old lady think she had dropped it in the collision?

"This isn't mine."

The old woman did not answer. Instead, she reached for Tanya's new scarf, the silky red fabric slipping easily through her fingers.

"A pretty color for a pretty girl. A wise choice too."

Tanya felt a shiver shoot up her spine.

"What do you mean?" Her voice emerged thin and scared. "Who are you?"

The woman ignored her questions and nodded at the compass.

"Guard it well...and use it wisely." Then she turned and shuffled from the shop, leaving an unnerved Tanya behind her.

Tanya stumbled out into the sunlight, visibly shaken. Fabian strolled toward her lazily. "You do realize that it's an hour-long wait for the next bus if we miss this one, don't you?" He glanced down at the compass in Tanya's hand and looked distinctly unimpressed.

"Surely you didn't just buy that old thing?"

"The old woman," Tanya said, her voice quivering. "The one in the shop. She gave it to me."

"What old woman?" said Fabian, searching the length of the street earnestly, but the old lady was gone.

"She came out just before I did," said Tanya, still clutching the compass stupidly.

Fabian's mouth fell open. "You don't mean Mad Morag?"

"*Mad Morag*? You know her?"

"Everyone knows her," said Fabian. He began to jog, and Tanya had to sprint to keep up with him, Oberon's bone clashing against her knees.

"How do *you* know her?" she panted as they sped into the square and on, past the marketplace.

"I don't really *know* her. I meant I know of her. I've just heard things."

"What things?"

"Like she lives in the woods in a caravan, and hardly ever goes out. And she barely talks to anyone, except when she tells them their fortunes. And she's supposed to be a witch."

The bus came into view, held up by a line of people waiting to get on.

"I wouldn't pay any attention to her," Fabian added. "The old girl's crackers."

But even after boarding the bus, Tanya could not help thinking of the old woman. She looked down at the compass, and for the first time noticed that the needle was spinning uselessly.

"It doesn't even work," said Fabian. "Throw it away. You don't know where it's been."

"I say," a voice interrupted from the seat behind. "Do you mind if I take a look at that?"

Tanya turned to look at the scruffy middle-aged man who was leaning earnestly toward her. He was dressed strangely, in a thin tattered raincoat that was inappropriate given the weather, and a wide-brimmed hat that left his face partially in shadow.

"I collect antiques, you see," the man continued. He whipped out an eyeglass and held out his hand. Tanya handed him the compass somewhat reluctantly. A sudden feeling she could not explain, that somehow the man was familiar to her, passed through her mind. She wondered if she had seen him on television, on an antique hunt program perhaps.

She tried to get a better look at his face, but the stranger had ducked his head as he was studying the compass and all she could see was the top of his hat. A moment later he looked up, and Tanya quickly lowered her eyes, not wanting to make it obvious she had been staring.

"How much did you pay for it?"

Tanya stared at him blankly.

"Five pounds," she lied.

"If it was working it would be worth around fifty pounds," said the stranger. "But obviously the fact that it's not lowers the value." Still clutching the compass with one hand, he reached into his pocket and pulled out a wad of crisp bank notes. "I'll give you twenty pounds for it."

For a moment Tanya was too surprised to answer. Luckily, Fabian came to her rescue.

"Why?" he said, doing nothing to hide his suspicion.

The man's smile never wavered. "I told you, I'm an antiques dealer."

"No, you said you were an antiques *collector*," Fabian retorted, quick as a flash.

The man's smile no longer reached his eyes. It was clear he was finding Fabian tiresome. "I'll give you thirty pounds," he said to Tanya. "That's a good deal, trust me."

"*I* don't trust you," Fabian said immediately. "How do we know what the compass is worth if we only have your word for it? For all we know you could be a rip-off merchant."

By now the conversation was attracting curious glances and whispers from other passengers. Tanya had barely said a word to the stranger, but the more insistent he became the more determined she was to hang on to the compass for herself.

"Thirty pounds is my final offer," the man said stiffly, all pretense of friendliness gone. He was undoubtedly riled by Fabian's last comment.

"Hey!" The bus driver called out. "If you don't stop harassing those kids you'll be leaving the bus at the next stop!"

The antiques dealer stood up, red-faced. "I'll get off now."

Tanya held out her hand for the compass, and was shocked as the man slammed it into her palm. A guttural growl sounded from his throat as he stalked to the front of the bus. The driver halted abruptly, even though there was not a stop anywhere in sight, and the man got off.

"Good riddance too," the bus driver muttered as they pulled away, leaving the antiques dealer behind.

"I think I must have had too much sun," Fabian said, shaking his head. "I could've sworn...no, never mind."

"No, what?" Tanya asked.

"Just as he got up, I thought I saw his watch ticking backward," Fabian said with a laugh. "Stupid, I know. Anyway, he was far too pushy. The compass must be worth something after all—and probably a fair bit more than he was offering."

He paused and scooped something up off the floor with a crow of delight. "Look! Silly old fool must have dropped this when he was flashing his cash!" He presented Tanya with a crisp twenty-pound note. "It must have come loose when he pulled that wad out of his pocket. Here, you have it. Buy yourself a new watch."

"I can't take that," said Tanya. "It's stealing... sort of."

Fabian rolled his eyes. "As if. You're never going to see him again, so it's not like you can return it.

Give it to charity if it makes you feel that bad. Or give it to me. I'll spend it. But I reckon it serves him right. I doubt he'll even miss it."

Tanya slipped it in her pocket, not knowing what else to do.

By the time they reached their stop the color had started to return to Tanya's cheeks. As they walked down the lane toward the manor she realized that for the first time, she was actually looking forward to getting back to her grandmother's house. However, when they reached it ten minutes later, there was a shock in store.

Warwick's Land Rover was parked in the courtyard, the trailer at the back stacked high with books. Tanya knew in an instant that he had begun clearing out the library without her, and it appeared that most of the job was already done. She raced inside, leaving Fabian behind. The library door was open, and Warwick was standing at the writing desk with his back to the door.

"Why didn't you wait for me? I said I'd help!"

Warwick glanced over his shoulder and shrugged. "I thought I'd get a head start."

He turned away from her again and continued to pack a large box. Tanya glanced around. Of all the books that had been in the library the day before, less than half of them remained. It was clear Warwick's "head start" meant he must have begun clearing the room the moment she had left the house. She moved aside as he strode past her, carrying books out to the trailer.

"What are you going to do with them, anyway?" she asked, unable to keep the anger out of her voice.

Warwick grunted over his shoulder, not even bothering to stop. "Charity shop."

Tanya surveyed the rows of remaining books. None of the titles there looked as if they would be of any use to her.

"What's going on?"

She turned and scowled. Fabian had appeared behind her.

"Your father has decided to get rid of every book in the house, *that's* what's going on!"

Fabian blinked. "What for?"

Tanya did not answer. Instead she left the library and ran upstairs: there was no point in staying to help now. On the way past the grandfather clock she heard the lodgers tittering, and forced herself to refrain from kicking it.

Once in her room she threw herself down on the bed, gasping as something dug painfully into the top of her leg. It was only then she remembered the compass. She pulled it from her pocket and stared at it dubiously. In addition to the needle not working, Tanya saw that instead of an "N" for north, there was an "H" where it should have been. She frowned, wondering what it stood for. And, as she slowly pushed the compass out of sight beneath her pillow, she wondered why the strange old woman had given it to her.

6

On Wednesday morning Tanya was awakened from a deep sleep by the sound of somebody shouting. She peered out from beneath the bedclothes toward the window, where the badly hung curtains were allowing several rays of light through. The clock on the dressing table read six o'clock.

The shouting continued. It was Amos, Warwick's father, calling him from his room on the second floor. The old man ranted on, getting louder by the minute.

"Warwick? Where are you? I want my breakfast! It's late! You're always late, boy!"

Heavy footsteps thundered up to the second floor as Warwick went to tend to the old man. For the last few years nobody except him and Tanya's grandmother had had any contact with Amos at all.

The old man was now a recluse; not even Fabian was allowed near him. Warwick single-handedly waited on him night and day, and if he happened to be out when his father called for him, Amos would shout incessantly until his strength was spent.

A door slammed from above and the shouting stopped. Tanya lay staring at the cracked, stained ceiling, knowing it would be useless to try to go back to sleep. Eventually she got up, then washed and dressed carefully in a pair of jeans, sandals, and a bright red T-shirt.

Breakfast was a somber affair of few words. Tanya stirred her coffee repeatedly, gazing into her cup in a daydream, while Fabian pushed a lightly nibbled piece of toast around his plate, still sleepy-eyed and not attempting to make conversation with anyone.

"Warwick tells me you were a little upset yesterday, Tanya," said her grandmother, taking a sip of tea. She never ate in the morning, although she insisted that everyone was present at the breakfast table, something that grated on Tanya immensely.

"I wasn't upset," said Tanya. "I just wanted to . . . help . . . or something."

"I see," said Florence, evidently not fooled for a second.

"I thought Warwick was just going to clean the room," said Tanya. "I didn't know he was going to get rid of all those books." She cast an accusing look in Warwick's direction, but he remained unperturbed.

"Actually, it was my idea to give the books away,"

her grandmother replied. "Nobody has bothered to read them in years."

"*I* would have read them!" said Tanya.

"I apologize," said Florence, not sounding sorry in the slightest. "If I'd known then I would have kept them." She paused, finishing the last of her tea. "I can't ask the shop for them back now, though. They would think it most uncharitable."

Tanya did not trust herself to speak. Her grandmother's haughty performance was really starting to get on her nerves. She was wholeheartedly glad when breakfast was over, and raced up to her room.

As she made her bed, the compass that the gypsy woman had given her slid from behind her pillow and dropped to the floor with a clang. Tanya transferred it to the hiding place under the floorboard, then reached within the folds of the scarlet blanket at the foot of the bed to retrieve the book from the library. She pulled it free and hugged it to her chest, thankful she had rescued it from Warwick. Right now, all she wanted to do was get out of the house and away from everybody.

She whistled to Oberon, who was waiting patiently at the foot of the stairs. Together they left the house through the back, heading out into the wildly overgrown garden. At the very rear, just to one side of the gate, there was a neglected rock garden with weeds and untamed shrubs spilling over the rocks. Today it seemed even more run-down than usual.

Then Tanya noticed something. Standing on the

rock garden were three of the ugliest, most realistic-looking garden gnomes she had ever seen. She frowned. It was out of character for her grandmother to bother with extravagances such as garden ornaments. One of the gnomes took a step in her direction. Tanya jumped.

They *were* real.

Oberon yelped and hid behind her legs. Curiously, the creature did not seem to be looking at her. Instead, it was watching Oberon with a hungry look that made Tanya feel decidedly nervous.

"Are you... are you goblins?" she asked carefully.

The goblin—or whatever it was—shook itself and regarded her as if it had only just noticed her—but did not answer. Tanya realized then that it *hadn't* initially seen her; her red T-shirt must have acted as a camouflage until she had spoken to it, forcing it to notice her. She could have kicked herself for her own stupidity.

The creature continued to stare at her, its eyes still in its fat, toadlike face. It stood just above knee height, and judging by the size of its teeth could probably give a vicious bite. Tanya eyed the other two. One was stooped over badly, having to crane its neck at an angle just to view her properly. The third hung back. He was the smallest, and would probably have had a pleasant face had he not been covered from head to foot with ugly bruises. Some were yellow and green, obviously old, and there were newer, fresher ones of blue and purple. The black eye he was sporting was evidently one of the latter. It was he who spoke first.

"Pray do tell . . . what have we here? A mortal child who shows no fear?" he said, in a singsong voice that was deep and strange.

"This is one born of second sight, aware of us by day and night," said the hunchback.

Tanya took a step backward. The strange little men were beginning to scare her. They were dressed curiously, wearing jackets and trousers fashioned from a combination of human castoffs: curtains, blankets, and old tea towels. In places there seemed to be holes that had been darned with leaves. Tanya's sharp eyes caught the neat, glistening stitches. It looked like something very close to spider's thread. Their feet were bare, filthy, and scarred.

"Are you goblins?" she repeated, but still they would not acknowledge that she had spoken. She thought quickly. "If I put my words to rhyme, will you answer me this time?"

For a moment she did not think it had had any effect, but then the toadfaced creature responded.

"'Tis not for mortals to question the fey. With our own kind our secrets stay."

Tanya racked her brains, struggling for another question. Usually she was quite good at making up poems, but trying to think of them instantly for use in a conversation was far more difficult.

"I ask again, I'd like to know, are you goblins,

yes or no?" she said after a couple of minutes had elapsed. She was unable to think of anything else, especially anything that rhymed with the word "goblin."

"Ask away! I cannot say! The answer lies with us today!" sang Toadface, and the other two creatures guffawed, dancing to the rhythm of his words.

Not to be outdone, Tanya pondered for a moment.

"I'm tired of playing your silly game. I'll never bother you again."

She made to move past them, but the hunchback blocked her path.

"This is no game, as you will see. We do not trust mortals easily."

Tanya retrieved a notebook from her pocket and scribbled some words down, trying to make sentences rhyme.

"Fairies lie and fairies steal, but humans think and humans feel," she began, looking in her notebook again. "I do not think what you say is just. In fairies I do not place *my* trust."

The creatures stared at her, seemingly taken aback that she was able to keep up with them. The one with the bruises stepped forward.

"You ask too much, we cannot tell. We goblins hide our secrets well."

"I see," said Tanya. "So you *are* goblins!"

The goblin looked stricken the moment he realized his error. His companions turned on him, their eyes wild with anger.

"Foolish cretin! Stupid fool!" said Toadface. "Trust you to break that simple rule!"

"Forgive me, it was not my intention to make this accidental mention!" said the culprit, trying to back away, but there was nowhere for him to go; he had backed up against the garden wall.

"Spare us your whines, half-breed. A good hard kicking's what you need!" The hunchback grabbed the bruised goblin's arms and pinned them behind his back.

The goblin howled as Toadface drove a heavy fist into his stomach.

Tanya flinched. "Stop it!"

But Toadface did not stop—and Tanya did not know how to make him. She watched, helpless as he delivered blow upon blow on his poor companion.

When Toadface had finished, panting and sweating from the exertion, the bruised goblin was left weeping in a heap on the ground. He had sustained several cuts to his face and was bleeding profusely, his lower lip split and swollen. Tears were streaming down his cheeks, mingling with the blood congealing in his beard.

"You brutes!" said Tanya, as the goblin's sobs gradually subsided into whimpers. Setting her book down on the rock garden, she pulled a crumpled tissue from her pocket and knelt down in front of him. He shrank back in fear.

"There's no cause for alarm. I don't mean any harm," she said, reaching for his bloodied face. He allowed her to dab at his cuts but continued to whimper softly.

Tanya handed the crimson-stained tissue to the goblin. It was quite clear now where the other bruises had come from. She stood up and turned to face the other two goblins.

"Touch him again and my dog will bite. And then we'll see how well you fight."

Oberon gave a timely growl, but remained hidden behind her all the same.

"Brunswick is not worth defending, his stupidity is never-ending," said the hunchback.

Toadface scowled. Tanya watched, waiting for him to attack the hunchback for letting the name slip, but he didn't, and she knew then that though he was the leader, he was also the kind of coward who chose the easy target. He saw her eyeing him disgustedly and grinned.

"You may be smiling smugly now, but you'll get what you deserve somehow," said Tanya, the words popping into her head from out of nowhere.

Toadface stopped smiling, and there was a horrible hawking noise in his throat. He spat in Tanya's direction, the yellow-green phlegm missing her by only inches.

"You've said quite enough today. Now leave us and be on your way."

Tanya looked into his hateful face and decided to leave. She picked up her book and flung the wooden gate open, sidestepping the goblins, and headed onward toward the forest. She had taken only a few steps when a hesitant voice called after her.

"The color red protects you here, but in the woods there's more to fear."

Tanya spun around. Brunswick hovered just inside the gate, still holding the bloodied tissue to his face.

"What do you mean? Is it something you've seen?" she called, but the hunchback forced Brunswick back into the garden and slammed the gate shut. She stood unmoving for a moment, but knew it would be pointless going back to question them. The warning had probably already cost Brunswick dearly.

❦❦

The morning dew glistened as Tanya kicked through the grass, the wetness seeping through her sandals and onto her toes. She settled beside a hazel thicket, listening to the trickling of the brook close by. Oberon flopped down beside her, panting heavily, and she fondly scratched his head.

From the depths of the woods a gunshot sounded. She looked up and knew it to be Warwick out hunting. More shots followed, fading farther into the distance. Behind her an animal rustled in the hedge. Oberon's ears twitched. He ambled over to the little stream and lapped at the crystal-clear water.

Tanya yawned and stretched, then opened the book. Remembering what she had read before, she went straight to the index, then frowned. What should have been a coherent list of contents and their corresponding page numbers was now a meaningless mass of words and figures, none of it making any sense. With increasing anxiety she thumbed through the book. Every page was the same: full of jumbled text.

The entire contents of the fat volume—with its invaluable information on fairies—had been completely scrambled. With a groan of despair, Tanya recalled placing the book down for those brief moments when she had tended to Brunswick. The hunchback must have tampered with it while she was preoccupied.

The book was useless.

A twig snapped crisply in the bushes, and she started.

"Hello?" she called.

Silence.

Tanya shook herself mentally. It must have been some wild animal, a deer perhaps. There was another snap, nearer now, followed by a rustle. Oberon sniffed the air, his ears pricking up.

A rabbit shot out from the bushes, darting right under the dog's twitching nose, then through the shallow part of the brook. Oberon barked delightedly, then took chase, dashing through the stream and into the forest.

Tanya sprang to her feet, still clutching the book in distress.

"Oberon! Get back here!"

But Oberon had no intention of returning, not until he had caught the rabbit at least. Then someone stumbled out from the bushes, startling her a second time.

"You!"

A sheepish Fabian brushed grass and leaves from his hair and clothes, his normally pale face flooded pink.

"Why are you spying on me?" yelled Tanya.

"I wasn't spying. I was looking for, er... butterflies and things."

"Is this what you call *observation*? You were watching me!" With an angry yell, Tanya flung the useless book to the ground. Fabian watched her, an eyebrow raised.

In the distance, another gunshot sounded. She looked toward the forest in alarm, giving Fabian one last glare before stalking in the direction of the trees.

"Surely you're not going in there?" he said.

"Thanks to you I don't have a choice," said Tanya, her temper rising further. "My dog is in there—and so is Warwick—with a gun!" She quickened her pace, leaving a stunned Fabian behind.

"Thanks to me? What did I do?"

Tanya turned back and rounded on him.

"I'll tell you what you did. You were so busy spying on me that you startled a rabbit in the hedge, and now Oberon has chased it into the forest!"

"Well…he didn't *have* to chase it," said Fabian, but then his voice trailed off. For a moment he looked as if he were struggling to make a decision, then he began to jog after her.

"I'm coming with you. But if Warwick finds out we've been in these woods—"

"You'll have a lot more than Warwick to worry about if anything happens to my dog! I'll…I'll…"

She broke off as tears began to sting her eyes.

"We'll find him," said Fabian. "Warwick wouldn't shoot him, anyway."

"How do *you* know? He could mistake him for a deer or something!"

"The dog's more like a donkey than a deer," Fabian muttered.

At that moment Tanya would have slapped him if it hadn't been for a further round of shots cracking in the air. She broke into a sprint. Fabian followed, pausing to use the stepping stones to cross the brook. Tanya ran straight through it, soaking her feet but not caring. They sped onward, Fabian eventually taking the lead. Gradually the trees grew thicker, taller, and closer together. It was cool and dark between them, and small creatures rustled in the undergrowth as they passed through and disturbed them.

"Oberon!" Tanya yelled. A flock of birds scattered above, squawking at the sudden noise.

"Do you think we ought to shout like that?" said Fabian. "Warwick's bound to hear us."

Tanya looked at him scornfully. "How else do you expect to find the dog?"

The woods were silent. They moved farther in, calling the dog's name, twisting and turning through the densely growing trees, dead wood crackling underfoot. Whispering came from all around, and Tanya knew that it wasn't just the trees. With each step she could feel unseen eyes upon them.

Looking up, she sensed movement above. On one of the lower branches, a birdlike fairy crouched at the edge of its nest, its bright black eyes fixed, staring straight at Fabian. From inside the nest, the cries of its young could be heard, demanding to be fed. Tanya quickly saw that, as with the goblins, her red T-shirt was shielding her from its attention. The creature saw only Fabian, and as he unknowingly blundered nearer, it began chattering a warning at him to stay away.

"We must be near a nest of some sort," Fabian whispered, looking around for the source of the noise. "I can't see a bird anywhere, though."

As he drew closer to the nest, the fairy's chattering escalated into a harsh, insistent threat. Tanya watched helplessly, knowing that to speak and warn him would betray her to the fairy and surrender the protection of her red T-shirt—but what followed left her with no choice. Momentarily, the creature left its nest and vanished into a nook in the tree bark. It reappeared seconds later armed with an assortment of ammunition that it proceeded to hurl viciously at Fabian's head.

"Look out!" Tanya cried, lunging forward to push Fabian to safety.

A spray of objects flew through the air, narrowly missing them to become embedded in the ground. Pebbles, acorns, pinecones, balled-up litter, a heavy silver brooch, jagged shards of broken glass, and bottle caps lay scattered around them.

"What happened back there?" Fabian gasped, as Tanya pulled him out of throwing range.

"A magpie," she answered. "We got too close. It must have disturbed the contents of its nest as it flew off." She looked back at the nest as they hurried away. The fairy watched her coldly. Its fierce chattering had stopped, but it continued to call out. Tanya did not need to be able to understand it to know that it was issuing a warning to any fairies nearby in the neighboring trees, communicating her presence to them. She was now defenseless—and exposed.

"Come on," she muttered. "Keep moving."

They headed onward and away. Above them, Tanya was aware of the furious whispering and calling in the trees, as the word of her presence spread throughout the woods. She forced herself to try and be calm, but the panic inside her was rising.

"Listen," said Fabian, stopping dead. "Do you hear that?"

"Voices?" Tanya whispered.

Fabian frowned and shook his head. "A dog."
Faint barking sounded from far away. "This way!"

Tanya battled to keep up with him; the sandals she was wearing were highly unsuitable for running through the woods. Already she had sustained several cuts to her feet. Branches snagged on her clothes and tore at her hair. The fairies in the trees mocked her.

"He went that way!"

"No, *that* way!"

"I saw him come this way!"

Tanya did not look back. She knew they were all lying. She did not dare to take her eyes off Fabian.

"There's something up ahead," he shouted.

Tanya saw him stop and stand still, and she quickened her pace until she drew level with him. An ugly metal railing was just visible through the trees. They walked toward it wordlessly, coming into a little clearing.

The railings went around in a circle, with a diameter of about four meters. Inside, there was a huge hole in the ground roughly three meters wide. A small tree was growing beside it, tilting inward. Half its roots were exposed and it looked unstable, as if a heavy gust of wind would send it tumbling into the cavern below. Fixed to the railings was a worn wooden sign that said DANGER! DO NOT ENTER!

They had found one of the catacombs.

Fabian began to circle the railings, his scientific mind automatically trying to estimate how deep the thing went into the ground. When he had done a full lap he stooped and picked up a pebble, then hurled it over the railings. They both listened as it plummeted soundlessly. Neither of them heard it hit the bottom. Fabian gave a low whistle, and then a strange look crossed his face.

"What?" said Tanya. Her heart missed a beat as she followed his gaze. Her worries about the fairies were forgotten instantly.

One of the metal posts was missing, leaving a gap in the railings large enough for a small person to squeeze through. Large enough for a dog to get through.

"No!" Tanya's voice choked in her throat. Suddenly her legs would no longer support her, and she sank to the ground in despair. Fabian stood rooted to the spot, his eyes glued to the gap in the railing.

"He...he wouldn't have gone through there... would he?"

"He might have. If he was chasing the rabbit, he might have..."

"*Oberon!*" Fabian shouted.

The woods remained silent.

"Let's keep looking."

Tanya shook her head, silent tears streaming down her cheeks. She didn't even care what Fabian might think.

"I can't. What if he's down there, injured? I can't leave him."

Deep down she knew that if Oberon had fallen

into the hole there was no way he could have survived it, but she could not bear to leave the spot.

Fabian studied the gap in the railings, chewing his lip. "He's not down there."

Tanya looked up through her tears, sniffing noisily. "You're just saying that."

"No, I'm not." He knelt beside her. "Think about it. He's a big dog. The gap is wide enough for him to get through, but only just. If he did come this way, he would have had to slow down to squeeze through it, and so he would have seen the hole in time. Dogs are intelligent animals, especially Dobermans. And the leaves and twigs around the hole are undisturbed. If he'd fallen down it there would be claw marks."

He gave her an encouraging smile.

Tanya gave him a rather watery smile in return, feeling a ray of hope. She scrambled to her feet and wiped her face, leaving a streak of dirt on her cheek.

"Come on, then," she said.

❧❧

They had been walking another twenty minutes when Tanya noticed something.

"Listen."

Fabian stopped and cocked his head to one side. "I can't hear anything."

"Exactly. The gunshots have stopped. Warwick must have gone back to the house."

"Good," said Fabian, looking relieved. "That means we can shout as loudly as we want. *Oberon!*"

They yelled until their voices were hoarse and their throats were sore, but still there was no sign of the missing dog. The hope that Tanya had felt earlier was steadily diminishing. She had been certain that they would have found him by now. All she wanted to do was find him and get out—the longer they remained in the woods, the more the chances of another attack by the fairies increased. Then another alarming thought occurred to her.

"Fabian? Do you know the way out of here?"

"I was hoping you would remember."

They stared at each other dumbly.

"Of course I don't know the way out," she said at last. "I've never been in here before."

"Neither have I," said Fabian.

"So we're lost then," said Tanya, feeling weak again as the clarity of the situation hit her. She envisaged wandering in the woods all day, then still being trapped at nightfall, and suddenly, she was glad she was not alone.

"We'll follow the stream," said Fabian. "The stream will lead us out at some point."

"At *some* point? Do you know how big this forest is? I can't even remember the last time I saw the stream; it was ages ago!"

"Have you got any better suggestions?" said Fabian testily.

Tanya scowled and shook her head.

They set off in search of the stream, ducking under low branches and listening for any sign of running water. As the minutes ticked by, even Fabian was beginning to look worried as the truth finally dawned. They were lost: completely, utterly, and hopelessly lost.

"This is impossible," said Tanya, sitting down on a tree stump to examine a bulging blister on her foot. "We're never going to find our way out." As she spoke, she saw, to her horror, a small mound of grassy earth scurrying along the ground to reposition itself at the base of a fallen tree. Moments later, a clump of weeds and tuft of wildflowers scuttled across her path to switch places.

She stifled a terrified sob. The fairies were deliberately losing them, drawing them farther and farther into the woods by confusing them. They must have begun doing so the moment she and Fabian had entered the forest.

"We're lost," she said in a small voice. "We're not going to find the way out!"

"We will," said Fabian. "It just might take a little longer than we expected."

"You don't understand," said Tanya. She battled to keep her voice from rising, and failed. "Before you know it there'll be a search party out looking for us. Then we'll be in even deeper trouble!"

Fabian sighed and looked at his watch. "We've still got plenty of time before it gets dark. Let's keep going."

Tanya hauled herself to her feet, and limped after him. As she did so a glint of silver caught her eye. "Wait."

Fabian paused, looking mildly irritated.

She pointed. "I think it's another one of the catacombs."

The metal railings came into view as they drew nearer. This hole was significantly smaller than the first, and did not look nearly so threatening. Tanya was relieved to see that the railings were intact the whole way around. There were no gaps in this, dog-sized or otherwise.

"How many of these are there, exactly?" Tanya wondered aloud.

"Seven." Fabian craned his neck to peer into the cavern. "I'd love to know how deep this thing goes."

Tanya made a face. "I wouldn't. Just think of all the—"

"Quiet," said Fabian, holding his finger to his lips. "There's someone over there. Look—in the clearing!"

A girl in a green dress with long, dark hair was walking slowly toward them, bending down every now and then to add a wildflower to the bunch in her arms. For a moment Tanya thought the girl had not yet realized she was no longer alone, but then she looked straight at Tanya, smiling as she approached.

Tanya's initial relief at seeing another human being was short-lived, replaced with suspicion as she recalled the passage on glamour in her grand-mother's book. She scrutinized the girl, searching for any clue that this might be some fey disguise, but there was nothing about her that suggested anything out of the ordinary.

"Why do you think she's here all alone?" Tanya whispered, trying not to move her lips in case the girl saw that they were speaking about her.

Fabian did not answer right away. "I don't know. She looks like she could be a gypsy—she might be a relation of the old gypsy woman. She lives in these woods."

"Mad Morag?"

"That's right. The one who gave you the compass. Which, by the way, I looked up in an antique book of Warwick's. It's worthless."

Tanya looked toward the girl. "Shall we ask her if she's seen Oberon?"

Fabian nodded. "Even if she hasn't she might be able to help us find our way out. She seems to know her way around pretty well." He stepped away from the railings and toward the girl, Tanya behind him.

The girl eyed them and smiled again. She looked to be in her early teens, with creamy skin and thickly lashed dark eyes. "Are you lost?" she asked softly.

"We're looking for our dog," Fabian said. His voice was quavering and unusually self-conscious. "He ran off, and we can't find him. And now...yes, we're lost," he admitted finally.

The girl nodded. "I saw a dog come this way." Her voice was quiet and well spoken, somehow sounding older than her years.

"When?" Tanya said urgently.

"Not long ago," the girl replied. "Just a few minutes."

"Was he all right? He didn't look hurt, did he?"

The girl trained her dark eyes on Tanya. "No, he looked fine. Come with me, I'll help you look for him. I know these parts well. Once we have the dog I can lead you out of the forest."

Tanya shot a relieved glance at Fabian; then they began to follow the girl, who was moving quickly ahead, weaving in and out of the trees. Once or twice Tanya thought she saw faces in the bark of trees, or the limblike movement of a branch, but no longer felt able to distinguish between that which was fey and her own paranoia.

She noticed that this part of the forest was very quiet, and the trees seemed bigger and older somehow, the colors richer and the woodland scents heavier. They neared a huge tree, with a hole in its trunk wide enough to walk through.

"I wonder if this is the tree," Fabian said. "It's sturdy enough."

"What tree?"

"You know, *the* tree!" He pulled a ghoulish face. "The one people used to be hanged from. There must be one. How else do you think the forest got its name? Go on, you go through first."

"I don't want to," Tanya protested, but Fabian's hand was between her shoulder blades, urging her through. Inside it was dark and smelled musty and damp, and she could hear the scuttling of creatures that were nesting there. In her haste to get out quickly she caught her foot on a root, and stumbled back through into the light.

A rough hand grabbed her shoulder.

Tanya yelled and kicked out as hard as she could. There was a horrible thud as her foot made contact, and her assailant gave a low groan. Fabian stumbled through, reaching for her blindly, then stopped dead.

"Warwick," he gasped.

Tanya looked up into Warwick's face. He was rubbing his shin with his free hand. Sitting meekly behind him was Oberon, a length of thin rope joined to his collar as a makeshift leash.

"That hurt," Warwick told her through gritted teeth. "Don't do it again." He turned to Fabian, eyes flashing with anger. "And it's *Dad* to you."

Tanya wrenched herself free of his grasp and fell upon Oberon. The dog licked her lovingly, not quite sure what all the attention was for but enjoying it all the same. Fabian reached over and patted him, relieved.

"How did you find him?" Tanya asked.

"You're both in big trouble," Warwick growled, ignoring the question. It was clear he was seething.

Tanya felt a sudden jolt of fear. She had never seen the man so angry.

"How many times have I told you, boy? These woods are dangerous!"

"It's my fault," said Tanya, before Fabian had the chance to speak. "Oberon ran off, and I panicked. I—I asked Fabian to come with me."

Warwick eyed her coldly. "You should have waited for me. This forest is no place to be if you don't know your way around."

"I'm sorry," she replied, hanging her head, which seemed to placate him a little.

"It's lucky you were wearing that," he said, jerking his head toward her red T-shirt. He gave Fabian a scathing once-over. "If you were wearing green like this idiot I wouldn't have spotted you so easily—even though you were making enough noise to wake the dead."

"Oh," Tanya muttered. For a moment she had thought Warwick had known the real reason she had chosen to wear red—not that it had done her much good in the end. Fabian looked down at his brown and green clothes uncomfortably.

"Best be getting back," said Warwick, although his tone was marginally less angry now. He turned and began to walk briskly.

She exchanged glances with Fabian behind Warwick's back. He was looking glum, and although she was glad he had been with her, she was sorry that he was going to get into trouble.

"Hang on a minute," said Fabian suddenly. He turned back to look the way they had just come. "Where did that girl go?"

Warwick spun around. "What girl?"

"There was a girl," said Tanya. "She saw Oberon a few minutes ago—she offered to help us find him."

"She can't have seen him," said Warwick. "He's been with me for the best part of an hour." He scanned the trees. "Where is she?"

"I don't know," Tanya replied. "She must not have seen that we stopped, and kept on walking."

"What did she look like?"

"Pretty," Fabian said, a hazy look in his eyes. "Really pretty."

Warwick said no more. Instead he turned and continued to stomp through the woods. Tanya and Fabian plodded after him in silence. Tanya watched as a tiny fairy, much like the one she had buried, landed gently on Warwick's back and collected a downy feather caught in his hair, then flew back up into the trees to make its nest. Tanya stayed close to him, feeling safer, but her dislike of Warwick left her confused and a little resentful of the feeling.

The journey back to Elvesden Manor was long and weary, but thankfully the fairies troubled them no more. For the second time in as many days, Tanya was glad to see her grandmother's house.

7

As soon as Warwick had closed the garden gate behind them, Tanya untied the rope from Oberon's collar, and then the four of them battled through the overgrown weeds toward the house.

"I suppose you're going to have to tell my grandmother about this," Tanya muttered as they trudged into the kitchen. Its familiar smell was oddly comforting.

Warwick turned to face her, his expression grim. "Under normal circumstances I would. But I understand you only went into the forest to find your dog, not out of disobedience, so the matter can stay between us."

Tanya stared at him in surprise. Fabian looked equally flabbergasted.

"There's one condition." Warwick's eyes bored into them. "You promise me now, both of you, that you'll never set foot in those woods again."

They both promised readily. Neither harbored any desire to repeat the experience. Apparently satisfied, Warwick turned up the volume on a small portable radio on the windowsill.

"Other news now. Reports are coming in of a suspected child abduction from the maternity ward of an Essex hospital. Security camera checks have so far proved futile, with evidence that the cameras had been tampered with prior to the incident. It's been confirmed that the child in question—a boy thought to be little more than a week old—had been abandoned near the hospital shortly after birth, and was being cared for by staff there.

"Police are asking for the mother to come forward, and have also issued a description of a teenage girl who was seen acting suspiciously in the reception area prior to the incident. She is now wanted for questioning. An eyewitness described the girl as—"

Warwick turned the radio off and rubbed a hand over his bristly chin.

"I hate the news," he said softly, then turned and left, leaving Tanya and Fabian alone.

"Oh, no," Fabian said in an exasperated voice. He was craning his neck to view his sleeve. "My best T-shirt. It's ripped! Look at it." He sighed in annoyance, then looked at her hopefully. "Are you any good at sewing?"

"Terrible," she answered.

"I'll leave it here later on," he said thoughtfully. "Maybe Florence will mend it."

"Thanks for coming with me," she said, after Warwick's footsteps had faded away.

Fabian shrugged. "It was partly my fault anyway. If I hadn't scared the rabbit it might not have happened."

"But you still came. Even though you knew we'd get into trouble if we got caught." She shuddered, remembering how easily they had become lost, and the mysterious black holes in the ground.

"I couldn't let you wander off alone," said Fabian, his eyes darkening. "People have disappeared in there."

"I know. I read about one of them, a girl with an unusual name. Something Bloom."

"It was Morwenna."

"That's it," said Tanya. "Morwenna Bloom. I read about her in a newspaper clipping that fell out of one of the books in the library."

"What did it say?" asked Fabian, interested all of a sudden.

"It just said she had vanished in the woods, and that people thought she had fallen into one of the catacombs," said Tanya. "Surely you know the story? You knew her name."

"I was just making sure it was the same person. So many people have gone missing it's hard to remember all of them." Fabian removed his glasses and polished them on his grubby shirt. "She was the youngest person ever to disappear in those woods. It was because of her that the railings were put up." He paused, and replaced his glasses. "I suppose you know she was Florence's best friend?"

"*What?*" said Tanya. "But I showed her the clipping—she didn't say anything about being best friends." She remembered the strange look on her grandmother's face—now it made sense. "She said they used to be friends but had drifted apart. Are you sure they were best friends?"

"Positive," said Fabian. "I've overheard her talking to Warwick about it more than once, but whenever I come into the room they stop. It probably brought back too many memories. Maybe it traumatized her—maybe she finds it too painful to talk about."

Tanya was silent, flooded with guilt. "How many people have disappeared in the woods, then?" she asked finally, unable to contain her own morbid curiosity.

"Loads," said Fabian. "Obviously not as many since the railings have been there, but still a few. Mainly it was poachers from Tickey End, or people passing through. There are probably numerous others that are unaccounted for though. Travelers, gypsies... too many cats and dogs to count.

"And the holes aren't really catacombs." Fabian walked to the sink to wash his hands. "A 'catacomb' is defined as an ancient burial chamber. The holes are actually called deneholes. There are quite a few of them scattered over the country, especially in the south of England. Over the years people began to refer to them as the catacombs because so many people vanished there."

"That's horrible," she said. She joined Fabian at the sink and caught sight of herself in a small tilting mirror on the windowsill. Her face was tearstained and dirty, and her hair hung in tangles.

"Listen," said Fabian, in a low voice. "There's something I want to show you, but you've got to promise not to say anything to Warwick or Florence."

"Say anything about what?"

"I found something up on the second floor. I wasn't sure if I could trust you until today."

"What did you find?" Tanya asked.

Fabian shook his head. "Promise first."

"Fine, I promise," said Tanya, irritated. "I barely speak to either of them anyway."

Fabian checked the hallway.

"Let's go up there now—it looks like Warwick's gone right back out again."

"Fabian," Tanya began, "after what we've been through today can you just tell me what it is first so I can decide if it's worth the effort? I'm tired, and fed up, and I'm not going on some harebrained mission before I've had a shower and got changed."

Fabian's blue eyes danced with mischief.

"It's worth the effort, I promise you."

"Give me ten minutes," she said with a sigh. "I'll meet you up there."

❧❧

The second floor was even dustier than the rest of the house, due to the fact that usually Amos and Warwick were the only people who ventured up there. Mounted on the wall at the top of the stairs was the head of a majestic stag. This was only the second time Tanya had seen it, but both times, as she looked into its sad brown eyes, it made her want to weep. She dropped her gaze, concentrating on the threadbare carpet until she reached the top of the stairs. Fabian was waiting in a small, darkened alcove in which a chair sat in front of a dingy wall tapestry.

"This is it."

Tanya examined the filthy old tapestry that hung from floor to ceiling against the wall. Apart from its size it was nondescript, and so faded and dusty that it was impossible to make out what it was actually a picture of.

"Wow," Tanya said, her voice dripping with sarcasm.

Fabian pursed his lips. "Not the tapestry, idiot. What's *behind* it."

Tanya gave him a look, and pulled the tapestry back. A door of solid oak lay behind it, set back into the wall.

"When did you find this?"

"Yesterday. I can't believe I never knew it was here before."

"Well, no one really comes up here," said Tanya. "Even when we used to search the house for the secret passages we never checked the second floor. We were always too afraid of coming up here. Where does it lead?"

"That's what we're about to find out," said Fabian.

"Oh, I get it. You were too scared to investigate on your own."

"Actually, no," Fabian said coolly. "The door is locked."

"So how do you propose we get through it?"

"With this." From his pocket, Fabian produced an ancient-looking key. "It's a skeleton key. It'll open every door in the house."

"I know what a skeleton key is," Tanya snapped. "But what are *you* doing with it?"

"I borrowed it. From Warwick."

"You mean you *stole* it. There's no way he'd let you use that."

"Whatever. Let's just make the most of it before he finds out it's missing."

He inserted the key into the door. It gave a soft click as he turned it. "See?" he whispered triumphantly. "Good as new. Come on."

As Fabian pushed the door open a waft of damp, musty air descended upon them. He stepped through the darkened doorway, beckoning for Tanya to follow.

"What is it?" she asked, moving forward. "A room?"

Fabian pressed a finger to his lips as Tanya came through the doorway into complete darkness. She stood waiting awkwardly as he carefully arranged the tapestry in its correct position and then closed the door softly behind them.

"Now we can't see a thing!" she hissed.

"Wait," said Fabian, and she could hear him fumbling in his pockets in the darkness. There was a small click and then there was light. Fabian stood grinning, holding a small but obviously powerful pocket flashlight.

"I knew this would come in handy one day."

As her eyes adjusted, Tanya could see that it was not a room they were standing in but a narrow passage that led off to the left and the right. To the right there was a set of stairs leading up.

Fabian shone the flashlight at the walls. "It's damp in here."

"And the air is bad too," said Tanya, wrinkling her nose. "I wonder what this passage was used for... maybe this is one of the secret passages."

"It would've been hidden a lot better than that if it was meant to be secret," Fabian said scornfully. "I think it's the old servants' staircase."

"But I thought it had been blocked off," said Tanya.

"It is. Or at least, the main entrance in the kitchen

is. Florence had it all closed up years ago—she said it would prevent so much heat escaping in the winter."

"I thought the entire staircase was blocked off, though," said Tanya. "I didn't realize that it was only partially filled in."

"Me neither."

"Which way should we go?"

Fabian aimed the flashlight at the flight of stairs. "We're already on the highest floor, so those steps must lead up to the attic. I think we should go this way." He pointed the flashlight at the corridor that led off to the left, lifting the light to the walls. Huge patches of mold had formed from years of moisture in the air. A flash of light dazzled Tanya's eyes.

"What was that?"

"The light from the flashlight reflected off a window," said Fabian.

"Window?"

"Look closely and you can see the ivy has grown over it—that's why there's no light."

He was right. As Tanya looked at the window, filthy with years of grime, she could see the mass of entangled leaves growing wildly over the glass from the outside, blocking out virtually all daylight.

Fabian took a step farther into the hallway. "Be careful. This passage is very old. It might not be completely safe."

They began to edge into the darkness tentatively, the wooden floor groaning under their weight.

Things scuffled in the woodwork, and Tanya found herself wondering whether it was mice or fairies—and trying to decide which would be worse.

They had walked only a short distance when he stopped.

"There's a door on my left." He rattled it. "It's locked."

"Try the key," Tanya suggested.

Fabian bent down and shone the tiny flashlight into the keyhole. "I think the key is in the lock on the other side."

"So use the skeleton key to push it out."

"That won't work," said Fabian. "Because we might need the key that's on the other side. Not all the doors have the original locks."

"Come on then," said Tanya. "Let's see if there are any more doors farther on."

"Wait." Fabian handed her the flashlight and began to rummage through his pockets again.

"What are you doing?" Tanya asked, watching as he removed a folded sheet of paper and a small reel of wire.

"Oldest trick in the book," Fabian muttered, unfolding the paper.

As Tanya looked more closely, it was evident that the piece of paper had been folded and unfolded many times. It was limp and the creases were well worn.

"What's that for?" she asked again, but Fabian did not answer. He was now busy unraveling the wire and twisting it into a thin prong of about four inches.

"That should do it."

He placed the paper at the foot of the door, then slowly slid it through the gap underneath and on to the other side, leaving an inch or so still visible. Carefully, he took the wire and inserted it into the keyhole very slowly. After he wiggled it around for a few seconds there was a small thud, then Fabian pulled on the sheet of paper until it reappeared under the door—with the key sitting neatly in the middle of it.

"That's brilliant!" said Tanya, staring at the key in amazement.

"Not really," said Fabian, with a modest grin. "I read about it once in an old detective novel. It's just common sense."

Tanya eyed the well-folded piece of paper.

"You've obviously done it before."

Fabian picked up the key and the paper, which he folded again and put carefully back into his pocket. "Once or twice. Although if the key doesn't land right, it can bounce off the sheet of paper. We were lucky this time." He fitted the key into the lock and turned it. The door opened, and the two of them stepped into a small, dark room.

As with the secret staircase, there was no light from the window; it was completely wreathed with ivy from the outside. An ornately carved wooden chest stood beneath the window, coated in a gray blanket of dust. There was a huge wardrobe in the corner, one of its doors open slightly as if someone had left the room in a hurry and never again returned.

In the center of the room stood a beautiful crib, complete with a crocheted set of bedclothes that had been hastily turned back. Abandoned in the crib lay a tiny, raggedy bear, and as Tanya reached in and gently picked it up, she saw a jagged rip through which a dirty lump of stuffing protruded.

"It was a nursery," she said.

Something moved within the bear's stuffing. With a surprised squeak, Tanya flung it back into the crib.

"What's the matter?" Fabian asked.

"I think there are mice nesting in here."

"Pretty creepy room, if you ask me," said Fabian, lifting the lid of the chest. A cloud of dust shot into the air, causing him to sneeze three times in quick succession. Inside the chest there was another bear, several dolls, and an old spinning top. A jack-in-the-box lay broken, its spring full of rust.

"You're right," said Tanya, feeling a sudden shiver. "It is creepy."

"I never knew this room was here," said Fabian, moving toward the main door. "I wonder where we are."

He opened the door cautiously, and Tanya heard him exclaim.

"Come and look at this."

She moved closer to the door and looked where Fabian was pointing the flashlight. The doorway was barred by a large area of solid wood.

"It's the back of the dresser . . . it's been moved in

front of the door. Someone went to a lot of effort to make sure this room was never found."

*"Because of the bad thing,"* a muffled, rasping voice said suddenly.

Tanya stood stock still, watching Fabian for a reaction. There was none; he had not heard. Turning slowly, she moved back to the crib. Her eyelids twitched as she drew nearer. There was a series of small movements, and then a small, pinched face appeared from within the stuffing of the bear in the crib. Its skin was dusty and gray, and Tanya found it impossible to tell whether it was male or female. Her eyes were drawn to the creature's protruding, rodentlike front teeth.

"Bad thing," it croaked, eyeing her reproachfully. "The bad thing that happened here." With one suspicious eye firmly on Tanya, the creature delved into the depths of its nest and pulled something out. "Long time ago. Long, long time."

Bile rose in Tanya's throat when she realized that the thing it had retrieved from its nest was a half-eaten mouse. "What bad thing?" she whispered to it, careful not to let Fabian hear.

"Not telling," it muttered nastily. The sound of crunching bones reached Tanya's ears and she backed away from the crib. The tangy, metallic scent of blood followed her.

"Let's get out of here," she said, as the creature chewed and sucked. "This room has a nasty feel to it."

Fabian closed the door quietly, and the two of them headed back to the servants' staircase. Tanya stepped through gladly but Fabian paused, shining the flashlight around one last time before leaving the room.

"What's that?"

"Fabian! Let's go!" Tanya hissed, but Fabian went past the crib and peered at something on the wall.

"Oh," he said. "It's just an old embroidery."

"What does it say?"

"I can't read very well in this light," said Fabian, removing his glasses and polishing them.

Tanya walked over, ignoring the muttering from the crib, and squinted at the cross-stitch on the wall. It was white, or at least it had been once, and embroidered on it were pale pink roses and the words, "Congratulations on the birth of your daughter," with a date underneath.

"That's unusual," said Fabian, once he had replaced his glasses. "The date of birth is the twenty-ninth of February, which means the baby was born on the extra day of a leap year."

Tanya frowned. "February twenty-ninth is my mother's birthday."

"Oh," said Fabian. "This must have been your mother's nursery then." He sniggered suddenly. "Does that mean you only have to buy her a birthday card once every four years?"

"No," Tanya replied, shaking her head. "We celebrate her birthday on the first of March, although she always jokes that I'm older than her."

In silence they went back through to the darkened passage. The next door they tried must have had a newer lock, and Fabian's technique was rendered useless as there was no key on the other side. They did manage to open a number of other doors, though most turned out to be empty rooms or contained nothing of interest.

When they came to Amos's room, the radio was blaring on the other side of the door. They crept past, trying to ignore the old man's rants and mutterings.

Down on the first floor there were fewer rooms that remained a mystery, as this was the floor where everybody except Amos slept. The last door they came to was just before a flight of steps leading down to the ground floor, and it was unlocked. Inside, the light streaming through the windows dazzled their eyes.

The ivy had been trimmed back and the room was well-maintained. Dust sheets covered every item of furniture, which Fabian immediately set about throwing off. A huge four-poster bed stood in the middle, surrounded by spectacular carved wooden furniture. A luxurious fur rug lay before the fireplace, and a double portrait of a stern-looking man and a young woman hung above the mantelpiece.

Tanya's eyes widened. "Whose room is *this*?"

"This must be the Elvesdens' room," said Fabian. "I've heard Florence talking about it before, but I've never been allowed to see it. It was the bedchamber of Lord and Lady Elvesden. That's their portrait."

Tanya studied the painting above the mantelpiece and took a sharp breath as she looked into the eyes of her ancestors. It was the first time she had ever seen a picture of them.

EDWARD AND ELIZABETH ELVESDEN, read the inscription in a brass plate on the frame. The man's surly eyes seemed to bore into her, and the woman looked as though she must have felt uncomfortable in his presence. With a jolt Tanya noticed a silver charm bracelet on the painted woman's wrist; the same one that was now fastened on her own, two centuries later. She looked down at it, sparkling in the sun. She'd polished it until it shone. Beautiful though it was, it was an unsettling feeling to be wearing the jewelry of a dead ancestor.

"How come it's been kept like this?" Tanya asked. "With all the original furniture and everything?"

"I don't know...I suppose because they were the first owners of the house. Elvesden was one of the richest men in the county; this house was even built to his specifications. Years ago Florence used to make a bit of money from showing people around—it's a historic building, you know. This must have been one of the most important rooms in the house."

Tanya stared at the portrait. "They made an odd couple."

"They certainly did," said Fabian.

"I wonder what they were like. I wonder if they were happy here."

"I doubt it."

Tanya looked at him curiously. "What makes you say that?"

"Well, you must have heard," said Fabian. "They hadn't been married long when it happened."

"When what happened?"

"I thought you knew," said Fabian. "About Lady Elvesden?"

"All I know is that she lived here when the house was first built, and that she and her husband had one son," said Tanya. "Why? What else happened?"

"She went mad in this house ... supposedly."

"What ... what made her go mad?" Tanya asked, unable to tear her eyes away from the troubled young woman in the portrait.

"There's a bit of a dispute as to whether she was mad at all," said Fabian. "She kept journals—split them all up into parts and stashed them around the house, apparently. And she was quite clever about it too. One part was found sewn into a dress she'd owned. Another was hidden behind a baseboard. But several parts were never accounted for. They're believed to have been found and destroyed by her husband."

"Why did he destroy them?" Tanya asked. "What did they say?"

Fabian shrugged. "Florence won't disclose exactly

what was in the journals to anyone—although thanks to a leak there's a pretty good idea. In fact, the diaries were a big part of the reason she stopped allowing the public to view the house.

"Do you remember when the old stables in the courtyard were pulled down, a few years back? Well, halfway through the job one of the contractors found a segment from the diary wedged into some of the old stonework. He was immediately removed from the premises with strict instructions not to repeat anything he might have read, though if you ask me I think Florence paid him to keep his mouth shut. Of course, it ended up getting out eventually."

"What did it say?"

"Put it this way, it didn't look good. Elizabeth had been visiting the local wise woman, or cunning woman as they were known back then, to learn about herbs and medicine and such. Apparently, she had a gift for healing and wanted to develop it— something that was frowned upon by a number of the townsfolk.

"There was always talk of witchcraft whenever the wise woman was mentioned. Although the worst of the witch hunts were over by this time, Lord Elvesden knew that it was only a matter of time before disaster struck.

"He forbade Elizabeth to have any dealings with the wise woman, but Elizabeth continued to do as she pleased. She never seemed to care what others thought.

"Eventually, as Elvesden predicted, something happened that placed the two women under suspicion. The wise woman was also a trusted midwife. But then a child she had delivered died shortly after being born. The death was followed by a series of illnesses. It was enough to make people talk witchcraft.

"The wise woman was run out of town and was forced to take residence in the woods. After that she was pretty much left to herself, except for a few townsfolk who sympathized with her and took her food when they could. Without their help she probably would have moved on. Mad Morag is said to be one of her descendants."

"So what happened to Elizabeth?"

"She wasn't so lucky," said Fabian. "Children called her names in the street. People crossed themselves when she passed them. She was even spat at. But through it all she appeared unfazed, even continuing to research the practice of healing by herself. Her husband could see what would happen if she didn't start to behave in a more acceptable way—but Elizabeth would have none of it. And so eventually, Lord Elvesden caved to pressure from his advisors, and had her committed."

Tanya was aghast. "He put her in an *asylum* for researching herbs?"

"It didn't take much in those days," said Fabian. "Lots of perfectly sane women were locked up and left to rot in an asylum on their husband's say-so...

and, well, if they weren't mad when they went in, they usually ended up that way."

"Did she ever get out?" Tanya asked.

Fabian looked almost apologetic then.

"I can't believe Florence hasn't told you any of this."

Tanya felt an impending sense of doom.

"Any of what?"

"Tanya, Elizabeth Elvesden never came out of the asylum. She died in there when she was only twenty-three."

8

Elizabeth Elvesden's death played on Tanya's mind for the remainder of the afternoon. After going back through the servants' passage, she made an excuse to Fabian that she was feeling unwell and headed downstairs, intending to go for a walk outside by the brook to clear her head.

A burning curiosity had ignited inside her. More than anything she wanted to see Elizabeth's journals, and to learn the secrets her grandmother was so eager to keep hidden. Did they have something to do with the "bad thing" the fairy in the nursery had spoken of?

As she passed the library she was so caught up in her own thoughts that she almost didn't notice the hushed voices that were coming from the other side of the door—that is, until she heard her name mentioned.

"...I don't *want* her here, you know that," said her grandmother.

"The sooner she leaves, the better," said another voice, unmistakably Warwick's. "We can't have her here; it's just not an option."

Something—possibly a chair—scraped over the floor, blocking out the next few words.

"...in the woods today," Florence hissed.

"It's lucky I found them when I did," said Warwick.

Tanya stood motionless outside the door. Her grandmother's low voice continued on the other side, oblivious to her new audience.

"I should have listened to you before."

"About what?" Warwick asked gruffly.

"Moving. I'll do it this time—once she goes back. It's getting too much. It's eating away at me. I've been a fool to stay here."

"You'd really move away?" Warwick continued. "Leave all this?"

"I think I'm going to have to," Florence said, and it sounded as if there were tears in her voice. "I don't want to, but I don't see any other way."

"But you love this house. I thought you'd never part with it."

"I do love this house—I always will. When she was born I had such dreams...how all this would be hers one day. But now...how can it be? How can I let Tanya inherit?"

"Have you ever thought about telling her the truth?" Warwick asked.

"How can I?" Florence was flustered now. "I'm a coward. I know I am. I was a coward then and I'm a coward now..."

Footsteps neared the door. Tanya crept back to the stairs in stunned silence. She remembered once hearing a saying that eavesdroppers seldom heard any good of themselves, and it had proved right. She wished with all her heart that she had not heard what had been said, but now she knew she would never forget.

She wasn't welcome. She had pretty much guessed that anyway, but to hear it actually being said was a different thing altogether. There was no going back. It could never be unsaid. She was not wanted. She was a nuisance. An inconvenience. Her grandmother hated her. Hated her to the extent that she was willing to give up a house she loved rather than see her only granddaughter inherit.

The landing was silent as she made her way upstairs, her walk forgotten. Even the lodgers in the grandfather clock did not utter their usual insults. Above, on the second floor, she could hear Amos pacing, as he often did at that time of day. She shut herself in her room and lay down.

Her head swam with her grandmother's words. She hugged her knees to her chest, trying to squash the sickening feeling away, but it remained, along with the haunted sensation she had brought back with her from the two rooms she and Fabian had seen.

Lifting her wrist, she studied the bracelet miserably, wondering why her grandmother had given it to her if she disliked her so. She remembered her grandmother's words about the belief that charms such as these would offer protection. In turn, she studied them, imagining that each had a story to tell about its original owner, and allowed her to glimpse through a window into the past.

Tanya picked through them one by one. Some were easy enough to make associations with; a heart for love, and a ring for marriage. A key for home, or security, perhaps. A mask...a love of the theater? Most were odd and a little unsettling, a sword and a dagger among them. And one made Tanya's throat constrict as though a strand of the manor's ivy had snaked around it: a tiny, engraved cauldron, for which there was only one association she could think of: witchcraft.

Whatever the mysteries behind the bracelet, there was one thing Tanya was certain of: that it could not have granted Elizabeth Elvesden any protection or luck at all.

※

At dinner, Tanya ate with a good appetite that was unexpected given the events of the day. Afterward, her grandmother transferred the plates to the sink and replaced them with a huge basin of fresh strawberries and a jug of thick cream.

"Oh," Warwick groaned, prodding his stomach but eyeing the strawberries longingly. "I couldn't eat another thing."

"Nonsense," said Florence. She set a bowl of strawberries in front of him and ladled cream over them.

Out of the corner of her eye Tanya noticed the lid to the tea caddy lifting, and then the wizened little brownie that lived there peered out. His screwed-up face was like a walnut, half hidden beneath a pile of shaggy, matted hair. The clattering of the dishes had woken him. He shot a disgruntled look in Tanya's direction, then leaned over and stirred the contents of the sugar pot with his cane before vanishing back into the tea caddy.

To Tanya's dismay, Florence then turned and reached for the sugar, sprinkling some on her strawberries and cream before passing it around the table. Tanya immediately handed it to Fabian. There was no way she was using it after the brownie had touched it—and no one present knew her well enough to know whether she would normally add sugar to her strawberries anyway.

Warwick was the first person to take a mouthful. His expression quickly turned to one of disgust. He spat into a napkin.

"It's *salt*!" he said, reaching for the water jug.

"Are you sure?" said Florence.

"Of course I'm sure!"

Fabian's hand was frozen in midair, his mouth slightly open. His eyes were fixed on the spoon in disappointment.

"Who was the last person to refill the sugar bowl?" said Florence.

"I was," said Tanya, guiltily. "I filled it this morning."

Florence snatched the ruined desserts away and began scraping them into the garbage. "For goodness' sake, try to be more observant!"

Tanya bit her lip in anger. She was only glad that Warwick had been the first to taste it. She was furious with him for telling her grandmother about the incident in the forest when he had given his word that it would go no further. She was furious with them both for the callous conversation she had overheard earlier.

Now in a foul mood, Warwick excused himself. Florence left soon after.

Fabian leaned over and prodded Tanya in the side.

"That was definitely sugar in the pot this morning. I had some on my cornflakes."

Tanya stared at him. A lazy grin spread across Fabian's face.

"So when did you switch it?" he asked.

"What?"

"To salt. When did you switch it?"

"*What?* You think... you think *I* did that?"

"Didn't you?"

"No," Tanya said coldly. "Why would I?"

Fabian smirked. "For fun?"

Tanya got up from the table, in no mood for dessert now.

"Yeah, that's right, Fabian. My idea of fun is being made to look like an idiot in front of everyone."

"Well, the look on Warwick's face when he took that mouthful was hilarious," he said gleefully. "And you didn't add sugar to your own bowl."

"I didn't do it." Tanya made for the hallway, but Fabian beat her to it and stood blocking the door.

"Get out of my way."

"You know," said Fabian, "It's funny how this sort of thing always happens when you're around."

Tanya narrowed her eyes, but inside her heart skipped a beat.

"What sort of thing?"

"Like the time when you were staying here because your parents were in France," Fabian continued. "On the first night we were all watching a film, and when it finished you got up and fell over because your shoelaces had been tied together. You blamed me, but you knew as well as I did that I couldn't have done it—I was sitting on the other side of the room all night. I never came near you.

"Then last summer you bought those flowers for Florence fresh from the market. And by breakfast the next day they were dead. Every one of them, withered up in water that was as stagnant as if it had been three weeks old.

"And then there was the time when—"

"Is there a point to any of this, Fabian?" said Tanya, trying hard to conceal the tremor in her voice.

"Yeah, there is. It's *you*. Weird stuff happens when you're around. You think nobody notices… but I do."

Tanya forced a hollow laugh. "You have a very vivid imagination. Now, if that's all then can you get out of my way, please?"

Fabian moved aside, smirking. "There's something about you that doesn't add up. You're hiding something. And I'm going to find out what it is."

Tanya stiffened. "Just leave me alone. I mean it, Fabian. Stay out of my way."

"Fine," said Fabian, airily. "Warwick's never liked me talking to you anyway. He says you're a troublemaker."

"I don't care what your father says." Tanya pushed past him angrily. "His words mean nothing— I heard him going back on his promise earlier. I heard him telling my grandmother about finding us in the woods today. He snitched on us. So why don't you have a good think about who the *real* troublemaker in this house is?"

It took Tanya a long time to fall asleep that night, such was her anger at Fabian and Warwick. She replayed the argument over and over in her mind, each time thinking of better comebacks she could have retaliated with, even mouthing the words in a half-whisper to a silent room. How *dare* Warwick say she was a troublemaker? And how dare Fabian accuse her of switching the sugar to salt?

The thing that was bothering her the most, however—bothering and unnerving her—was that all the time Fabian had been noticing the little oddities that had happened around her. Everything he'd said had been true, from the wilted flowers to the shoelaces tied together: all things that the fairies had done. It shocked her that he had noted it all and never said a word until tonight.

In the end Tanya knew she was just winding herself up, and made herself force it all from her mind in an effort to get some sleep. But when sleep finally came, it was not to last.

She awoke with a start and the unshakable feeling that she was not alone in the room. Her initial thought was that the fairies had come, but as her sleep-fuddled brain came into focus she neither saw nor heard anything that would suggest their presence. The room was silent. There was no fluttering of wings, no whispers, no strange earthy smell. Just her, and the sparse, unwelcoming room.

Unsettled, she allowed herself to lean back into her pillow, trying to shake off the weird feeling and relax. It must have been a dream. What with the upheaval of the past few days, it wasn't surprising she was having trouble sleeping. She closed her eyes and took a shaky breath, forcing herself to exhale slowly.

Then she froze as she heard something in the

darkness, like the soft hiss of a snake—or was it slithering? Something was sliding slowly along with precision, with caution. It was the noise that had woken her, she was sure of it.

She couldn't move, couldn't breathe. Trapped by fear, a prisoner in her own body, she could only listen as the slithering continued. She couldn't even work out where it was coming from. It seemed so close that it had to be in the room with her... and yet something told her that it wasn't. But wherever—*whatever*—it was, it was close. Very close.

Something snapped in her then, pulling her out of the frozen state she was in. Choking back a cry of terror, she threw back the bedclothes and leaped up. A small noise stopped her in her tracks. She froze a second time—but this time it wasn't with fear. It was to listen. For what she had heard had been unmistakable. The slithering had stopped. But she had heard something—something distinctive.

Someone had *sneezed*.

In that instant, Tanya understood. She strode over to the wardrobe, opened the doors, and swept aside the few clothes that were hanging up, then gave the back of the wardrobe a sharp tap. It was hollow.

She took a step backward as her suspicions were confirmed.

Her wardrobe had been constructed in front of the old doorway to the servants' staircase. Where, right now, someone was creeping along the passage on the other side. Suddenly, Tanya had a very good idea of who that someone was. She banged on the back of the wardrobe again, hard.

"I know you're there, Fabian," she hissed. "And let me tell you—"

Her words stuck in her throat as a horrible noise started from behind the wardrobe: a high-pitched, desperate mewling, like a kitten being slowly strangled. It chilled Tanya's blood to hear it. Then there was a gurgle and the noise seemed to muffle and grow lower, before stopping altogether. Then the slithering began again, accompanied by the barely audible footfall of someone who was trying to be very, very quiet. It faded as the passage continued past the room and by the next.

Tanya never remembered how she ended up on the opposite side of the room, backed up against the wall as far as she could go. When she woke at four to the bleak morning light, she was huddled cold and stiff in the corner, and as she crawled back into bed all she remembered was thinking one solid thought.

*Perhaps the person on the servants' staircase wasn't Fabian.*

9

At six o'clock the following morning Amos's ranting woke the entire household. Tanya shielded her ears from several clatters and clangs from above—the old man had either dropped his breakfast or thrown it. The latter was confirmed when Warwick stomped past her room swearing under his breath.

Moments later, the events in the night came flooding back. In the daylight, the fear she had felt from hearing the noises seemed ridiculous, funny even. It must have been Fabian, she decided. It was too coincidental that the two of them had discovered the old staircase only a short while before, and their quarrel would have been reason enough for Fabian to want to get back at her. But she had foiled him—and would relish pointing it out the first chance she got.

She hauled herself out of bed and got dressed,

pondering over what to wear. Her red T-shirt was in the wash and the beaded scarf she had bought from Tickey End made her neck itch. Instead she had wrapped it around the shoebox containing the list of fairy deterrents, the compass, and her one remaining diary that was hidden beneath the floorboards. For now, she decided to try another method of protection from the fairies from the book in the library; she turned her socks inside out, figuring that no one would see them under her sneakers anyway.

When she went downstairs her grandmother was seated at the breakfast table opposite Warwick, grumbling about the amount of food the household was getting through. A huge pot of porridge was steaming on the stove. As Tanya passed by, deliberately ignoring it to spite her grandmother, the hearth-fay skittered out from under the pot and hid behind the toaster.

"Good morning," said Florence.

"Is it?" said Tanya. "My mornings don't usually begin for at least another hour. I should still be in bed."

Warwick looked up, acknowledging her presence for the first time.

"Then why aren't you?"

"I couldn't sleep," Tanya said pointedly.

Florence lifted her teacup from the saucer.

"Perhaps we could put you in another room if Amos is causing a disturbance. I'm sure Warwick wouldn't mind clearing one of the rooms on the opposite side of the landing for you."

"It's fine," Tanya muttered. "I wouldn't want to cause you any further *trouble*." She deliberately placed an emphasis on the final word, looking her grandmother directly in the eye as she did so. She was gratified to see the teacup in Florence's hand wobble a little. Her grandmother averted her eyes.

"It's no trouble," she said quietly.

*Liar,* Tanya thought. Outwardly she said nothing. She helped herself to a slice of toast cooling in the rack and began to spread it with butter.

"There's hot porridge, freshly made—" Florence began.

"I don't like porridge."

"Funny," said Warwick, gruffly. "I seem to remember you eating bucketloads of it last year."

"Well, maybe that's why I can't stand it now."

Silence.

"So would you like to do that, then?" said Florence, eventually. "Change rooms, I mean?"

Tanya munched noisily and took her time in replying. She was beginning to enjoy herself in a twisted sort of way. If her grandmother and Warwick had thought her a pest up until now, then they had a shock coming to them. For at that moment Tanya made up her mind to be as much trouble as possible. With a bit of luck she might even get sent back to London; then her mother would have to deal with her. She had to stop herself from grinning at the thought.

"No, don't bother," she said finally. She swallowed the last mouthful of her toast and took another bite. Much as she would have savored making Warwick clear out one of the dusty old rooms, she decided against it on the basis that she might end up with something even worse than she already had. Out of the corner of her eye she saw Warwick visibly relax and fought the rising urge to giggle.

She helped herself to a second piece of toast and headed for the kitchen door, half expecting her grandmother to call her back to the breakfast table. But the room behind her stayed silent.

❧❧

Later that afternoon Tanya caught sight of a movement in the back garden through the kitchen window. She got up from the table and stepped outside the back door, trying to see past the overgrown bushes and shrubs.

Brunswick was sitting in the rock garden alone. Tanya edged over slowly and sat down. The goblin was sitting with his head in his hands, staring miserably at the ground. She reached over and gently touched his arm.

Brunswick jumped. Evidently he had not heard her approaching. He glanced up at her, and then put his head back in his hands. The glimpse at his face revealed that he had been hit again, even worse this time than the last. His right eye was a swollen, purple bruise, completely closed. One of his earlobes looked as if it had been bitten. As she watched, a tear rolled onto his bulbous nose.

Tanya pulled her notebook out. She'd had the sense to write down a few questions that she wanted to ask the goblins, if and when she got the opportunity.

Another fat tear slid down Brunswick's cheek. He mumbled something that Tanya did not catch, and she noticed then that he was missing a few of his teeth. Before she could ask him to repeat himself, he lunged toward her feet and seized something.

She caught sight of a caterpillar wriggling frenziedly between his thumb and forefinger before he dropped it into his mouth. There was a slight squelch as his jaws chomped down, then he swallowed noisily and coughed. She watched in pity and revulsion as he picked caterpillar hairs out of his remaining teeth, now tinged with green.

"Wait a minute, stay right there," said Tanya. "Perhaps we've got some food to spare." She ran back into the kitchen, raiding the cupboards and fridge for anything that wouldn't be missed. Her grandmother had been right; there was hardly any food left. She made do with a little bread, some cheese, and a handful of grapes.

As she closed the fridge door she became aware of a lapping sound and turned to catch a flash of movement as the hearthfay scurried behind one of Warwick's boots. Curious, she drew nearer to where it had darted from and saw a shallow bowl on the quarry-stone floor. It held milk swimming with matted clumps of ginger fur and a chewed-up spider. The surface was still rippling slightly, and a few telltale drips leading to Warwick's boot belied the culprit.

Full of pity for any creature who braved the wrath of Spitfire for a few drops of milk—for even Oberon stayed well away—Tanya took a clean saucer and poured fresh milk into it before setting it down by the coal bin—the hearthfay's favorite place—then hurriedly slunk back out to the garden.

Brunswick looked as if he didn't know whether to laugh or cry as he fell upon the food. Tanya watched as he shoveled every last crumb into his mouth then settled back and burped contentedly. It was clearly the most substantial meal he had eaten in days. She waited patiently, wondering how, or indeed if, he would respond to her questions.

The goblin eyed her expectantly.

"Brunswick, may I ask you, please, what's to fear within those trees?" she said, pointing in the direction of the forest.

Brunswick shuffled his feet. "With regret, all I can say is protect yourself and stay away." He hopped off the rock and headed toward the bushes.

"Where are you going?" Tanya called. "You can't leave me not knowing!"

Brunswick turned back to her, his eyes full of tears.

"You have treated Brunswick well, but there's no more that he can tell."

With that, he darted into the bushes.

"Don't run away!" Tanya waded into the nettles. "Brunswick! Please stay!"

The goblin had vanished. Tanya winced as she inspected the sore red lumps on her ankles where the nettles had stung her. She stared gloomily at the rock garden, stooping to pick up a cracked tooth lying amongst some breadcrumbs; it had obviously belonged to Brunswick. She pocketed it and then started to walk back to the house. The goblin's warning was all very well, but how was she supposed to protect herself if she didn't know what she had to protect herself from?

❦

"Who were you talking to?"

"When?"

"You were talking to someone over by the rock garden earlier."

As usual, Fabian had sneaked up on her when she least expected it. It was late afternoon, and Tanya was outside walking Oberon by the brook. This time she carried his leash with her, and jangled it every now and then so as to warn him not to run off again.

She was not willing to get lost in the woods a second time, nor to ask for Warwick's help.

"I wasn't talking to anyone." She peered at Fabian's brown leather book, in which it appeared he had been sketching something. He saw her looking and snapped the book shut.

"You were. I saw you."

Tanya shrugged. She was annoyed by his whole stance—the way he was so secretive about his silly book, and more so that he always seemed to be watching her.

"I was probably just talking to myself."

Fabian raised his eyebrows, as if she were some deranged animal that needed to be put out of its misery.

"Whatever you say."

He strolled off, book in hand.

"Well, it's better than talking to you!" Tanya yelled. "And by the way, if you must insist on sneaking around in the servants' staircase in the middle of the night, then at least have the decency to be quiet. It's bad enough being woken up every morning by Amos!" She stalked after Oberon, jubilant as she imagined Fabian's smug face falling.

"What are you talking about?"

Tanya stopped and spun around. "You know exactly what I mean. Slithering through the servants' staircase by my room last night like a little snake, making weird noises. It'll take a bit more imagination than that to scare me!"

Fabian shook his head. "Whatever you heard, it wasn't me."

Tanya stared after him as he walked away. Even though he had sounded truthful, she had no choice but to disbelieve him. For if it wasn't Fabian, then who else could it have been?

❦

The day dragged on with little improvement. Out of sheer boredom, Tanya decided to have a snoop up on the second floor. After poking around a couple of empty rooms she eventually found something of interest: a box of photographs wedged into a cupboard full of junk. She transferred the box to her own room, groaning under the weight of the thing, before tipping its entire contents out messily.

She picked up a handful of pictures and began leafing through. There were a great many of her mother and herself, at various stages through their lives. She smiled to see herself as a chubby toddler, her face smeared with ice cream, and then years later waving to the camera from a carousel at a fairground.

There were several pictures of her parents' wedding day. Tanya put them all to one side. She scowled when she came across photos of Fabian and Warwick, immediately tossing them back into the box. Soon she fell into a routine of filing the pictures into categories, and only then did she notice a significant

❦ 129 ❦

majority in one particular area: herself. For the first time, she realized that she couldn't remember ever seeing a picture of herself on display at her grandmother's house. None of them had ever been framed and mounted on the wall in the sitting room alongside Fabian's or her mother's. They were all here, in a box that had been hidden away in a musty old cupboard.

An hour later the carpet was strewn with photographs. Tanya found herself distracted each time she came across one of the many photographs of her grandfather, who had died before she was born. He looked like a happy, jolly man with twinkling eyes, and Tanya wished again that she had had a chance to know him.

She sighed and picked up the next dog-eared picture, uninterested until she saw that it was of her grandmother, taken when she was not much older than Tanya was now. But Florence was not alone in the photograph. The sepia picture was of two girls, standing side by side in front of the gate in the back garden. A young Florence smiled into the camera, happy and carefree. Next to her stood a strikingly pretty girl of about the same age with long black hair. Tanya stared into her dark eyes and recognized her immediately. She flipped the photograph over. Something was written on the back.

*Florence and Morwenna, age fourteen.*

Her heart began to pound and her breathing became shallow. There was no mistaking it. The girl in the photograph was the same girl that she and Fabian had seen in Hangman's Wood the day they were lost. It didn't make sense.

The girl in the forest was Morwenna Bloom... her grandmother's childhood best friend who had been missing for more than fifty years.

Tanya scrambled to the door, sliding on the piles of photographs scattered everywhere. She ran downstairs and outside into the back garden. The night air was warm and balmy, yet her teeth had begun to chatter.

"Fabian! Are you out here?"

For a few seconds she heard nothing, then there was a faint rustle from the oak tree.

"Fabian!" she called, louder this time. "I need to speak to you."

"So *now* you want to talk!" crowed Fabian, popping his head out from the branches. "I thought you preferred talking to yourself?"

"I'm serious! This is *serious*!"

The urgency in her voice told Fabian she was not messing around. He climbed down lazily, by which time Tanya was shivering uncontrollably.

"What is it?" he asked.

Wordlessly, she handed him the photograph.

"So? It's Florence... only less wrinkly."

"Not her. The other one," said Tanya.

Fabian's face went white. "The girl... that girl... in the woods... but we *spoke* to her..."

"There's more." Tanya snatched the photograph

and pointed to the name on the back. "It's her. The missing girl."

"It can't be," said Fabian. "It was fifty *years* ago. It's impossible. There must be some logical explanation."

They stared at the photograph. There was no doubt in Tanya's mind that the girl standing with her grandmother was the same girl they had seen in the woods, and the expression on Fabian's face told her he was just as convinced as she.

Fabian looked troubled. "There's . . . there's something I have to tell you."

"What?" she asked weakly.

*"Fabian!"* Warwick's voice echoed in the hallway.

"Not here," Fabian said. "Meet me on the second-floor landing in half an hour."

10

The next thirty minutes seemed the longest of Tanya's life. After Fabian left to find his father, she slipped the photograph into her pocket and walked to the stairs in a detached, trancelike state, feeling as if she were trapped in a dream that she couldn't wake from. Only it wasn't a dream. It was real, and it was scaring her.

Her mind was racing. Who was Morwenna Bloom? What had really happened to her that night in the woods? And what else did Fabian know about her disappearance?

As she crept up the stairs she heard her grandmother cough over the sound of the television in the living room. She went to her room and sat in silence, the time crawling immensely. After twenty minutes had elapsed, the floorboards outside her door creaked as someone stepped over them. Tanya edged toward the door and listened. There was nothing. No footsteps, no voices. Opening the door just a tiny crack, she peered out onto the empty landing.

"Fabian?"

Only silence answered her. She slipped out of the room, deciding to head up to the second floor. Fabian should be along any minute now.

All was quiet on the second floor of the house, though this did nothing to quell her nerves. She made her way to the darkened alcove with the tapestry concealing the servants' staircase, and sat down, waiting.

Seconds after she had sunk into the chair, a door flew open at the other end of the landing. Slow, unsteady footsteps came padding in her direction. She did not have to see the person to know it was Amos; the labored breathing that grew louder with every step confirmed it was him. She watched from the alcove as the old man's elongated shadow stretched before her, edging forward until his stooped frame came into view.

She was not prepared for the sight of him. Since the last time she had seen him he seemed to have aged more than a decade. His face was sunken, his cheeks hollow and his body wizened. He had several days' worth of gray stubble, and many years' worth of scraggly white hair.

He moved with difficulty, his mad eyes fixed and staring. He did not see Tanya, motionless in the shadows. She did not even realize she had been holding her breath until he passed her, slamming the bathroom door, and it was then the thought occurred to her how odd it was for someone so frail-looking to have so much pent-up aggression.

"Tanya! Over here," came Fabian's voice.

Tanya eased herself out of the chair cautiously, hardly daring to move.

"Where are you?"

"Over here, quickly!"

His voice was coming from a gloomy corridor just beyond the bathroom. Hastily, Tanya tiptoed past, knowing that any second Amos could open the door and see her. She found Fabian waiting anxiously behind a door adjacent to the bathroom.

"In here," he said, opening the door wider for her to step through. He closed it just as the toilet in the bathroom flushed.

"Why are we standing in the dark?" Tanya asked, her eyes flitting about nervously.

"Quiet," Fabian whispered. They listened to the floorboards creaking as Amos went back to his room. Once Tanya's eyes adjusted to the darkness, she glanced about the room. It had not been used in some time. There was no carpet or curtains, and the lightbulb was bare. The only furniture was a rickety bed and a crooked old wardrobe with one door.

"Why are we in the dark?" Tanya repeated, still shivering slightly. She could not seem to get warm.

"Because we're not supposed to be up here," said

Fabian. "If I put the light on it could be seen from under the door or through the window." He sat down on the floor, motioning for Tanya to do the same.

"What's going on?" she said.

Fabian closed his eyes tightly. "The newspaper clipping you found—what exactly did it say?"

"I told you," said Tanya.

"Tell me again."

"It said that a fourteen-year-old girl named Morwenna Bloom disappeared in Hangman's Wood, and everyone thought she had fallen into the catacombs. Oh, and that she was a reverend's daughter."

"That's all?"

"It's all I can remember."

"It didn't mention anything about a boy...who saw her?"

Tanya went quiet for a moment.

"Yes," she admitted at last. "I remember now. There *was* something about a local boy. It said he was the last person ever to see her, and that she was standing by the catacombs. Then it said he was questioned by the police but released without charge." She stopped and watched Fabian in the muted moonlight streaming in through the window. His pale face was troubled.

"What's all this about, Fabian? Do you know who he was?"

Fabian lowered his head and gave an almost imperceptible nod.

"Yes. Only I wish I didn't. It...it was my grand-father. It was Amos."

A terrible silence hung in the air. Outside, an owl hooted. Downstairs, a door slammed in the hallway.

"Fabian!" Warwick bellowed.

Tanya glanced at Fabian in alarm. He held a finger to his lips, his eyes glittering in the dim light.

"Fabian!"

Footsteps thundered on the first-floor staircase. A door slammed. Then another.

"What does he want?" said Tanya. "He only saw you a few minutes ago!"

"Don't worry," said Fabian. "He won't come up here."

The creaking of the second-floor staircase told them he was wrong. Keys jangled and more doors opened and slammed shut. Warwick's voice grew nearer—and angrier.

"FABIAN!"

Amos began to shriek in his room, disrupted by the noise.

"Get under the bed!" Fabian hissed.

The two of them scrambled beneath the low bed with difficulty and huddled together. The floor-boards in the narrow space underneath were coated in a heavy layer of dust, and to Tanya's horror an enormous black spider lurked in a cobweb right in front of her face.

"I can't stay under here!"

"We don't have any other option!" Fabian said fiercely.

"But—"

*"Quiet!"*

Tanya bit her lip and forced her eyes away. A broken spring dug into her head and tangled in her hair, and she could smell the musty dampness of the mattress above. It smelled like it had been peed on, but whether by animal or human Tanya could not tell. Fabian tensed up beside her as Warwick entered the room next door, leaving seconds later. His footsteps drew nearer. Tanya's breath caught in her throat as Warwick slowly, deliberately paused outside. The door swung open violently, and the light from the hallway streamed in.

Warwick entered the room breathing heavily, coming so close to their hiding place that Tanya could see the clumps of mud on his boots. He snapped on the light switch. Fortunately it was broken. He swore and turned it off again, taking another slow step toward the bed. It was then that Tanya knew what it was to be paralyzed by fear. All she could feel was her heart thudding in her rib cage, pounding erratically until she was convinced she could hear it. For a split second, the ridiculous notion that Warwick too could hear it entered her mind. She waited, not even daring to breathe; expecting any minute now for him to kneel down and see them. Instead he turned abruptly and left, banging the door behind him.

Tanya released the breath she had been holding, and felt Fabian sag with relief next to her. They listened as Warwick strode across the landing from room to room, checking each one. Eventually he went downstairs, where his footsteps faded altogether. All that was left for them to hear was Amos's ranting.

Tanya eased herself out from under the bed, glad that Warwick was safely out of the way for the time being. Fabian, however, did not look at all relieved. He raked a hand nervously through his straw-colored hair.

"We don't have much time. He won't stop looking until he finds me."

"Hurry up and tell me what this is about, then," said Tanya, her teeth starting to chatter.

"All right," said Fabian, looking uncomfortable. "Here goes. On...on the evening Morwenna disappeared, nobody was concerned when she was a little later to return home than usual. She'd lived in these parts her whole life, and she knew the woods well enough not to get lost in them. It was only when it started to get dark that her parents began to worry, because Morwenna hated the dark and never stayed out after nightfall.

"When they found out she wasn't with Florence, they panicked. They got a search party together of friends and neighbors, and went into the woods to look for her, thinking that maybe she had hurt herself and couldn't make it back.

"After hours of searching the hunt was abandoned. The next day rescuers were lowered into the catacombs to look for her, but there was no sign. Then the police had a tip-off. A churchgoer had seen Morwenna entering the woods on the evening of her disappearance with a boy a couple of years older than her."

Fabian paused. "Amos fit the description exactly. He was even wearing the same clothes when they came for him." He stopped speaking and looked down at his hands. Tanya followed his gaze and noticed for the first time that his fingernails were bitten back.

"They questioned him," said Fabian. "They wanted to know why he hadn't come forward. He told them he was scared of what people might think, what they might say. He said he had been passing through the woods and seen her, but that was all there was to it. He didn't know any more than anyone else. In the end they had to release him; they had no other evidence to link him to her disappearance.

"As for Morwenna, well...you know the rest. It was like she just vanished off the face of the earth. Her family moved away a few years later, when it was clear she wasn't coming back. And things changed for Amos after that, too. People began to avoid him."

"But why?" Tanya asked. "You said there was no evidence against him."

"That doesn't stop people talking, or insinuating, or accusing. There were rumors, suggestions that he was involved somehow—that he'd pushed her ... or killed her first then disposed of her body in the catacombs."

"But why?" Tanya asked. "What would his motive be?"

"It was common knowledge that Amos had ... had a thing for her. They'd been seeing each other for a few weeks, apparently. But Morwenna had broken it off—and broken his heart." Fabian hung his head miserably. "People thought he was angry and frustrated, that he might have followed her, tried to get her to change her mind. Maybe they had a fight. Or maybe he wanted ... he tried to ... oh, I don't know. I don't *know*."

But he did know, and so did Tanya. But neither of them wanted to say it.

"For the people of Tickey End suspicion was just as good as proof, because an accusation sticks. People will always look at you wondering if there's a possibility you really *did* do it."

"Why didn't he just leave?" said Tanya. "Move away, and start over again?"

"Why *should* he?" said Fabian. "Why should he leave when he did nothing wrong?" His voice faltered. "Besides, it would only have fueled the rumors. He didn't want to appear to be running away." He looked into Tanya's face, his eyes pleading for understanding.

"Can you imagine how it must feel to have people look at you, wondering if you're a killer? Can you imagine how Warwick must have felt, growing up known as the son of a murderer? I've seen the looks he gets from people in Tickey End. All his life he's had to put up with the stares...and the comments. They still talk about it, even now."

It was a terrible thought. A small part of Tanya suddenly pitied Warwick. No wonder he was so curt and unfriendly. People had made him that way. And now she could see why Fabian never brought any friends back to the manor: no one wanted to be associated with those living there.

"Amos never found another job after that. Nobody wanted to employ him. That's why he ended up staying at Elvesden Manor for so many years. When he eventually married, it was to a Danish girl called Elsa who didn't speak much English, and the marriage only lasted until just after Warwick was born. As soon as she heard the rumors she left, leaving Amos to raise my father alone. And now he grows older and madder with every day."

Tanya felt an unexpected lump come to her throat.

"The thing is," said Fabian, "I was always convinced of his innocence. But after today, I—I don't know what to believe anymore."

Tanya stared at him in horror.

"You can't be serious? You think...you think he did it? That he killed her?"

"I don't know what to think," said Fabian. "Ever

since I saw that photograph all sorts of things have been going through my mind."

"What things?"

Fabian bit his lip. "Horrible things. Do you . . . do you believe in . . . ghosts?"

"You think the girl in the woods was a ghost?"

"All I do know is the girl in the woods was the same girl in the photograph—which doesn't make sense. If Morwenna Bloom was alive she would be in her mid-sixties by now."

"Maybe it was just a girl who looked a lot like her," Tanya suggested, not wanting to accept Fabian's explanation.

Even though he was clearly worried, Fabian still managed to give Tanya the scornful look that always made her feel about five years old.

"She would have to be her *twin* to look that much like her. Which still wouldn't make sense." His brow furrowed. "For argument's sake, let's say she *was* a ghost."

"All right," said Tanya reluctantly.

"She was taking us somewhere. Maybe she was trying to show us something?"

"She said she was helping us to find Oberon."

"She can't have been," said Fabian. "He was already with Warwick."

"Then it must have been another dog—she was mistaken. . . ."

Fabian was not listening. "Ghosts linger on earth

because they have unfinished business, right? Morwenna Bloom vanished all those years ago, and still, nobody knows what happened to her. What if she *did* die in those woods? What if the girl we saw *was* Morwenna's ghost? Maybe she was trying to tell us what happened to her... or lead us to her... her... remains."

"She didn't look like a ghost," said Tanya. "She looked as real as you and me. And anyway, why now? Why *us*?"

"I've been thinking about that too," said Fabian in a small voice. "And the only reason I can think of why she would show herself to us is because of the family link—I'm Amos's grandson. Maybe the rumors were true. Maybe she's trying to tell us that he *did* kill her all those years ago. Maybe she can't move on until justice is done."

Tanya fell silent. In a horrible way, what Fabian was saying made sense. Plus she could think of nothing else to explain the mysterious girl. A shiver ran down her spine.

"What are we going to do?"

Fabian gritted his teeth. "We'll have to go back into the woods. If she found us once she can find us again."

Tanya paled. "We can't. We'll get into so much trouble if we get caught—you saw how angry your father was!"

"We won't get caught," said Fabian. "We'll plan it all first."

"I really don't know about this...."

"Do you have a better idea?"

Tanya shook her head.

"I'm not going to rest until I find the truth," said Fabian. "We're going back into the forest the first chance we get. And this time we'll find out what *really* happened to her."

11

Moonlight streamed through the open curtains and spilled into the room, penetrating its darkness and washing it with silver. The night had grown warmer in the past couple of hours, and the window was thrown wide open in an attempt to draw any kind of breeze in, but there was none. The scent of the roses in the courtyard below was heavy and sweet, drifting up from the gardens to sit sluggishly in the room.

Tanya lay on top of the bedclothes, in thin pajamas that were turned inside out. They were sticking to her uncomfortably. She was wide awake, though this had less to do with the heat and more to do with what Fabian had told her earlier in the evening. In addition, Warwick had fixed the grandfather clock on the landing once more; for all night its mocking chimes had kept her awake while reminding her of how little sleep she was likely to get. The last set of chimes had marked two o'clock in the morning, and she knew that even if she got to sleep now it would only be about four hours before Amos woke her.

Her skin crawled at the thought of him, shuffling about on the floor above muttering to himself and goodness knew what else. It had been years since he'd had any real contact with the outside world. Horrible thoughts began to crowd her mind.

What if Amos *had* been involved in Morwenna Bloom's disappearance? What if the old man upstairs was a murderer? And then another idea popped into her head. Maybe she and Fabian were not the only ones to have explored the servants' staircase recently. Maybe Amos had realized Tanya was visiting and had decided to take a little wander...

All of a sudden the moonlight was not enough. Tanya fought the urge to turn on the bedside lamp, and then did it anyway, berating herself for being so babyish—but the light never came on. Cursing, and no longer bothered if anyone were to see the light under her door, she got up and crossed the room, snapping the main light switch on. Nothing.

The realization hit her that this had happened before, more than once. Power outages were all too common at the manor, and she knew from experience that it was usually hours rather than minutes before the electricity was reconnected. Her grandmother was usually well prepared, stashing a generous supply of candles in the rooms most often used, but Tanya already knew with a sinking feeling that in this room there were none. It wasn't used often enough, and she had not seen any when she had unpacked her things and put them away.

She clenched her eyes shut and tried to think. There would be candles downstairs in the kitchen. Florence always kept a supply under the sink, along with a few spare boxes of matches. She would go down, grab a few, and then return to her room and read until she was sleepy. And she would remain in bed until she was good and ready to get up, whether her grandmother liked it or not and whether or not Amos shouted the place down. If it came to it she would say she was feeling unwell. That way she could get some rest and avoid them all: her grandmother, Warwick, and Fabian.

More able to focus now that she had a plan, Tanya located her slippers and crept out of the room. In the silence of the sleeping house every noise she made seemed monumental. Every step, every creak of the floorboards beneath her made her cringe and pause.

In the kitchen, Oberon thumped his tail in greeting and rose from his blanket by the hearth. Tanya knelt and made a fuss of him, briefly comforted. He smelled of marrow bone, and there were pieces of a chewed-up boot of Warwick's in his basket.

She gave him an extra pat while making a mental note to dispose of the evidence, then began to search under the sink for the candles and matches. She gathered several, and after locating a brass candle-stick shoved to the back of the cupboard, pushed a candle firmly into it and lit the wick. Instantly, the kitchen was lit with a golden glow. Tanya took a step toward the door, ready to creep back upstairs—but something made her pause. Frowning, she held the candle aloft.

On the countertop there were four pieces of bread, placed neatly in a square on the chopping board. Three of them had been buttered. Next to them was a tub of spread, with a knife wedged half-way in at an angle. As Tanya took another step she saw a small parcel of tinfoil, partially opened to reveal that it was full of beef left over from dinner. A ripe tomato sat on the chopping board, waiting to be sliced. Tanya placed her hand on the foil containing the meat. It was cold, like it had not been out of the fridge for long.

She took a sharp breath and scanned the kitchen. She had interrupted someone, that much was clear. And whoever it was wouldn't have had time to go far. But who would bother hiding over something as trivial as making a sandwich?

"Who's there?" she whispered. "Fabian?"

A dark figure sprang from the alcove where the servants' staircase had been blocked off, and darted from the kitchen. With no time to think through what she was about to do, Tanya followed. As she moved through the kitchen into the pitch-black hall, the candle in her hand sent shadows scattering across the walls, the flame flickering wildly before going out.

In the sudden darkness she paused, trying to get her bearings. Light footsteps padded slyly away from her. A nearby door opened, then closed softly. The library. Hardly daring to breathe, Tanya relit the candle and pushed the door open. By now she knew it wasn't Fabian, and knew she should go and wake someone. She also knew there wasn't time.

Warily, she stepped into the library, scanning the now-empty bookshelves and the writing table near the window. The door closed behind her, and there was a scratching of claws and a small whine from outside. Oberon had followed her. She ducked down, looking beneath the table, and jumped as a single yellow eye glared back at her. Spitfire. The cat hissed, then curled itself into a ragged ginger ball. Tanya stepped back, surveying the room. It was empty and open. There was nowhere else to hide.

She set the candle down on a nearby bookshelf. Perhaps she had been mistaken. The intruder must have gone into one of the other rooms nearby. She knew she would have to go and wake her grandmother and Warwick—but what if the intruder was out there, waiting for her? She stood, contemplating her next move.

Something gleamed in the flickering candlelight. She lifted the candle once more. On the edge of the bookshelf at eye level, the tiniest smear of something pale and shiny was lodged into the complex pattern in the woodwork. It was a moment before Tanya recognized what it was. Butter.

Her fingers traced the engravings in the old, dark wood. Amidst ornately carved ivy there were several small circular panels. It was on one of these panels the butter had been smeared. Three small indents were part of a triangular shape within the pattern. Almost in a trance she lifted her hand and placed her thumb, forefinger, and middle finger into the indentations, and instinctively turned her wrist clockwise.

Soundlessly, effortlessly, the circular panel began to turn with her hand. After rotating the panel a half-turn to the right she withdrew her fingers and thumb, then replaced them so her wrist was straight and turned clockwise again. After another half-turn the panel resisted slightly before clicking into place. Several seconds passed before anything happened. Then slowly, the end partition of the bookcase began to revolve in the wall.

Tanya could hear her own blood rushing through her ears as her eyes struggled to comprehend what they were seeing. As the bookcase revolved farther it revealed a narrow gap in the wall. The other side was completely black. She lifted the candle. Already, she knew this was not the servants' staircase. This was something else. A steep set of stone steps spiraled downward. The air was cold, damp, and moldy. She leaned forward, trying to get a glimpse down the staircase. It looked positively treacherous.

Tanya took a few steps into the passageway,

nearing the staircase. Fabian had been right all along. Elvesden Manor was home to secrets that she had never imagined possible. There *were* hidden tunnels—and clearly, the intruder that had been in the house knew about them and was using them. But why?

Too late she heard the soft scrape of the partition being pulled back into place by whatever mechanism controlled it. There was a dull click of finality, and then the tunnel was sealed like a tomb...with Tanya still inside.

Horrified, she began searching desperately by the candlelight for any kind of latch or lever on the inside. There was none. Stricken, she forced her fingernails into the tiny gap of the door. It was shut tight as she knew it would be, still sturdy and impenetrable; truly built to last. She guessed then that the tunnel was only designed to get out of the house, and that there must be others for getting in. Her one candle continued to burn, her only source of light and comfort.

There was no way back. She was trapped.

She drew a breath, ready to scream for her grandmother; for Warwick, for anyone. But sense flashed a warning into her mind. The person nearest—who would hear her cries and reach her first—would be the intruder. As it was, whoever had entered the tunnel probably had no idea that they had been followed through the secret entrance. Her only chance was to try to follow at a distance and find the way out.

There was no choice but to go on. Her heart was

pumping wildly, and her breath was now coming in short gasps that she fought to control. She had never been more terrified. She started down the steps, winding farther and farther beneath the house. As she did so, the temperature plummeted. Tanya could feel her skin, covered only in the thin cotton of her pajamas, prickle with gooseflesh. The candle began to shudder in her hand.

The stairwell ended and opened out. She came to a halt, and with shock and dismay counted four possible tunnels she could take. Each spiraled off in a different direction and appeared as terrifying as the next.

Through thick green mold, small areas of gray stone were visible. Then, on the ground, Tanya spotted something: a large, flat pebble, trussed and knotted with dirty string that led off into one of the tunnels. Its purpose, she realized, was to mark the way in this underground labyrinth. She was then faced with her most difficult task yet. Knowing that her candle was burning low, and that its light would alert the intruder to her approach, she knelt and took hold of the cold, damp string that was tied to the pebble and allowed it to run through her fingers, leading the way.

Bracing herself, she blew the candle out and began to move along in the pitch-black, following the only path she could in the hope it would lead her out. What was it Fabian had told her? The tunnels led out in a couple of places . . . somewhere in Tickey End—a pub . . . and the little church nearby.

*Let it be the church,* she begged silently.

She walked for several long minutes, imagining in her mind's eye the tunnel becoming narrower, like the darkness was closing in. The musty dankness caught in her throat and crawled down her airway. Her own tremulous breathing was all she could hear. The darkness was swallowing her.

And then the air changed, became thinner and fresher—and colder still. She sensed that the tunnel had opened out into something: some kind of underground room—or perhaps a way out. She fumbled for the matches, then jumped in terror as a distinctive click echoed in her ears. A strong light shone in her eyes, blinding her. Weakly, she lifted her hand to her eyes, realizing her mistake too late.

"Nice of you to join us," a voice hissed, horribly close.

The flashlight went out and light footsteps moved away from her. Then came the sound of a match being struck. Tanya blinked repeatedly as white lights danced in front of her eyes. From what little she could see at the edges of her vision it was apparent that she was in an underground cavern of sorts.

Now lit by candlelight, the outline of a figure stood about ten feet away. She squeezed her eyes closed, willing the dazzled feeling to pass. Her vision was clearing. The figure by the wall shifted slightly, though the person's face remained hidden in the darkness.

"Who are you?" said Tanya. Her eyes darted

around. In the farthest corner was an old-fashioned bed, heaped with blankets and a meager pile of clothes. A dark-colored bag had been half-emptied on it. A tiny wooden table and chair stood next to the bed. Flickering on the table, the flame of a single candle was caught in some underground draft. The intruder stepped away from the wall toward her. As the shadows were chased away by the candlelight a face came into view.

The girl looked young, not much older than Tanya. She was tall and athletic, flat-chested and boyish in shape with a plain, unreadable expression. Even in the muted light Tanya could see the mane of red hair tumbling to her waist, wild and unkempt. It glowed through the darkness, brighter than the candles, as though it were flaming all by itself.

The girl took another step in her direction, silent and as sure-footed as a cat. She wore a simple, short, dark dress and worn but sturdy hiking boots. Strapped to her slim, freckled thigh was a knife. Tanya met her gaze, and knew with absolute certainty that if she needed to, the girl would use it.

"Who are you?" Tanya asked again. "And what were you doing in my grandmother's house?"

The girl simply stared at her with unblinking green eyes.

"I need some answers of my own. First, your name."

"Who do you think you are?" Tanya whispered. "That you can just—"

The girl had crossed the cavern and was upon her in one swift movement, her face inches from Tanya's, lips drawn back over her teeth in a snarl. Tanya was forced backward against the cold cavern wall. All the calmness about the girl had gone. She looked feral, demented. Her breath was sour and rank, and her clothes reeked of sweat. She clearly hadn't washed for days.

"You've cost me a great deal tonight, and lost time I can ill afford. Now we can do this the hard way, but I would advise against it. Or I can ask you once more, *nicely*. Your name."

"Tanya."

"Good. Now, Tanya. Did anyone else hear me tonight?"

Tanya hesitated. Something in the girl's unfaltering gaze told her it would be a mistake to lie. "I don't think so."

The girl relaxed and leaned back a couple of inches.

"How did you know about the secret passages? Have you used them before?"

Tanya shook her head. "No. I'd...I'd heard stories...but I never really believed they existed."

"So how did you find this one?"

"I followed you. You left a smear of butter on the panel that triggers the mechanism. It was just a fluke..."

The girl gave a cold smile. "So you followed and got trapped in the tunnel. Quite the little detective, aren't you? Who else knows about the passages? You said this is your grandmother's house."

Tanya felt her head start to spin as she was hit by a wave of nausea. The girl's breath was making her feel ill.

"I don't know. My grandmother hasn't ever spoken to me about anything like this. Please, I just want to get out. Tell me how to get back into the house—I won't say anything about you."

The girl ignored her. "How soon is your grandmother likely to notice you're missing?"

"When I don't show up for breakfast. About eight."

The girl swore.

"What do you need?" Tanya began. "If it's money you want, maybe I could—"

"Money?" The girl's tone was incredulous. "I'm not here for money! You think I'm a thief?"

"You were taking food."

"I only took what I needed. And not out of choice."

"You're hiding here, aren't you?"

The girl's face twitched involuntarily.

"That's it, isn't it? You're using this place as a hideout." Tanya stared around the cavern, trembling. "And you're not alone."

"What?"

Tanya met the girl's emerald gaze. "Nice of you to join us. *Us.* That's what you said when I found you. There's someone else with you."

Before she had even finished speaking, a terrible, bloodcurdling sound filled the cavern. Tanya froze as the noise grew louder. There was something horribly familiar about that sound . . . she had heard it before.

Something was moving on the bed beneath the pile of clothes. No. *Within* the clothes. Tanya's back was pressed against the cold stone wall as the red-haired girl moved soundlessly toward the bed and pulled the bundle into her arms. Tanya watched, transfixed, as a tiny hand reached out from the bundle and stretched toward the girl's face; a clenched little fist slowly unfurling as the noise continued.

"A baby? You're hiding down here with . . . with a *baby*?"

The girl did not answer. Tanya wondered if she'd even heard. Instead the girl sank down on the bed whispering to the child, who did not appear to be taking any comfort.

"Why is it crying like that?" Tanya asked, wincing at the terrible noise. The wails had now escalated into piercing shrieks that echoed through the cavern and filled her heart with dread.

"He's crying because he's sick," the girl replied unexpectedly. "He needs medicine. And I have none."

Steadying herself with a hand against the freezing wall, Tanya's fear was momentarily quashed by her desire to see the child. She took a slow, quiet step toward the bed. The girl didn't notice. Emboldened, she took another.

"If he's sick then why isn't he in a hospital?"

"He was," the girl muttered. "But it wasn't safe."

"Is he yours?"

The girl did not reply. Tanya took another step. The baby continued to writhe in the girl's arms, tiny limbs flailing beneath the fabric it was wrapped in. Still she could see nothing of it, except for that weak little hand.

"What do you mean it wasn't safe? How can a hospital not be safe compared to this...an underground...underground *dungeon* with no warmth, no light, no fresh air..."

"Shut up, Tanya!" the girl whispered. "And get back where you were."

Tanya retreated. But she could not shut up. Something was wrong here, something was niggling at her. "Why would you take a sick baby out of a hospital?"

"I said shut up! Shut *up*!" The girl's face crumpled, and for a second it seemed she had been about to sob, but then she composed herself.

From the depths of Tanya's memory something was stirring, hovering just on the edge of recognition. As she willed it, the memory began to materialize, slowly at first, and then without warning it cascaded upon her with such force she felt as if she'd been punched in the stomach.

"I remember. I heard it on the radio. A baby, stolen from the hospital..." Her voice was shaking. "It was you. *You* did it."

The girl's eyes were wild with anger.

"You took that baby away," Tanya whispered, horrified. "And now you're holding him here when he's sick and needs medical attention..."

The nausea that had been threatening finally took hold. Tanya bent double, gripped by pain, and vomited. Yet even when her stomach was empty she was still retching out of sheer fear. She knew then that she would have to outwit or fight this girl to escape. At that moment, neither seemed likely.

Minutes passed, and along with them, so did Tanya's nausea. Still she bent over, pretending to gag and spit. She was buying time while her mind raced and wrangled with ideas of escape. She glanced at the girl out of the corner of her eye. She had risen from the bed and was now stuffing clothes into her bag.

By now the child had exhausted himself and was lying quietly in his blankets. Tanya watched as the girl zipped up the bag and then collected a plastic bottle about a quarter full of water from the table. Unscrewing the lid, she walked over to Tanya and offered it. Tanya eyed it warily.

"Take it," the girl said impatiently. "Unless you like the taste of your own vomit."

Tanya took the bottle and swilled a large mouthful of water around before spitting. Then she took another smaller mouthful and swallowed.

"I know what you're thinking," the girl said suddenly.

Tanya put the bottle down and regarded her. "What am I thinking?"

"That I'm a bad person. And you're probably trying to think of a way to escape. Correct?"

Tanya nodded.

The girl was silent for a moment.

"What if I told you I'm not a bad person? That I've just done some bad things in the name of trying to do something else, something good. Would that make a difference?"

"I don't know," Tanya answered. "Why don't you tell me? Tell me why you stole the baby. Then maybe I'll understand."

"You wouldn't. You'd just think I'm even madder than you do already." She gave Tanya a long, hard look. "You're just trying to keep me talking so you can distract me and try to escape. I don't blame you. I'll do whatever else I have to in order to get away from here with that child—and not you or anyone else will stop me. So go ahead. Draw your conclusions."

"If you're so convinced what you're doing is right then why not tell me?"

"Because you wouldn't believe me," the girl replied simply. "And because I have to leave, now. Before it gets light."

"So where do I fit in with this?"

"You don't. When I'm a safe distance away, I will send message of your whereabouts to the house."

"You can't leave me down here!" Tanya gasped. "How do I know you'll keep your word? Or that you won't get caught by the police? Or...or run over and killed? Anything could happen! And then no one would find me!"

"No," the girl said. "I don't suppose they would. But maybe this will teach you a valuable lesson about minding your own business in the future. After all, you know what they say about curiosity. And if you're thinking of following me, or attempting to find your own way out of these tunnels, don't.

"If you follow me I'll hear you and I'll make sure you can't follow any farther. As for finding your own way out, there's not a chance. These tunnels are an intricate maze, and parts of them have caved in. Of those that remain, only a few actually lead some-where." She paused and looked Tanya straight in the eye. "The rest are decoys, looping back on them-selves to prevent anyone from being followed. It's what they were designed for when the property was built. Pretty ingenious, really."

Tanya bit back tears and a torrent of abuse.

"What are you going to do with the baby...sell him? Hold him for ransom?"

"Neither. He was abandoned in the first place, so who'd pay the ransom? And selling him would be impossible given that it's probably been all over the news."

The baby began to howl again. Tanya jumped at the sudden noise. It was a horrible, gurgling wail. "Can't you stop him from crying?"

"We'll be gone in a minute."

The child screamed even louder. This time even the redheaded girl flinched. For a moment she paused, then reluctantly stopped what she was doing and looked up.

She gave a small cry and flew to the bed.

From between the folds of the blanket the child's hand was visible. Blood ran in rivulets from minute crescents in the baby's palm: he had pierced his own skin with his fingernails. At the girl's touch, the shrieks subsided as he was comforted. The girl wrapped him up tightly and gathered him in the crook of her arm. On her other shoulder she hoisted the bag. She strode over to Tanya.

"I'll need a couple of hours before I notify anyone of your whereabouts. I'm warning you again—don't try to follow me. If you get lost down here you will die." She tossed a blanket on the floor. "Here. You'll need this to keep warm."

Tanya did not answer her. She was staring at the child, lying quietly in the girl's arms. It was the moment that changed everything. The moment when she saw the child for what it truly was.

The child stared back at her, unblinking. What happened next turned her stomach with fear. As the baby watched her its features warped and then morphed. The tips of the ears elongated and pointed and the skin took on a greenish hue. The eyes in their entirety flooded black, as if with ink, sparkling eerily. All this in the briefest of moments before the ghoulish vision was gone—but Tanya knew what she had seen.

And so did the redheaded intruder.

"You saw." Her voice was a throaty whisper.

Tanya lowered her eyes to the thing in the girl's arms and swallowed a scream.

"I don't believe it," the girl murmured, eyes fixed on Tanya. "You *saw*. You can see them too."

Tanya stared back. A moment of clarity and quiet understanding passed between them as the girl whispered something softly.

"You have the second sight."

Tanya recoiled. "Who *are* you?"

There was a short pause.

"You can call me Red."

Tanya nodded toward the fairy child. "What are you doing with that baby?"

"Good question," Red replied. "Sit. I'll tell you my story. I'm sure it's one you'll find interesting."

12

Red leaned across the table, her eyes fixed on the candle. Light and shadow flickered across her face as she held her hands to the warmth of the flame. Numbly, Tanya watched her pale, slender fingers moving up and down, absorbing the heat as gracefully as a butterfly would dance in the sunlight. They looked like they should belong to a pianist. Or an artist or a musician. The reality now seemed quite different.

She did not trust the girl an inch.

"How did you get past Oberon?" Tanya whispered tentatively. "I...I don't get it. He would've barked."

"The dog? That was easy. He did start to growl the first time I got into the kitchen, but after a few scraps of food we were practically best friends."

Tanya's eyes widened in fear. "You'd better not have...have—"

"What? Drugged him? Poisoned him?" Red finished. "No. I'm not lying. I bribed him with food. Simple. And anyway, I happen to like animals. A lot more than I like people, that's for sure."

Tanya did not react.

"So," said Red. "You've never met anyone else with the second sight before. That much is obvious."

Tanya dared to look up. It did not feel as if what was happening was reality.

"I always thought... *hoped* there must be others," she said at last. "But I don't think I ever allowed myself to believe it, not fully."

"There are plenty of others," said Red. "Just like I was. Just like *you*. All thinking they're alone, abnormal. A freak. It takes time to recognize the signs, but you'll pick up on them eventually. You'll learn to see when someone shares your ability."

"But why?" Tanya asked shakily.

Red narrowed her eyes. "Why what?"

"Why can we see them? Who are we? *What* are we?"

"Do you know what a changeling is?"

A feeling of dread engulfed Tanya as she recalled the passage from the book in the library. "It's a child that's been stolen by fairies."

Red nodded. "The stolen human child is replaced by a fairy child, often with similar characteristics. Usually, the children are too young to be told apart. It probably wouldn't be recognized by anyone other than the mother, and even then it's not always noticed."

Red cast her eyes upon the baby, now sleeping peacefully. "They like to take the ones that won't be easily missed: orphans, or babies that are abandoned. By the time he was found, the switch had most likely taken place already." Red got up and began to pace the cavern, clearly agitated.

"The human child will be long gone by now; vanished into the fairy realm. Sometimes they get brought back, sometimes not. It all depends on the reason they were taken in the first place. Sometimes they're replacements for fairy children that are born sick, or ugly. A healthy fairy child may be traded in for an exceptional human child: one that will grow up to be beautiful, or possess a rare gift or talent.

"Sometimes they're taken for no reason other than to cause havoc and misery." She spat the last three words and Tanya flinched. "Whatever the motive, the more time that passes after the switch, the less likely it is that either child will ever find their way back. It will be obvious early on whether they can adapt or not."

"What happens if they don't adapt?"

"A human child will usually be returned, more often than not to the same place it was taken from. But with a fairy child it's not quite so simple." Red closed her eyes tightly for a long moment. "Again, it depends on the circumstances. Mainly on whether the glamour lasts or not. In this case I'm guessing it probably won't." She paused again. "Do you know what glamour is, or do I have to explain that as well?" she said sarcastically.

"No...I mean yes," Tanya stuttered. "I know what glamour is."

Red nodded toward the child. "What you see there is what appears to be a human child. Yet you glimpsed—the same way I could—what really lies beneath. And the only reason you and I could see that is purely because we have the second sight and because the glamour is not one of the child's own creation.

"An ordinary person wouldn't know any different unless it wears off. Then they'd see exactly what we saw. The child would be exposed for what it really is, as it doesn't have the knowledge or ability to protect itself. And I can't let that happen."

"What...what would happen to it?"

"What do you think?" Red hissed. "If people saw him for what he really is? He'd be taken away! Put under observation in a laboratory somewhere—analyzed, poked, prodded, and experimented on. Just like they all are." Her voice weakened. "It's what humans do. If something's different. If we don't understand it. Once they go in those labs... well. They never come out. And it's all hushed up by people high up."

"You mean...you mean he'd probably die in a

laboratory somewhere, being experimented on?" Tanya choked.

"More than likely." Red's face was as hard as her voice. "So now you know why I did what I did. Why I do what I do."

Tanya closed her eyes. "This isn't the first time you've done this."

Red shook her head slowly, her catlike eyes unblinking as she studied Tanya. "It won't be the last, either."

"It . . . it happened to you, didn't it?" Tanya said quietly. "They took someone close to you. Someone you loved."

Red nodded. "James," she whispered. "My little brother."

Tanya averted her gaze as Red's eyes clouded. "So what happens now?"

"I wait."

"For what?"

"To see if the glamour on this child is one that's intended to last."

"How soon will you know?" Tanya asked.

"If it's only a superficial glamour—not intended to last—it'll weaken and show signs of the child's true nature very quickly. It could be anything from a couple of hours to a few days. A week at the most."

"What sort of signs?"

"The eyes will be the first to change," said Red. "They start to go dull until eventually they're completely black. The ears will be next, lengthening and pointing. Then finally the skin will take on a green-ish hue. These are the changelings that take priority. It's essential that they're returned to the fairy realm as soon as possible."

"And if the glamour isn't superficial?"

"Then the illusion will have been created to last a lifetime. Although the fairy children may look every part human, there will be certain...unusual quali-ties about them. Despite their best attempts to mimic human behavior, they'll be seen as different. In addi-tion to this, the lifespan of changelings in either instance will vastly vary from the norm. A human living in the fairy realm will surpass the average life expectancy by many years, whereas a fairy living in the mortal world will have a much shorter life."

"How much shorter?"

Red smiled a wry little smile.

"They are lucky to live much beyond their thir-ties. Just old enough to have settled down, started a family perhaps." She paused before adding, "A fam-ily with a *human*. Which brings me to your question: what are we?"

At this Tanya's heart began to thump.

"Are you starting to catch on yet?"

Tanya gave a dry swallow.

"I think so. You're saying that we're...people like us, we've..."

"Somewhere along the line, someone in your family—and mine—was switched. Someone was a changeling. It could be from either side; your mother's or father's. The second sight comes from having fairy blood. Like a gene, it won't occur in all of the changeling's descendants. In fact, it's quite the opposite. It's rare. It's like having blue eyes, for example. They wouldn't be passed down to every member of a family, just some of them. It's like that with the second sight."

"Fairy blood," Tanya repeated, stunned. "*Fairy blood.*" Instinctively she knew it to be true, along with everything else Red had told her. Fairy blood ran through her veins.

"So...now you know what you are," said Red. She glanced at a watch on her wrist, and gathered up her bag once more. "The sun will be rising soon. I need to leave."

Tanya watched her, trying to digest the sickening truth that she had just been fed. It swam inside her uneasily, like oil on water. For so long now, she had yearned for someone to believe her; for someone to understand. For even longer she had craved information. Knowledge, she knew, was power. And this girl—this strange, unbalanced girl whose obsession with the loss of her brother had driven her to these acts of desperation—had given her both. And Tanya knew that she could not afford to let her leave.

"Wait," said Tanya. "I..." She trailed off.

Red stopped moving. "Something you want to say to me?"

"I believe you," Tanya said quietly. "Everything you've told me. I believe it."

"What makes you think I care?"

"Because the fact that I believe you means that you don't have to run—not yet," said Tanya, an idea forming in her mind.

Something ignited behind Red's eyes; a small spark of interest.

"Go on," she said quietly.

"You need to lie low. People are looking for you... the police. It's been all over the news. I'm the only one who knows that you're here. And if I keep quiet, then nobody else will find out. I can help you."

"Why would you want to help me?" Red asked, suspicion all over her face.

Tanya looked at the changeling. "Because I know you don't mean him any harm. And because you have something that I want."

Red stared at her incredulously. "What could you possibly want from me?"

"Information," said Tanya. "You know things... things about fairies. I want you to share them with me. If you do then I won't tell anyone that I've seen you. I'll keep you a secret. And I can bring you food and water—you won't have to risk being seen in the house. With a bit of planning, you might even be able to sneak a shower."

At the mere mention of a shower Red's eyes took on a hungry look.

"A hot shower," she whispered. "Sounds like heaven." She lowered her head toward her armpit and sniffed suspiciously. "And is long overdue." Her eyes snapped back to Tanya. "If I agree then there's something else. If you want information, it'll cost you. I'll need you to do something for me."

"Like what?"

From her pocket Red pulled out a small piece of paper. "I need what's on this list. As many items as you can get. When you bring food and the items, leave them behind the passage opening where you got in. *Don't* come into the tunnels. If I hear anyone down here then I'll assume you've ratted me out— and I'll leave. Once you've got me the items I'll give you information. And then I'm out of here."

"All right," said Tanya, warily. "But in return, you keep out of the house until I say so. Stay down here, out of sight, until I say it's all clear for you to come up. I'll put food in the passage but you can come up when I've got the stuff on the list."

Red nodded curtly and held out the list. Tanya took it from her filthy, clammy hand.

"I'll take you back," said Red. "It's quite a way through the tunnels—and it's not the same way we left the house either."

"How did you find out about the secret passages in this house?" Tanya asked. "By accident?"

"No. Someone told me about them, someone I trust. I have a number of contacts—people doing the same thing as me. We swap information about hide-outs such as these. There are quite a few, dotted all over the country. Houses, churches, inns. Some of them, like this house, are connected to others a short distance away."

"I heard that there's a tunnel linking the house to a pub in Tickey End, and one leading to the church," said Tanya. "Is that true?"

"Yes. I got in through the one at the church. The entrance is through a grave."

"A *grave*?"

"It's a fake. Nobody was ever buried there. It was constructed solely as an entrance to the tunnels."

Tanya stood up. "Are all the tunnels one-way? Either into or out of the house?"

"No. Just one. The others go both ways. The only reason the one behind the bookcase doesn't is because of a fault. It was meant to allow access to the house from the tunnels too."

"So where's the way back in?" Tanya asked, clasping her arms about herself for warmth.

"The quickest way from here leads to a room up on the first floor: a guest room that was never intended for use. Because of that, the door has no lock. The way in is through a tiny crawl space in a section of the wooden wall paneling. We'll go that way."

Red moved off toward the opening in the cavern that led to the tunnel. As they approached, she stopped abruptly and spun around to face Tanya.

"There's something I forgot to mention. Something that might change your mind."

"What?" Tanya asked.

"The fact that you're helping me," said Red. "The fairies aren't going to like it. They aren't going to like it at all."

"How are they going to find out?"

"Surely you're not that naive?" Red hissed. She gestured wildly to the darkness surrounding them. "They're probably here, now. *Watching*."

"I can protect myself," said Tanya. "I'm not afraid."

Red eyed her with an expression that was half admiring and half scornful. Wordlessly, she spun around so her back was to Tanya, pulled her thick, tangled hair aside, then reached behind and yanked the neck of her dress down so the top of her back was exposed.

Even in the poor light, the shape of the girl's spine jutting through her flesh was clear to see. On her skin, at the top center of her back, Tanya could make out an ugly, burnlike mark that was about the size of a fist. It was not just any mark. The silvery scar tissue was in an oddly familiar shape: a set of wings. *Fairy wings*. They had been branded into the skin.

At Tanya's horrified gasp, Red pulled her dress back into place and turned back around to face her. "*This* is what happened when I made the mistake of underestimating them," she said bitterly. "I consider myself lucky to have escaped with only this scar."

"H-how...did you get that?" Tanya asked, all attempts at bravery gone.

"I hope for your sake you never have to find out," Red said grimly. "If you're not afraid of them, then you should be."

13

Avoiding Fabian the following day was to prove more difficult than Tanya anticipated. Since her discovery of Red and the knowledge of the truth behind her ability, Tanya now had her own agenda, and it was one that did not involve Fabian or his plans to go gallivanting in the woods.

When she finally came out of her room shortly after midday, stiff and exhausted, the first thing on her mind was to find out who the changeling in her family might have been—and she had no idea where to start. She wondered who had been switched: someone from her mother's side of the family, or her father's, and whether they had lived many years ago—or whether it was someone alive now, someone she knew. This possibility disturbed her deeply.

Her second concern was the list of items that Red

had asked her to get. This, she knew, was going to be problematic, for she only had a few pounds left over from what she'd spent in Tickey End. Unless she figured out a way of getting some more money then she would have to risk filching most of the items from around the house, and this would take time and planning. Until the list was complete, there was little Tanya could do except supply Red with food and water through the passage behind the bookcase.

Her grandmother was nowhere to be seen when she went downstairs, although a note had been left on the fridge bearing the message that her mother had telephoned earlier that morning. Tanya scrunched it up and chucked it into the trash. If her mother was trying to ease her conscience for dumping her out in the countryside, then Tanya had no intention of making it easy for her.

She filled a bowl with cornflakes and sat down at the kitchen table. Florence had not been at all happy when Tanya had refused to come down for break-fast. She had spent several minutes banging on the bedroom door before finally giving up and stomping back downstairs.

Halfway through her breakfast Tanya got up and switched on the radio on the windowsill, listening for the news. There was a brief mention of the stolen child, and a further description of Red. When the bulletin ended, Tanya was tense. The thought of Red in the tunnels below the house left her ill at ease, and not for the first time, she wondered if keeping quiet was a mistake she'd come to regret.

A torrent of conflicting thoughts fought inside her. Red was unstable, desperate. Desperate people did desperate things. *Dangerous* things. There was nothing to guarantee she would keep her word and stay out of the house. Yet she was also the only person Tanya knew of that shared her ability, and this was a bond she could not ignore. They had both suffered at the hands of the fairies, but now it was evident that so far, what Tanya had experienced was torment. Red, it seemed, had endured something like torture.

She turned the radio off in the middle of a weather forecast that was predicting summer storms, and was staring dismally into her soggy breakfast when Fabian slouched into the kitchen. Wordlessly he picked up the cereal box still on the side where Tanya had left it, delved inside with his hand, then withdrew it and shoved a fistful of cornflakes into his mouth.

"You are disgusting," snapped Tanya. "How about a bowl, some milk, and a spoon?"

"Tastes better this way," Fabian mumbled, between munches. As he turned to leave Tanya saw an angry bruise on his temple, glaring out against the paleness of his skin.

"How did you get that?" she asked immediately. "What happened to your face?"

"Nothing." Fabian's tone was sullen, his blue eyes lowered. "I fell."

"You *fell*?"

"Yes. I fell, all right?"

Tanya narrowed her eyes, but said nothing more.

"Oh, and thanks for mending my T-shirt," he said suddenly, and Tanya sensed his eagerness to change the subject. "The stitches are perfect. I thought you said you were terrible at sewing?"

"I am," she said, puzzled. "I didn't mend it."

Fabian blinked, his eyes huge and owl-like behind his glasses. "Then who did? Florence says it wasn't her, either. And it definitely wasn't Warwick."

Out of the corner of her eye, Tanya became aware of the hearthfay's creepily long fingers wrapping themselves around the coal bin. The movement was followed by a simpering little sigh. She glanced at it suspiciously. It shot out of sight, and a reel of green cotton rolled a little way along the hearth before being hastily snatched back.

Tanya turned back to Fabian and shrugged. She was wise enough to know better than to take credit for a fairy's work—even if it left her with no answers.

"Anyway, we need to talk," he said.

Tanya stared at the bruise on his temple, the hearthfay forgotten. "About what?"

"About what we discussed last night—going back into the forest."

"Oh. That," Tanya answered, unable to hide her lack of enthusiasm.

"We have to get organized," said Fabian. "We'll

need to take a few things with us. Warm clothing, a map, a flashlight, a compass, food and water—"

"Food and water? I'm not planning on a picnic!"

"Neither am I," said Fabian. "It's just a precaution in case we get lost again. Now, I've already got a thermos, a map, and a flashlight, so—"

"Hang on a minute," Tanya interrupted. "Why do we need a flashlight...I hope you're not suggesting what I think you are?"

The absence of an answer confirmed her suspicions.

"You're not serious? I'm not going into those woods at night!"

"Keep your voice down!"

"Well, I won't go!"

Fabian's nostrils flared in annoyance.

"Look, I'm not ecstatic about the idea myself. But in case you haven't noticed, Warwick hardly let me out of his sight yesterday—it's as if he knows we're up to something. The only chance we've got is when he's not watching. And the only time he's not watching is when he's asleep." He glared at her, but there was a desperation about him. "I have to find out what happened. I have to *know*. If you want out then say so. Otherwise, don't waste my time."

"What if we find out that your grandfather *did* do...do something to Morwenna Bloom?" Tanya said quietly. "Have you thought about how that'll make you feel? It could change everything. You've lived with not knowing up until now. Maybe you're better off staying that way."

She regretted her words instantly as she saw the look in Fabian's eyes. They were haunted.

"I'd probably agree with that if we hadn't seen her... or whatever it was that looked like her in the woods," he whispered. "But now... things have already changed. I *can't* just forget. And whatever happened can't be worse than I've already imagined in my head. Whatever happened can't be worse than the not knowing."

Tanya bit her lip. And even though her mind was screaming the opposite, she heard herself say, "I'll... I'll do it. I'll come with you."

The look on Fabian's face told her heart she had done the right thing. Her head, however, remained unconvinced. "So... when?" she asked.

Fabian looked solemn. "Tonight."

***

It was the first time Tanya had seen Fabian's room. He was intensely private about it, and now it was clear to see why. The best way in which it could be described was a hybrid of a science laboratory and a small museum. On the desk over by the fireplace was an enormous globe of the world, along with various papers in Fabian's scribbled handwriting. Skulls and teeth of animals covered the shelves, and there were thick books on every scientific and historic subject

Tanya could think of, plus many she had never even heard of.

There were detailed drawings, diagrams, and observations on natural forms and the like, plus the weird magnifying device Fabian had been using on Tanya's first day at the manor. She also noted with disgust a glass of milk that was so old it was turning to cheese, and was unsure whether it was an experiment or just the result of Fabian's general untidiness.

In the corner of the room stood a life-size human skeleton, which probably would have looked eerie had it not been wearing Fabian's school tie and blazer.

"That's not real, is it?" she asked.

"It's plastic."

"Where did you get it?" Tanya asked.

"School," Fabian replied. "Now, about this map—"

"You didn't steal it, did you?" said Tanya, swallowing a surge of laughter as she envisaged Fabian smuggling out a fully clothed skeleton under the pretense of it being a real person.

Fabian's nostrils were beginning to flare in the way they always did when he was annoyed about something. "It's for a project. Now shut up for a minute and listen." He took the map and spread it out. After flicking a dirty sock out of the way, Tanya sat at the foot of the bed.

"This map shows the whole of Hangman's Wood and its surrounding areas," said Fabian, pointing to the church and Tickey End. "All the catacombs are

clearly marked. This is where we entered the forest."
He tapped the clearing by the brook. "This is the
first catacomb we came to, see? The big one. This
smaller one here is where we saw the girl. It's actually
not that far from the first one—but we were so lost
that day that we must've been walking in circles, so it
seemed farther away.

"We should follow the same route as before—it'll
be easier with the map. I've got everything we need
except for a compass, but Warwick has one, so I just
have to think of a way—"

"I've got a compass," said Tanya, thinking of the
one that the gypsy woman had given her. She felt
more than a little disturbed as the thought occurred
to her how coincidental it was that she now needed
to use it.

"You don't mean that lump of junk Mad Morag
gave you?" Fabian rolled his eyes. "All right. It might
come in handy if I can't get hold of Warwick's. I'm
going to hide my backpack with all this stuff in the
garden in a few minutes, while no one's around.
Meet me there and bring the compass. I might be
able to fix it."

"Maybe this isn't such a good idea..."

Fabian gave her a hard look. "You're not having
second thoughts, are you?"

Tanya squirmed. "No...it's just, well, I heard
the weather forecast for this evening. It's not good.
There's going to be a storm. Maybe we should leave
it until another night."

Fabian shook his head. "No. The forecast isn't always right anyway. Plus, if there is a storm it could be an asset to us."

"How?"

"Because nobody—not even Warwick—will be expecting us to sneak off in the middle of a storm. If he's guessed we're planning anything, he'll think that the storm will deter us."

Tanya was silent as she pondered his words. In a way, he was making sense, although this did nothing to comfort her. "We might not even find anything," she said in a small voice. "Maybe the girl we saw wasn't her..."

Fabian scowled. "That girl was Morwenna Bloom. You know it as surely as I do." He folded the map and shoved it violently in his rucksack, then stalked over to the window. On the window ledge, Tanya noticed for the first time, was a framed photograph of Warwick with his arms around a woman who was holding a small baby. For once, he looked happy.

"Is that your mother?"

Fabian would not look at her. "You'd better get the compass," he said abruptly. "Meet me in the garden in five minutes."

Tanya left quietly, feeling foolish for mentioning his mother. The subject was obviously still raw—and always would be. She collected the compass from beneath the floorboard in her room and took it out to the back garden.

She had to trample through a substantial amount of weeds before she found Fabian sitting on a tree stump with his head in his hands. Balanced on his knees was his brown leather book, which he was reading so intently he had not noticed that his glasses were nearly falling off the end of his nose. He jumped up when he saw her approaching and snapped the book shut.

"Did you bring it?"

Tanya reached into her pocket and fished out the compass, thankful that his mood seemed to have improved.

"Here. I don't think it's going to be of much use, though."

Fabian took the compass and examined it. "Seems all right now," he said, giving Tanya a strange look. "Maybe it was just damp that day, or something. Lucky you didn't sell it to that dodgy fellow after all."

"But the needle wasn't working," she argued, snatching it back from him. "It—oh . . . that's funny."

Sure enough, the tarnished hand on the old compass was pointing steadily to the bottom, back the way she had just come.

"What did you do with that money he dropped, anyway?"

"Nothing," Tanya replied. In truth she had completely forgotten about the money she had pocketed that day—but she could have hugged Fabian for reminding her of it. Now she could use the money the antiques dealer had dropped to buy the items on Red's list. She suddenly became aware that she was starting to smile to herself, and quickly pulled herself back to the task at hand before Fabian noticed her expression.

"I've never seen a compass like this before," she said. "What does the 'H' stand for? And where are all the other directions, North, East, South, and West?"

Fabian grabbed it out of her hand and scrutinized it.

"That's odd. This 'H,' where the 'N' for north should be...if we turn this way, toward the house, the needle meets it perfectly."

"So?" said Tanya.

"It's wrong," said Fabian. "I know for a fact that the house, from the back door to the woods, faces northeast. So facing back in the opposite direction, the compass should read southwest, but it doesn't. It reads north." He thrust the compass back into Tanya's hand. "You're right, it *is* useless. And as Mad Morag gave it to you it's probably cursed anyway. I'd get rid of it."

"Oh, don't be so ignorant. The things people say about her—about her being a witch—it's probably just made up to keep kids out of the forest."

"I doubt it," said Fabian at once.

Tanya glared at him. "It's a *rumor*. And you're the last person I would have expected to believe rumors, especially with what you told me about Amos."

"If Amos is innocent, then he was in the wrong place at the wrong time. But that gypsy woman... people have been saying things about her for years."

"I think she was trying to help me," said Tanya.

Fabian ignored her. "Only last week old Rosie Beak, who owns the tea shop, told my dad that Morag got rid of her warts last winter, all three of them. Two weeks after the last one had gone, Ned Baker called Morag an old fraud because she refused to tell his fortune. And do you know what? Within days, he had three warts. Never had a wart in his life before, he said."

"Shut up," said Tanya, exasperated. She lifted the compass to face the house, her face screwed up in thought as the needle swung to "H" and sat there, perfectly still.

"She knew," Tanya whispered.

"Knew what?"

"She knew I was going to need this."

For finally, she understood what the "H" stood for. Home.

14

It was ten minutes before midnight. Outside, a wild wind howled, and torrential rain hammered at the windows. Tanya was growing increasingly jittery. She had dressed warmly in a woolen sweater, jeans, two pairs of socks, sneakers, and an old raincoat that she had left at the manor two winters ago. By a stroke of luck, it also happened to be red. This, she hoped, combined with a rusty iron nail she had pried loose from her doorframe, would protect her from any fairy activity. It would not be enough to prevent her getting soaked, however. In the pockets she'd found a crumpled ten-pound note that she had completely forgotten about. She immediately tucked it into her purse to go toward the items Red needed.

For the past two hours she had been asking herself exactly what she expected to find in the woods, aside from seven catacombs and an old witch who gave away magical compasses. The possibility of discovering a fifty-year-old skeleton was at the forefront of her mind; for if Morwenna Bloom *was* out there, then her bones would surely be all that was left of her.

She ran her thumb over the compass in her pocket. Since discovering its true use Fabian had remained oddly quiet, occasionally muttering about anomalies in the earth's magnetic field. Tanya however, was feeling increasingly troubled by the old gypsy woman's involvement and the nature of her intentions.

The minutes slipped away until she could put it off no longer. Her heartbeat quickened as she stepped out of her room into the dim hallway. If she was caught now, her time at the manor was sure to become very unpleasant indeed. She crept down the stairs, with only the light of a small lamp on the telephone table to guide her.

"Some-body's-in-trou-ble!" said a sly, singsong voice from inside the grandfather clock.

"Shut up!" Tanya whispered.

She was to instantly regret speaking as a light snapped on from above. Someone was making their way across the second-floor landing with slow, shuffling footsteps.

*Amos.*

Instinctively, she dropped to the floor and crouched in the shadows. The old man's slow pace continued onward toward the staircase. At the top of the stairs he seemed to pause for the briefest of moments before hobbling on. She waited for the sound of the bathroom door closing, then hastily slipped down the rest of the stairs.

She wiped the back of her hand across her forehead. It was cold and clammy. In the kitchen, the back door was rattling from the gusty wind. Tanya looked longingly at an umbrella propped against the wall. There was no point taking it. The gales would render it useless.

Oberon got up from his bed and padded over to her, his claws clicking softly on the tiles.

"Come on, boy," she said. "How about a nice walk?"

The dog's ears pricked up at her suggestion, and then he lowered his head, allowing her to slip his leash on.

The back door had been left unlocked, as Fabian had planned.

"Here goes," she whispered to herself, and then stepped outside.

Even though she tried to brace herself for it, the wind and rain hit her hard. The sheer force nearly knocked her off her feet. Had she not been wearing the raincoat she would have been drenched in seconds. As it was, her legs were soon soaked below the knee where the raincoat ended. Oberon, however, did not appear overly bothered by the wetness of it all. He just seemed glad for an extra walk.

She stumbled through the garden, the utter darkness from the combination of the weather and the towering trees preventing her from seeing any farther than a few feet ahead. She slid through puddles of mud, soaking her feet completely. By the time she reached the gate she was half-drenched, cold, and miserable. Already, she knew her decision to come was a mistake.

"What took you so long?" Fabian asked, his lips blue with cold.

"Amos," said Tanya, through chattering teeth. "He decided to take a little walk across the landing just as I was on my way downstairs. I had to wait in case he saw me."

"And what did you bring him for?" he said, looking at Oberon in disgust.

"Protection. I always feel safer when he's at my side."

"Hiding behind you, more like. He's a coward."

"He'd defend me if he needed to!"

Fabian gave a disbelieving stare, then looked toward the forest, squinting through the rain.

"Let's get going. Better not waste any more time. It should be drier in the woods, once we're under the trees."

They set off toward the forest, unsteady on the waterlogged ground. The squelching of their footsteps and the tumultuous pouring of the rain filled their ears. Then a low rumble of thunder began in the distance. There was no moon or stars to guide them; no streetlights glowed as they would in the city. The darkness was a heavy, suffocating vacuum. Only the silhouette of the forest stood out ahead, one shade of black darker than the sky.

Tanya's courage began to fail her.

"This is stupid," she said, stopping suddenly. "Anything could happen on a night like tonight. What if we get caught? Or what if one of us gets injured? We could get hypothermia by the time help arrives! And what if the ground caves in like it did in Tickey End—"

"The ground isn't going to cave in!" said Fabian.

"It might; it's happened before! You told me yourself!"

Fabian lost his temper. "If you're going to whine like a baby then I don't know why you bothered coming. You might as well go back. Otherwise, shut up! We're nearly there!"

Tanya opened her mouth to reply, but was struck dumb as a large, black shape swooped soundlessly through the air toward them. With a small cry she ducked out of the way, narrowly avoiding being hit by the flying object—but Fabian was not so fortunate. She heard him wince as the thing grazed the top of his head before it disappeared into the night.

"What was *that*?" he exclaimed, rubbing his crown.

"I don't know!" Tanya gasped, scanning the dark sky. The swirling mass of rain thrown into her eyes by the wind was blinding her. Her hair whipped around her face. "A bat, I think!" Before she had even finished the sentence, she saw another dark swoop—and this time Fabian yelled, clutching at his scalp.

"What?" Tanya cried.

Fabian pulled his fingers away from the top of his head. They were smeared with blood. They both watched as the lashing rain washed it away in seconds.

"It's attacking me!" Fabian managed. "Whatever it is . . . it's *attacking* me!"

"Look out!" Tanya shouted, as the thing swooped silently once more, seemingly out of nowhere. Oberon lunged into the air with an enthusiastic snap of his jaws, but the creature was long gone before his teeth had even clicked together.

Fabian ducked, then stumbled and lost his balance, falling down onto the waterlogged earth. He emerged wearing a suit of mud, shaking violently. There was no time to speak, or even to think of what was happening before the creature launched another assault—and this time it did not fly off. Instead, it hooked onto the back of Fabian's mud-drenched clothes with long, black talons, and began a frenzied attack on the back of his head.

Suddenly, Tanya was able to see the thing for exactly what it was: not a bat but a bird. A large, black bird. *A raven.* Tearing and jabbing at Fabian's hair and scalp for all it was worth—because, she realized, it could not get to *her.* By speaking, she had surrendered the protection of the red raincoat—but she was still protected by the iron nail in her pocket.

"*Get it off!*" Fabian yelled, batting at his head to no avail. "Make it stop!"

Oberon growled, jumping up at Fabian in an attempt to get at the bird. Ultimately, he only served to make things worse. His huge bulk collided heavily with Fabian's gangly frame—and Fabian went down for a second time, the wind knocked out of him. The raven, sensing its vulnerable position, released its hold on Fabian and soared up, above them.

Tanya hauled Fabian out of the mud. He was shaking with rage or cold or fear—or perhaps all three. A thin line of blood trickled down his forehead. Glancing fearfully above, Tanya quickly pulled her left arm out of her raincoat and bundled it around Fabian's mud-soaked shoulders, doing the only thing she could think of to project the protection of the nail in the raincoat pocket onto Fabian as well as herself. All the while her mind worked furiously to come up with a lie that she hoped would convince Fabian to do as she instructed.

"What are you doing?" Fabian said weakly.

"Put this on," said Tanya. "Put your left arm through—that's it—and now put your other arm around me."

"What use is that?" Fabian spluttered. "This is no time for a cuddle, you know!"

"It's to fool the bird, you idiot! Don't you see? It's been driven mad by the storm, and for some reason it's attacking you! If it thinks you and I are one person, we might be able to make it back to the house with your head intact!" She hoped she sounded convincing enough. For a moment, Fabian's expression led her to fear the opposite.

"Back to the house?" he said, looking toward the forest.

Tanya followed his gaze. Water was trickling down her spine, and her hair was plastered to the sides of her face. "We can't do this, Fabian. Not tonight; it's all wrong. We have to go back."

They stared at the woods, and Tanya felt Fabian slump with defeat next to her. They started to turn to go back when a flash of lightning lit up the sky. In that instant they both saw it. A shadowy figure was standing perfectly still by the brook. Even though it was no more than a split second, the outline of the figure was unmistakable.

"Warwick," Tanya whispered.

They stood, rooted to the spot in fear.

"What are we going to do?"

"Run," said Fabian, sounding choked. "And pray he hasn't seen us!"

They turned and ran as fast as they could back toward the house, jostling and bumping together in the raincoat like some kind of four-legged and two-armed mythical monster. Oberon galloped along beside them happily, his tongue hanging out like a slice of ham. To him it was all a game.

Tanya turned to look over her shoulder. The raven was gone, successful in its attempts to prevent them from venturing farther. There was only the more imminent danger that was Warwick. All she could see through the sheets of rain was the outline of the forest against the sky. "Do you think he saw us?"

"I don't know," Fabian gasped. "But if we saw him, then there's a good chance he saw us too!"

"I told you this was a bad idea!" Tanya yelled. "We should never have left the house!"

They neared the gate, wheezing for breath. Fabian shrugged out of the raincoat and fumbled with the latch. A clap of thunder made them jump.

"Quickly!" said Tanya. "Before the lightning strikes again!"

The latch lifted and Fabian swung the gate open and slipped through with Oberon, then Tanya stepped half into the garden, pausing to stare back toward the forest.

"Come on!" Fabian pulled her through. "Hurry!"

"Wait." Tanya peered around the edge of the gate. The lightning flashed a second time, illuminating the sky. It was enough to see that there was no sign of Warwick anywhere near.

"I can't see him," she said, closing the gate. "Let's just get back inside the house." By now her face was numb, frozen by the relentless rain.

They hurried through the garden, skidding dangerously in the mud. Fabian knelt down outside the back door and retrieved the key, hidden beneath an upturned flowerpot. It was only when they entered the kitchen and Oberon trotted over to his basket that Tanya realized that getting upstairs quickly was not going to be possible.

"Oh, no... the floor... look at the floor!"

Fabian looked down in dismay at the trail of muddy paw prints leading from the door to the dog's bed, then at his own mud-caked shoes and clothes. What little color was left in his face drained right then.

Tanya thought quickly.

"Take off your shoes and carry them upstairs. Hide them until you get the chance to clean them." She scanned the kitchen until her eyes rested on a damp cloth at the sink. "I'll clean up this mess, and any drips of water you might leave in the hallway."

"But what about Warwick?" said Fabian. "He could be here any second!"

Tanya's stomach churned. "There's still a chance he didn't see us. If we do this properly we might get away with it. If he did see us it'll make no difference if he catches me—he'll know it was us anyway."

"I just don't get it," said Fabian. "How could he have known?"

"He must have heard us talking somehow and decided to wait for us," said Tanya, removing her sodden sneakers. "But we don't have time for this now—go, and I'll see you in the morning." Spying a roll of paper towels, she tore off a handful and threw it at Fabian. "For your head. Now go."

Fabian pulled off his muddy boots and crept upstairs. Immediately, Tanya set to work on the floor, frantically wiping up all traces of mud. When the floor was spotless, she began to rub at Oberon's dirty paws. The dog lay there and let her do it, eyeing her lazily. Her heart thudded in her chest as the door rattled in the wind. With every gust she thought Warwick was back and the game was up.

When she was convinced there was no evidence that anyone had been outside, she took a towel from the draining board and carefully made her way upstairs, drying any drips that Fabian had left. Luckily, the first-floor landing was carpeted, so there was little else she could do except hope that any damp spots dried out by morning.

By the time she got back to her room Tanya was exhausted, but with the kind of nervous energy she knew would not allow her to sleep. She had no idea whether Warwick had seen them or not, although the fact that they had made it back unchallenged gave her hope. And the raven...she shuddered. The fairies had sent Raven in her bird form to scare Fabian as well as Tanya. It had been warning them. But about what? Warwick—or the woods?

She stuffed the filthy cloth and towel under the bed with her saturated clothes and shoes before pulling on her pajamas and jumping into bed, winding herself into the covers and desperately trying to warm her freezing hands and feet.

One thought was chanting in her mind.

*How could Warwick have known?*

She did not remember falling asleep that night, but when sleep came it was far from restful. When the yelling began shortly before six o'clock the next morning, it did not wake her as quickly as usual. After she finally opened her eyes, it was several seconds before she realized that the noise was not coming from Amos, but from the very same room she was in.

The person shouting was her.

15

At first, Tanya thought she must have still been dreaming as the room came into focus, for what she saw was the stuff of nightmares.

In the night, her hair had grown—a lot. It had grown at least four times as long as Tanya was tall. The room was full of hair. Thick, shiny chestnut waves spilled over the bedclothes, pooled on the carpet, and lapped at the walls and door like a dark brown sea. It was everywhere, and there was so much of it that it had even begun to climb the walls and wind itself around the doorknob, as well as snaking up the chimney in the same way ivy crawled up the walls of the manor. As a thick tendril inched its way slyly toward the window ledge, Tanya realized the worst of it.

Her hair was still growing.

Terror gnawed at her like a rat. She couldn't think. She couldn't move. She was frozen, helpless. This was her punishment for attempting to enter the woods last night.

She barely had time to register the telltale creak of the floorboards outside on the landing before there was a loud rapping on the door.

"What's going on in there?" Her grandmother's voice was harsh and insistent.

Tanya's mouth opened and closed wordlessly.

"N-nothing," she managed finally. "I'm fine."

"I heard shouting. Is everything all right?"

Tanya's eyes widened in horror as the doorknob began to turn. She heard her grandmother's exasperated tut as the door remained firmly shut—and closed her eyes in temporary relief. She did not even remember locking it.

"I had a nightmare," she croaked. "But I'm all right now."

"I don't like locked doors in this house," said Florence. "Not when there are people behind them."

Tanya stared at the door, stricken. There was absolutely no way she could afford to open that door to her grandmother, but if Florence really wanted to come in there would be no stopping her. If Warwick had a skeleton key then her grandmother was sure to have one too.

"I didn't mean to lock it," Tanya said quietly. "It won't happen again." Another lie.

"If you've wet the bed or something I won't be

cross." Florence's voice was firm but not unkind. "We can clean the sheets now and no one else need know. But if you leave it—"

"No, I *haven't* wet the bed!" Tanya practically shouted. "I just had a nightmare, that's all!" Panic was bubbling up inside her, threatening to turn into hysteria. She fought the urge to scream.

"Very well." Her grandmother's tone was back to its usual standoffish manner. "Breakfast is at eight. I expect you to be at the table promptly."

*Go away, go away, go away!* Tanya shrieked inside her head—but all she could do was listen as Florence retreated along the landing to her own room.

With the threat of her grandmother no longer imminent, Tanya jolted into action. She pushed back the bedclothes with difficulty, the movement hampered by the extra weight of the hair cascading over the covers. As she stepped out of bed, her feet disappeared into the mounds of hair. Every step she took felt like she was wading through thick brown syrup.

The hair was enchanted, of that she held no doubt. Its weight and the way it clung to her limbs was not normal; it was like the hair itself was trying to prevent her from escaping. Carefully, she slid her way toward the adjoining bathroom and rummaged through the cabinet for the nail scissors.

They were not there.

Something gurgled behind her. Tanya turned slowly, with a sickening feeling of understanding, and peered into the plughole in the bathtub. Her gaze met with a pair of huge, gleaming eyes. The rotten-egg stench of drains wafted up as the drain-dweller stretched its hand through the plughole and mimed a scissor movement with its froglike fingers.

"*Snip, snip,*" it gargled. "*Oh, snip, snip!*"

"Give them back!" Tanya whispered angrily. She lunged for the creature's hand but it slid out of her grasp. "Please," she begged. "Just for a minute, give them to me . . . you can have them back afterward, I promise! You can keep them!"

The creature belched and danced gleefully in the drain, spurting murky water through the plughole. It was clearly enjoying itself.

"Snip, snip! Findings, keepings! Trickings and treatings! Shiny, glittery, snippetty, snappetty . . . oh, snip, snip! *Snippetty* SNIP!"

Tanya would have gladly snipped the creature's thieving little fingers off had she been able to get to the scissors, but they were well and truly out of her reach, no doubt with her missing watch deep in the drain creature's lair.

"*Hairy, hairy, crossed the fairies, how does your bonnet grow?*" the fairy cackled. "*With dandruff, lice, it's all very nice, and . . . oh!*"

"I *don't* have lice," Tanya said furiously, scratching at her suddenly itchy head. "Or dandruff!" Several white flakes floated past her face. She stopped scratching in alarm. "You! You just did that, you . . . you—"

She broke off as she realized the creature had

ceased its taunting and was now gazing at something in utter adoration. Its beady eyes were trained on the silver charm bracelet her grandmother had given her. It was sparkling even in the murky light of the bathroom. A sudden plan formed in her mind, one in which the bracelet could play a part in protecting her after all.

"You like this?" she said. "You do, don't you?"

The creature nodded vigorously, its bald head bobbing up and down in the drain. "Shiny. *Twinkles*!"

"I'll make a deal with you," said Tanya. She lowered her voice. "These charms are magical," she lied. "Each of them has a special power."

The creature's eyes widened in excitement. Scanning the charms, Tanya selected her least favorite, the cauldron, and tugged at it until the link weakened and finally snapped. She held it aloft. "This cauldron will fill with anything you wish for. You could fill your whole drain with shiny, glittery treasures. You can have it in exchange for the scissors."

"Yes, yes," the creature gurgled, reaching its arm through the plughole once more. "Mine now, mine!"

Tanya shook her head. "First, the scissors."

The creature pouted and sulked, but Tanya held her ground, lifting the charm higher to catch the light. The drain-dweller's eyes grew wide and it licked its lips in anticipation. Finally it admitted defeat and squelched into the depths of the plughole.

A moment later it emerged with the slime-covered scissors and placed them in Tanya's palm, before snatching the charm she offered from her other hand and sliding back into the safety of the drain.

Tanya collapsed on the bathroom floor as the fairy crooned with glee over its new possession. Her sense of relief was to be short-lived. As she lifted the scissors to her hair and began to hack, it became clear that nothing was happening. She tried harder, with fewer strands, but not one single hair could be severed from her head. In frustration she tossed them aside. She already knew it wasn't the scissors, knew that they were sharp enough. It was her hair, or rather, the *spell* on her hair. It couldn't be broken with scissors alone.

She sat on the cold tiles, her hair rippling around her. She had no idea how she was going to get out of this one. Her only hope was Red. If only she could find a way of getting to her unseen. She felt her eyes well with tears at the thought. She was the one meant to be helping Red, not the other way around. Clearly she had overestimated her capabilities. She screwed her face up in determination. What would Red do?

"Salt," she murmured. "The color red. Running water. Iron. Turning clothes inside out." She repeated the list of deterrents over and over, hoping that a solution would present itself, but nothing did. The only thing she could think of was to wash her hair under the shower hose . . . but getting all of her hair into the bathroom would prove tricky, if not impossible. Besides, she had a feeling that the running water the old book had been referring to would be something like a stream or a river, not a running tap.

Tanya held her head in her hands, defeated.

"You knew the scissors wouldn't work, didn't you?" she whispered, knowing the creature in the drain was still there, listening. "You tricked me."

"*Tricketty, tricketty.* Tricketty trappetty!"

"I'll give you more charms...I'll give you the whole bracelet if you just break the spell!"

"Not my spell, oh no. Not mine to break."

Somehow, Tanya knew it to be true. The spell was too sophisticated, and the drain-dweller had never bothered her in this way before, even though it had added to the spell by giving her lice and dandruff. It simply contented itself with stealing away anything shiny.

The drain-dweller emerged from the plughole, brandishing the charm at her. "Not magical," it said crossly. "Tricketty girl!"

Tanya shrugged, careful not to let on that she had been untruthful. Despite the fact that the creature had lied to her, it would be unwise to admit her own deception in case it angered the fairy and incurred further punishment.

"Perhaps the magic doesn't work when the charms are separated," she said at last. "Perhaps the charms' power is linked—they have to be together to work."

The drain-dweller scowled. "Tricketty," it muttered one last time, before skulking back into the sink with the charm.

Not knowing what else to do, Tanya left the bathroom, dragging her hair behind her. She sat down on the bed. Red was her only hope. Somehow, she had to get to her, but deep down she knew she hadn't a chance. It was just a matter of time before her grandmother forced the door open. She did not want to think what would happen beyond that.

Breakfast time drew ever nearer. Tanya's stomach felt as though it was turning itself inside out as she waited for the inevitable call from her grandmother. She did not have to wait long before Florence was hollering up the stairs, and by the fourth time she was sounding very annoyed indeed.

Tanya pictured her thin mouth twisting in anger, and suddenly felt strangely detached. She would be taken away when they opened the door and saw her, of that she was sure. Taken away...and asked questions and experimented on by people in white coats. Just like a changeling.

Footsteps clomped up the stairs. Tanya drew in a slow, deep breath. Someone tapped on the door.

"Tanya? What are you playing at? Florence wants you downstairs now—she's had enough! And so have I. My breakfast is going cold!"

"Fabian?" Tanya whispered.

"Yes," came the impatient reply. "What are you doing in there? Open the door."

"I can't. I'm not coming down."

"You have to. Florence knows something's wrong. She says if you don't come down now she's coming up and letting herself in with the skeleton key." Fabian lowered his voice. "Is it something to do with last night? Warwick hasn't said anything—I think we got away with it."

"No...it's not that." Tanya got up off the bed and shuffled to the door. "I can't tell you. You might as well go downstairs."

"Just tell me. I might be able to help."

"Trust me, you can't."

"I'm not going anywhere until you open the door and I see that you're all right."

"No!"

"Fine."

There was scrabbling from the other side of the door.

"I hope you're dressed," Fabian said. "If you're not, then now's the time to get back in bed!"

"What? Fabian—"

There was a distinctive sound of a key being inserted into the lock, and the key on Tanya's side popped out and fell to the floor.

"Fabian, how *could* you!" she cried. She hurled herself against the door as the lock clicked. "How dare you do this? I'll...I'll tell Warwick you've been using his skeleton key to look all around the house!"

"It's not Warwick's." The doorknob began to turn. "It's mine. I found it in one of the old servants' rooms."

Fabian began to push the door from the other side. Tanya pushed back with all her might, but already she knew she was not strong enough to hold him off for long. The hair on the floor was impeding the grip of her bare feet as it was.

"I mean it, Fabian!" Tanya shouted. "I'll never forgive you if you do this!"

The door began to inch open. She shoved back, panic fueling her supply of strength.

"It's...for your own...good," Fabian panted. "Once I see...you're all right...I'll go. Florence... is going to...come up here...anyway!"

"I don't care!" Tanya roared. "You're not coming in!"

But whether she liked it or not, Fabian *was* coming in. He had gained another two inches in the last few seconds, and Tanya's stance was weakening. Already, it was clear he could see something was very wrong.

"What's that? On the floor...what is it? It looks like...like..."

Tanya's strength was all but spent. She managed a few more seconds before she slid backward into the room and Fabian fell clumsily but quickly through the door, skidding on the piles of hair like a newborn foal. He landed in an awkward heap beside the bed.

Tanya jumped forward and grabbed the skeleton key from the outside, and then closed and locked the door from the inside. She turned to face Fabian, sensing that he had been stunned into silence.

He was sitting rigid on the floor, with one ankle at an uncomfortable-looking angle from where he had fallen—and was too shocked even to move. He stared at a fistful of hair in his palm, then slowly flexed his fingers and followed the strand of hair with disbelieving eyes until his gaze met with Tanya's.

Strangely, she felt calmer now that Fabian was actually in the room than she had at the thought of him being in the room. She felt oddly out of control, like her life was no longer her own, and yet somehow she accepted that whatever happened next depended entirely upon Fabian's reaction. She was too tired to fight, too tired to lie. Bizarrely, all she wanted now was to tell the truth—and now that he had seen her, Fabian *had* to listen.

"I need to tell you something, Fabian." Her voice was quiet, and calmer than she anticipated. "You were right about me. I *was* hiding something. All those things you noticed about me, the strange things that happen when I'm around . . . well, they all happen for a reason. You might find it hard to believe at first—"

She stopped speaking as she noticed that Fabian hadn't heard a word. His mouth was moving slowly, although no words seemed to be coming out. His eyes were wide, and still fixed on her in horror and utter confusion.

"Witch," he said quietly, but clearly enough for her to hear this time.

"What? No, Fabian, listen to me—"

"The gypsy witch," said Fabian. His eyes trailed from her head, following her hair around the room for the umpteenth time. "She did this. She's cursed you! She cursed you when she gave you that compass!"

Tanya was struck dumb by his words. In a split second she considered Fabian's theory. It was one she had not even entertained: that this could be the work of the old gypsy woman. Certainly it seemed she would be capable of it. Yet somehow Tanya doubted that the old woman would go to the trouble of pretending to help her only to do something like this.

It seemed unlikely... and yet it was still possible. And Fabian's absolute conviction that this had been the turn of events also gave her an easy way out. She would no longer need to go through the humiliation of trying to convince him of the fairies' existence if this was what he believed.

"I think... I think you could be right," she said slowly.

"Of course I'm right!" Fabian spluttered. "The old hag has hexed practically everyone in Tickey End at some point, and you're next on her list! We should have sold the compass to that man on the bus!"

"What am I going to do?" Tanya gestured helplessly. "I can't let anyone else see me!"

"I don't know... I don't *know*," Fabian muttered. "But you're right. We can't let them see you like this. We'll have to get something to cut it. Haven't you got any scissors?"

Tanya shook her head.

"I've only got nail scissors. They didn't work."

"Well, what about if I can get the kitchen scissors... or Warwick has some garden shears... or an axe, maybe?"

"It's not just about a sharp object," Tanya said. "We need to do something that will break the spell."

"Oh," Fabian said gloomily. "Any suggestions?"

"I once read...somewhere...about a list of things that are supposed to...break spells and curses," Tanya said carefully. "The list was: being near running water, like a stream or a brook, the color red, salt, turning clothes inside out, and iron. So if we can think of something that links to one of those things, then maybe there's a chance it will work." She lifted her hand to her hair subconsciously. The movement caused a dazzle of light to shimmer off one of the charms on the bracelet. The dagger.

"Can you think of an object, say, a knife, with a red handle?" she asked.

Fabian brightened. "Florence has a letter opener with a sort of orangey handle. That's nearly red. And it's sharp. Maybe that would work."

Tanya shook her head. "It has to be *red*. Bright red."

They stared at each other in silence, dismal expressions mirrored in one another's face.

"A knife," Fabian repeated slowly.

Florence screeched up the stairs, making them both start.

"Will you both come down this instant! This is the last time I'm going to tell you before I come up there and drag you both down by the scruffs of your necks!"

"Well, that's it, then," said Tanya. "The game's up."

But Fabian had the start of a frown on his face; the kind of frown he wore when he had an idea . . . or when he was about to do something devious.

"Hold on." He sprang to his feet, barely wincing at his twisted ankle. "I've just remembered something that may or may not work, depending on whether or not I can actually get hold of it."

"What is it?" Tanya asked, her face lit with hope.

"Something that's going to be tricky to get to," said Fabian. He unlocked the door and slipped into the hallway. "So don't get your hopes up. And whatever you do, don't open the door to anyone else but me."

"Aren't you forgetting something? My grandmother is bound to have a skeleton key!"

Fabian grinned slyly. "She does. Only, she doesn't realize yet that she's *mislaid* it." He reached around the door and gave the key in the lock a gentle stroke.

"You said you found that in one of the old servant's rooms!"

Fabian's smile widened. "I know what I *said*. But I lied."

⚬⚬

In the kitchen, Warwick was kneeling by the hearth, scraping mud from his boots. Fabian watched him carefully. His father looked haggard today: old and tired. His skin was gray and his hair hung in tangles, evidence that it had been rained on and dried before he'd had the chance to comb it. His eyes were blood-shot and dragged down by the dark shadows beneath them. He had not shaved in a couple of days.

Florence stood with her back to them, washing up. From the amount of noise she was making it was clear she was in a temper. On the table two untouched cooked breakfasts were wafting heavenly smells into the air. Oberon sat under the table, the tip of his nose protruding guiltily from beneath the checkered cloth. Twin strings of dribble hung from his chops. Fabian's stomach growled. He understood exactly how the dog felt, but he forced away his hunger and walked casually to the sink to stand beside Florence.

"What is it?" she snapped.

"Can I get a glass of water?" he asked meekly.

Warwick glanced up and gave him a sharp look. "There's a jug on the table. Eat your breakfast."

"I will in a minute," Fabian said. He filled a tumbler with water and set it on the side. "It's for Tanya. She's been sick. I think she's got some sort of . . . bug."

"Then why didn't she just say so?" Florence said, her eyes narrowing.

Fabian shrugged and moved toward the back door. He had spied what he was looking for. His father's coat hung from the middle peg—limp and very, very damp.

"Come on, boy," he said to Oberon, and whistled. The dog reluctantly squeezed out from under the table and lumbered outside as Fabian opened the door.

"The dog's already been out," said Florence, exasperated.

"Oh, sorry," Fabian replied. His hand brushed against the hunting knife in the belt of the coat. It was Warwick's prize possession—and the entire thing was specially crafted from iron. He had seen his father use it to gut rabbits that he had caught in the woods more times than he cared to remember.

As the door was pulled back, shielding Fabian's hand from view, he slipped his fingers nimbly under the belt and unsheathed the blade. It was cold, heavy, and brutal, certain to cut through the hair. Deftly, he slipped it into his sleeve and held it there, his trembling fingers curled over at the ends, and then shut the back door. His other hand nearly knocked over the glass of water he had poured as he snatched it up in his haste to get out of the kitchen.

"Back in a minute," he mumbled.

"Do be quick," said Florence, wringing out her dishcloth with the kind of relish that told Fabian she was imagining it was his neck.

By the time he reached the bedroom Fabian was out of breath. He placed the glass of water carelessly on the mantelpiece and drew the knife out from his sleeve.

"This should work," he said.

Tanya eyed the knife apprehensively.

"What is that thing?"

"It's made from iron," said Fabian. "It should break the spell." He knelt at her side and began hacking at the hair. "Warwick's coat was by the door. His boots are caked with mud and the coat was soaked. It was definitely him we saw last night."

"He must have seen us," said Tanya.

"I don't think so," said Fabian. "If he had, he would have gone berserk. What I want to know is why he was skulking about out there in the storm."

He continued to cut at the hair, which was now coming away easily.

"It's working. Warwick certainly keeps this thing sharp."

"It's *Warwick's*? You stole his knife? You really are a crook!"

"Just as well I am, for your sake!"

Minutes later Tanya's hair was waist-length, and only slightly longer than it had been before the incident in the night.

"You'll have to trim it," said Fabian, apologetically. "It's really uneven."

"I will," said Tanya. "But later." She pulled her hair back from her face and secured it into a ponytail. "There. No one will be able to tell when it's like this. We'd better get downstairs before my grandmother flips."

"And before Warwick notices his knife is missing," said Fabian, not looking quite so brave now. He inspected the knife, ensuring that no telltale hair was snagged on the blade.

"What about the hair?" Tanya gestured to the floor. It was covered.

"Shove it under the bed for now," said Fabian. "We'll have to put it in some garbage bags after breakfast and figure out a way to get rid of it."

On all fours, the two of them scrabbled around on the floor, stuffing the hair under the bed with great difficulty. It was very soft and slippery, and kept sliding out into sight.

"There's so much of it!" said Tanya.

"It's making me itch," said Fabian. "Just push it under and pull the covers over the sides of the bed so it's hidden. That'll have to do for now. Come on."

They raced downstairs, taking them two at a time, and bounded into the kitchen just as a fuming Florence was about to scrape their breakfasts into the garbage.

"Don't!" Fabian yelped.

Florence froze, and did a double-take when she saw Tanya.

"I thought you were feeling unwell?"

"I was," she answered, not daring to look her grandmother in the eye. "But I'm better now." She sat at the table, and Fabian followed suit. Florence placed the plates in front of them.

"It's probably cold now," she said.

"That was a speedy recovery if ever I saw one," Warwick remarked dryly. He was now vigorously buffing his boots to a shine.

Tanya did not answer, nor did she look at him.

She knew that those icy blue eyes of his would be trained on her, unflinching and accusing. The thought made her skin prickle.

She tucked into her breakfast, which was still rather good, even lukewarm. She saw Fabian fidgeting on the other side of the table and guessed correctly that he was trying to maneuver the knife discreetly out of his sleeve and conceal it under the table while he ate.

"Still warm too," he said happily, between gulps.

"Mine isn't," Tanya began, but then stopped as the hearthfay slipped out from underneath Fabian's plate. It had warmed his food, and, for the first time, it remained still for a couple of seconds to bashfully bat its ugly little eyelids at him before scuttling off to hide again. Fabian tore off a chunk of bread and dunked it in his egg, oblivious to the hearthfay's attentions. Tanya stared after it, bristling with indignation. And after *she'd* been the one to give the ungrateful little wretch a saucer of milk too!

"You'd let *mine* go cold, then?" she muttered under her breath, forgetting herself. "Floozy."

"I beg your pardon?" Florence snapped, and Tanya looked up, alarmed. Fabian was looking at her strangely too.

"I said . . . I don't mind if mine's cold," she said, thinking quickly. "I'm not choosy."

"Hmm," said Florence. She pursed her thin lips, then began loading laundry into the machine.

"Warwick, could you take a look at the guttering by Amos's room at some point today?" she said. "I think it's coming loose."

Warwick grunted his acknowledgment.

Tanya wondered again how two such miserable people as her grandmother and Warwick had managed to live under the same roof for so long without killing each other.

"This house is falling to pieces," said Florence, slamming the washing machine door.

"Then move somewhere smaller," said Fabian, shoveling bacon into his mouth at an impressive speed.

Florence looked uncomfortable. "This house has been in the family for decades." She poured herself some tea from the pot and sat down at the table.

"I think a nice little cottage would suit you," Fabian continued, with a maddening grin. "One made of gingerbread."

He was swiftly dealt Florence's most withering look, while Tanya almost choked on a mouthful of eggy bread.

"Don't get lippy," Warwick growled.

Tanya felt a stab of annoyance. It seemed that the only time Warwick ever paid any kind of attention to Fabian was when he was scolding him. For the first time, it occurred to her that a substantial amount of Fabian's behavior might simply be a device for gaining his father's attention. His insistence of using Warwick's name certainly demanded it—and also provided a means of lashing out at him.

A small whine came from under the table, and Tanya lifted the tablecloth and peered beneath. Oberon was sitting in front of her grandmother with his head on her knees.

"You like it here, don't you?" Florence murmured, fondling the dog's silky ears. Oberon gave a contented little groan. Florence smiled faintly and reached over to one of the drawers to remove a dog biscuit from a packet she had bought especially for him. Oberon gently took it and proceeded to crunch away happily from under the table. Tanya watched jealously. For some reason, Oberon plainly adored Florence.

"Finished," Fabian announced. He let his cutlery fall to the plate with a clatter and got up from the table, his cheeks full with a huge mouthful of food.

"Oh, no you don't," said Florence. "For goodness' sake, Fabian! You look like a hamster. Sit down until you've finished properly."

"I have," Fabian insisted, his eyes bulging as he swallowed painfully. "See?" He moved toward the back door, and Tanya's own food got stuck in her throat as she saw what he was about to do. In plain view, Fabian began rummaging through the coats hanging on the kitchen door. He frowned as he took his father's coat off one peg and transferred it to another, but in the process he knocked several coats—Warwick's included—to the floor.

"What are you doing now?" Florence snapped.

"I can't find my jacket," Fabian said. "The gray one. I thought it might be hanging up here."

"It's in the closet under the stairs, where you always leave it," said Florence, clearly puzzled. "I saw it yesterday. What do you want a jacket for in this weather anyway? Really, Fabian. I don't know what's got into you this morning."

"Neither do I." Warwick stood up, boots in hand. Suspicion was all over his face.

"Nothing." Fabian replaced the coats back on the door and skipped back to the breakfast table. Tanya saw his face and relaxed. Fabian had succeeded. She caught his eye and the two of them shared a look; it was the kind of look children wear when they know they've gotten away with something.

At the same moment, Warwick and Florence also shared a look. Theirs was the kind of look adults wear when they know that somehow they have been well and truly hoodwinked, but are clueless as to the how and why, and know only that there's absolutely nothing they can do about it.

❧❧

The summer thunderstorm had cleared the air, and the day was bright and warm, but still scented with the rain that had fallen so heavily the night before. Soon after breakfast, Tanya and Fabian filled six garbage bags with hair and hid them beneath the bed once more.

Already, Tanya was concerned about how she would go about disposing of it without it being discovered. Tanya's instinct was to burn it in the fireplace in her room, while Fabian had suggested throwing it into one of the catacombs where it would never be found. Both presented problems. Burning the hair would be time-consuming and risky. If smoke was seen coming from the chimney in the middle of summer it would no doubt raise Florence's and Warwick's suspicions. And to get back into the woods was proving difficult enough as it was, let alone without the added problem of carrying six heavy sacks of hair. In the end she decided that burning the hair was her best option—and that once again, the cover of night would be needed for such a task.

It was early afternoon by the time Tanya was finally alone. After much talk of Mad Morag's curses on various townsfolk, Fabian shut himself away in his room, music blaring from the other side of the door. When he had gone, Tanya sketched a detailed plan of the house on a scrap of paper. Beneath the diagram she scrawled a short message:

MY ROOM, ANY TIME AFTER MIDNIGHT. I WILL HAVE THE THINGS YOU ASKED FOR, AND I WANT WHAT WAS PROMISED IN YOUR PART OF THE BARGAIN.

She folded the note twice and pocketed it. She would slip it through the secret door behind the bookcase, along with another supply of food and water for Red to find.

She lifted the loose floorboard beneath the carpet

and retrieved the list Red had given her. She scanned through it, mentally calculating the cost of each item. Unfortunately, she had little or no idea about the price of many of the things on the list.

Her eyes wandered to a small wooden box on the dressing table. It contained the twenty-pound note that had been dropped by the man on the bus who had tried to buy the compass. She had stuffed it inside the box as soon as she'd gotten home that day, and it had remained there ever since, untouched.

It took three attempts for Tanya to pry the lid off the little wooden box to retrieve the money. When she did, she discovered not a crisp twenty-pound note bearing the Queen's face, but rather a large brown leaf curled tightly into a roll in much the way money does after it has been wedged in someone's pocket. Other than that, however, the box was empty.

16

A heady fragrance of shampoo filled the air as Red emerged from the bathroom, a towel wrapped around her head. With her freshly scrubbed face and gleaming green eyes, she looked like an entirely different person from the grubby miscreant whom Tanya had encountered only a few nights earlier. Now, in the warmth of the softly lit room she appeared almost wholesome and decent, and even closer in age to herself than Tanya had originally thought.

"Is the baby all right?" she asked, peering anxiously at the child sleeping peacefully on Tanya's bed. "He didn't wake up, did he?"

Tanya glanced at the changeling, watching his tiny chest rise and fall with each breath. His cheeks had but the merest hint of color, which had only become apparent once the two girls had bathed him carefully and quickly, washing away several days' worth of dirt.

He had allowed them to wash him without complaint, all the while watching them solemnly with his huge black eyes. Afterward he had fed hungrily upon the warm milk that Tanya had smuggled up to her room in a flask, then fallen into a deep, exhaustive slumber almost immediately, not stirring since.

"He's asleep," she said.

Red sat down on the bed, pulling Tanya's bathrobe around her more tightly. "I'd almost forgotten what a hot shower feels like."

Tanya handed her a tote bag full of items. She had spent most of her afternoon buying them in Tickey End using the money she had found in the pocket of her raincoat. "Here are the things you asked for... well, most of them. I didn't have enough money for everything on the list."

Red poked through the contents of the bag with her long, delicate fingers.

"That doesn't matter. I can see you got what was most important."

From the bag she withdrew two items, a cheap toothbrush and a box of hair dye. Quickly she skimmed the instructions, then glanced at the shade Tanya had selected. It was mousy and dull, somewhere between dark blond and light brown.

"Bland, average, and forgettable. Perfect."

She ripped the box open and removed the contents, then pulled on two thin plastic gloves. Next, she connected the dye to the bottle of developer and shook the bottle until the fluids mixed, slowly becoming grayish in color.

"I see you managed to get ahold of some newspapers," she said, eyeing a pile on the dressing table. "How far back do they go?"

Tanya gathered the stack in her arms and set them down next to Red.

"Back to the day you took him. My grandmother hoards newspapers for lighting fires with, and I bought a couple in Tickey End too. There's a local one there as well as the national ones."

"Anything in them?"

Tanya lowered her eyes, nodding.

"I've folded the pages over of everything I've found. There are six articles total, all of them in the national papers...except this one." She pulled a three-day-old *Tickey End Gazette* bearing what appeared to be a gravy stain on the front from the selection. "It's not good." She flicked to a few pages in, then passed the newspaper to Red, who stopped shaking the plastic bottle and began to read.

Her lips moved soundlessly as she followed the words on the page. The article was a short one, but by far the most incriminating that Tanya had seen. As well as labeling Red a ruthless, coldhearted kidnapper, it had issued a detailed description of her from an eyewitness: sixty-six-year-old Rosie Beak, the owner of Tickey End's most successful teashop and the town's biggest gossip.

Red finished reading and nodded thoughtfully.

"So they know I'm in the area. What I look like. What I'm wearing. That old battle-axe. She seemed the nosy type, asking questions about everyone and everything. Gossiping with every person who came through the doors. Good thing I left when I did."

She got up from the bed, pulling the towel off her head. Tanya followed her to the bathroom and stood in the doorway. Red leaned over the basin and began to rub the dye into her hair. For the next twenty minutes Tanya watched her, speaking distractedly of the morning's events with one nervous eye fixed on the bedroom door. She was fully aware of the terrible risk she was taking by having Red in the room, and of the consequences if anyone should find out.

"So how did the fairies get your hair?" Red asked.

"What do you mean?"

Red stood up straight, piling her hair on top of her head, and then took off her gloves. "To do something on that scale—to enchant your hair in that way—they must have had some of it." She paused and gave Tanya a suspicious look. "When you brush your hair, what do you do with the stray hairs that get caught in your brush or comb?"

Tanya looked away sheepishly. She did not want to admit that leaving hairs in her brush was a bad habit of hers.

"Show me," Red snapped. She took Tanya's elbow and marched her back into the bedroom, where Tanya guiltily pointed to her brush on the dressing table.

Red stared at it in disbelief.

"Disgusting. You might as well have sent them a written invitation!" She grabbed the brush and began pulling Tanya's hair from it in clumps.

"You don't leave your hair lying around for them to find. You get rid of it, right away."

"All right," said Tanya, bewildered. "I'll...I'll throw it away."

Red shook her head. "Wrong. You don't throw it away. You *destroy* it. You burn it. The same goes for anything else that they could use to control you."

"Like what?"

"Blood. Saliva. Fingernail and toenail clippings. Teeth. All the stories of witchcraft, of people being controlled by a witch in possession of a lock of their hair or a tooth—it all stems from the truth. You don't leave anything to chance."

From her pocket she pulled out a box of matches, lit one, and placed it carefully in the empty grate of the fireplace. Then, with a flick of her hand, she threw a tangled ball of hair from Tanya's brush to the flame. It was swallowed immediately with a hungry hiss, leaving the little match to burn out.

"I think my mother has some of my baby teeth," Tanya said slowly. "But you can't burn teeth, can you?"

"Anything you can't burn, you bury," said Red. "Either in a bag of salt or on consecrated ground.

If you cut yourself, burn any tissues you may have used to wipe up the blood along with any bandages or dressings. Don't lick envelopes. Use water. Clip your nails straight into a fire. Do whatever you can to protect yourself." She paused. "What did you do with the hair you cut off?"

Tanya pointed to the bed. "It's under there, in garbage bags. I thought burning it would be the best way to get rid of it—I was waiting for a chance to do it without being discovered."

Red bent down and began pulling the sacks out from beneath the bed. "It's not a question of the best way," she said grimly. "It's the only way." She used her knife to slit a hole in one of the bags, and pulled out a handful of hair, which she handed to Tanya along with the matches. "Burn it. Now."

Tanya threw the hair into the grate and set fire to it. It fizzled and hissed, eaten by the flame in seconds. She reached into the sack and pulled out another fistful, repeating the process, then looked on dismally as Red removed the sixth and final bag from beneath the bed. Tanya gestured helplessly. "It's going to take hours to burn it all."

"I suggest you get on with it, then."

Tanya shoved another pile of hair into the grate. "How...how do you know all these things, Red? How come you know so much, and I know so little?"

Red shrugged. "Most of it I learned from others—others like us. The rest I learned the hard way—from experience."

"I want you to teach me what you know," Tanya said. She gestured to the tote bag of items. "I've kept my side of the bargain. Now it's your turn. I want information—I want to know what *you* know."

"I can't teach you everything in the time we have," Red said. "But I can teach you a little. The good news is that you already know many of the things that are most important. You know about changelings and the link to the second sight. You know a little about glamour. And you know of ways to protect yourself. But to really understand the fairies' connection to us, we need to go back to the beginning. So that is what I will do now.

"The fairy realm is ruled by two opposing courts, the Seelie Court and the Unseelie Court. The Seelie Court is known to be the most benevolent, or help-ful, toward their own kind and to humans, whereas the Unseelie Court is known to be vicious and cruel. Each court detests the other, yet each must tolerate the other in turn."

"But how can the realm be ruled by two oppos-ing courts?" Tanya asked, pausing to wince after let-ting a match burn down to her fingers. "That doesn't make any sense."

"They take turns to rule," Red answered. "They are bound to honor an old agreement that ties in with a little-known legend. The two courts were once one great court made up of the thirteen wisest and most powerful fairies in the realm. Upon its formation, each leader put forth a special gift of great power that was to be bestowed predominantly upon the human race whenever—and upon whomever—the court deemed worthy. These gifts were known as the Thirteen Treasures."

Tanya frowned. The words sounded familiar... then she remembered the book from the library. It had mentioned the Thirteen Treasures, but the goblins had scrambled the contents before she'd had the chance to read it properly.

"They were the Halter, a ring that would render its wearer invisible," Red continued. "Glamour, a mask of illusion to fool an onlooker for as long as one wished. The Light, a magic candelabrum that would never diminish. Next, the Sword, which would allow only victory and never defeat. The *Book of Knowledge* would open to answer any question the reader might want answered. A Key that would open any door, including doorways to other worlds. There was a Goblet, said to bestow eternal life on any who should drink from it. A Platter that would remain full, never allowing its owner to go hungry. A Staff for strength; the Dagger, dripping blood that could heal any wound. There was a Cup of divination. A Heart of courage. And finally, the Cauldron, which could restore the dead to life.

"The power of each gift could be given freely by its maker, provided that the rest of the court was in agreement that the recipient was deserving. From the beginning, one of the treasures caused unease and excitement in equal measures: the Cauldron. Six of the members of the court agreed that death should be respected, not toyed with, and pointed out the chaos it would create if it could be reversed. The remaining seven members—including the Cauldron's creator—believed that if a life ended prematurely—the life of a child, for instance—then the Cauldron was a way to give the deceased another chance, as well as easing the pain for those mourning."

Red paused momentarily to check her watch.

"Another ten minutes and I need to wash this dye out. Don't let me forget."

"I won't," said Tanya, impatient to hear the rest of the story. "Go on."

"The stage was set for a division in the court," Red continued. "And it came to pass when the Cauldron's creator was fatally wounded by an arrow fired by a human. The court split into two. Six members pressed for the death to be reversed, declaring war and hatred upon the human race. The other six refused to let it happen. Without a united decision from the appointed court, the Cauldron, like the other twelve treasures, could not be used.

"Neither side of the court would back down, each believing their stance to be correct. As the division grew, the chances of reconciliation diminished. Bitter negotiations took place. Eventually, a compromise was reached. There were to be two courts, each ruling for one half of the year as they wished, with no intervention from the other side. The Thirteen Treasures remained in the great court, forever unused, for neither court could bring itself to consult with the other to gain a united agreement, such was the intensity of their hatred.

"And so, for six months of the year, one court—the court that opposed the resurrection of the dead—governed the realm and its inhabitants and led them in order, peace, and goodwill. The fey people named them the Seelie Court, for under their rule the earth was as fruitful and productive as it is today."

"Today?" Tanya interrupted. "You mean—"

"The seasons of spring and summer."

"So autumn and winter are when the Unseelie Court is governing?"

Red nodded. "The earth withers and dies. Chaos ensues. Banquets are held in which prisoners are taken, tormented, and made to suffer for the court's entertainment. More often than not, these prisoners are humans who have got lost or been lured into the realm. Most of them never return. Of those who do, few are sane."

Tanya shuddered.

"Many fairies flee the realm when it is the time of the Unseelie Court," Red continued. "They fear for their safety, and the safety of their young. The Unseelie Court finds the changeling trade amusing. To switch the children of their enemies—supporters of the Seelie Court and humans—is commonplace.

"Most of those who leave return when it is safer for them. Some of them never return, preferring to stay out of the realm altogether."

"Where do they go?" Tanya asked.

"They come here. To our world. Where they can live as they please, with their own rules."

"So...so the ones we see here are the ones that have left their own realm?"

"Yes. Either that, or they've been banished by the courts."

"Banished?"

"For wrongdoing," said Red. "Those are the ones you need to watch out for. They're usually the most dangerous of all. Luckily, they're also easy to spot. A common method that's used to punish them upon banishment is for them to be cursed with the ability to speak—and be spoken to—only in rhyme. It discourages them from communicating with humans and other fairies. The alternative is having their tongues cut out."

Tanya grimaced, thinking of the goblins. Now their strange way of speaking made sense.

Red glanced at her watch again and got up, stretching. "It's time."

Tanya nodded mutely as Red shut herself away in the bathroom. She heard the faint rush of water as Red began rinsing her hair. The sound continued for several minutes, then was replaced by the distinctive sound of scissors cutting hair. Other than that there was only one sound, and it was that of the changeling's breathing as he slept.

As Red had predicted, the glamour had begun to wear off. One of the child's ears had elongated, and the tip was now pointed. His hair had grown at an alarming rate since Tanya had last seen him, and his skin had begun to take on a pale, greenish hue. He had grown weaker, too. He needed medicine, she knew, but it was the medicine of his own people, not humans.

Abandoning the sack of hair, Tanya got up and went over to him, reaching out to gently stroke his cheek. He smelled of baby shampoo and milk. His skin was soft and cool. Instinctively the child stirred a little, nuzzling her hand in his sleep, and she felt unexpected tears pricking her eyes. What became of him depended entirely on Red—and her. Yet he had no idea, no concept that he was merely a pawn in the cruel war between his own kind.

"I'll take good care of him," Red said softly from behind her.

Tanya wiped her eyes.

"I didn't hear you come out of the bathroom," she muttered. She looked up—and started. For Red did not look like Red anymore.

Tanya's eyes lingered on the scruffy men's trousers and shirt. She had bought them cheaply in a charity shop that very afternoon. They fitted Red's boyish figure perfectly, as did the scuffed brown boots on her large feet. Her long hair had been cropped severely. It was now the color of straw.

"How do I look?" Red asked.

"Like . . . a boy."

Red nodded. "Good." She looked up and caught sight of Tanya still staring at her head. "It'll grow back," she said matter-of-factly. "They're looking for a redheaded girl with a baby boy. So I need to be the opposite of that." She threw a handful of her own tresses into the grate and burned them, then rummaged in the tote bag and removed a pile of pink baby clothes. "And so does he."

Together they began to dress the changeling, as slowly and carefully as possible so as not to wake him. Managing the bottom half proved the easiest, but when it came to pulling his arms through the sleeves, the child gave an angry squawk of protest. Tanya winced in alarm and quickly pulled the rest of the arm she was holding through the sleeve. Red fumbled as she fastened the buttons on the little pink cardigan. The child's eyes flickered open and for a moment it looked as though he was about to howl, but then he settled back into his slumber without further ado.

"How long are you going to keep doing this, Red?" Tanya whispered.

"We'll be gone within the hour. Then you won't have to cover for us anymore."

"I didn't just mean this one. I meant all of them. Why do you do this? Why do you take it upon yourself to save them? Don't you have a family to go to?"

"No," Red answered. "Not anymore."

"Why not?"

"My parents died in a car crash eighteen months ago. The rescue services managed to cut my little brother and me out of the wreckage....I had a broken arm, but James escaped without a scratch."

"That was lucky," Tanya commented.

Red shook her head. "Luck had nothing to do with it. He was saved from further injury by a fairy."

"A fairy saved him?"

"It was a funny little thing, really odd to look at—almost like a rodent of some kind. Followed me everywhere...I never knew why. And the strange thing was that it never bothered me—not like the others. It was almost like it was...looking out for me. When the accident happened all I could think about was protecting James, and it seemed to realize that. It sort of swelled up on the moment of impact and cushioned him from everything."

"Where is it now?" Tanya asked.

"It died in the accident," Red answered, and her voice was sad. "It gave its life to save my little brother. Afterward, we were placed in the children's home in Tickey End. We'd been there for about a month when I noticed what was going on. Children were being switched—the younger ones, babies and toddlers, and changelings were being left in their places.

"I tried to tell them, but they wouldn't listen. But then the fairies got more daring. They took a couple of little kids without even bothering to leave a changeling replacement. Understandably, there was uproar and a huge investigation. Arrangements were quickly put in place to close the place down and transfer all the children to other children's homes. But on our last night, one more child was taken. James."

"What did you do?" Tanya asked.

"What could I do? No one would listen to me. I was transferred to London. As soon as my arm was out of the cast I ran away. It was easy to disappear. They didn't try very hard to find me. This is what I've been doing ever since. And hoping that maybe one day I'll get my brother back."

Tanya shook her head. "I don't get it. How is this going to get your brother back?"

"Because it's a *trade*. I don't just give the changelings back. The fairies have to give me something in return."

"You mean human children that have been stolen?"

"Exactly."

"But what if the fairies don't want the changelings back?" Tanya asked. "If they've been switched because they're unwanted in the first place, then surely the fairies would be reluctant to give back the human replacements?"

Red nodded. "They'll only willingly return the changelings that have been switched out of mischief or spite. If they were taken for any other reason then it's more complicated."

"What does that mean?"

"It means that not all of them can be returned easily...but there are still ways. There are always ways."

Tanya fell silent. Suddenly it all made sense. "You're hoping that one day it will lead you to your brother, aren't you? That you can trade one of them for him."

Red's eyes glazed over. She seemed lost in a daydream.

"If I could only find a way in..." she said softly.

"A way in?" Tanya asked. "Into where?"

"Into the fairy realm," Red said, still with the same dreamy look on her face. "I'm sure...I'm sure I could find him."

"Wait...you're saying you actually *want* to get into the fairy realm, knowing what goes on there?" Tanya asked, incredulous. "Even if you did find him, you'd probably never find your way out again!"

Red said nothing, but the sadness in her eyes answered for her. She didn't care, Tanya realized. All she cared about was finding her brother.

"Have you tried to find a way in?"

"Yes. But it's complicated. It seems the more you look for it, the more elusive it becomes. The conditions have to be right to get in."

"What do you mean?"

"If you're not tricked into going in, you have to be invited. Or bargain. Or answer riddles. It's never simple. They know I'm looking for him. That's reason enough for them not to want me to get in. James would be three by now."

A note of stiffness had entered Red's voice. Tanya knew then not to push the matter any further.

For what remained unsaid was something they both knew; that the chances of Red ever finding her brother were very slim indeed.

"So what will you do after tonight?" said Tanya. "Where will you go?"

Red began to pack methodically.

"There's a circus that'll be passing through tomorrow night, in a village a few miles from here. I have a contact who travels with them, a fey man who arranges the trade. Last year, after much persuasion, the circus folk allowed me to travel with them too. After I've traded the child they'll give me food and a place to sleep in return for my working for them, looking after their animals and such. They don't ask questions, and neither do I. It's perfect."

"Perfect for what?" Tanya asked.

Red crammed the last of her belongings into her bag.

"Disappearing," she said softly.

17

It rained for the next two days. The third day dawned to a gray drizzle that reluctantly eased off around lunchtime, and by late afternoon a hazy sun had begun to break through the clouds. Tanya stood by the window in the kitchen, staring out at the swollen, marshy fields stretching toward the forest beneath a leaden sky. An image of Red and the changeling huddled cold, hungry, and wet somewhere presided in her mind. Red had promised to send word to her once she had safely taken cover with the circus folk. Tanya had checked the mail thoroughly every day since they had left. So far there had been nothing.

She sat down at the table and changed the station on the radio yet again, fiddling with the tuner until she found another news bulletin. Beneath the table, Oberon grunted and fidgeted, before settling heavily on her feet. She listened nervously, but there was no mention of anything connected to Red or the changeling. Nor had there been anything further in any of the papers. She allowed herself to relax a little. It seemed that the trail had gone cold.

Fabian entered the kitchen, yawning widely. Since Red had left, Tanya had seen hardly anything of him. Warwick had been present almost constantly, leaving them unable to speak properly except for a couple of snatched moments in which she was able to tell Fabian that she'd successfully destroyed the hair.

He sat down, pouring some tea from the pot. "This is cold," he said in surprise.

"Make some more then," said Tanya, vaguely wondering where the hearthfay was. It was unusual for a pot to go cold.

"I don't know how," he confessed. "I've never made tea before."

"You start by boiling a kettle," said Tanya sarcastically. "I'm sure you can figure out the rest. You've got books in your room on Einstein's Theory of Relativity, for goodness' sake."

Fabian shrugged. "I'll wait for Florence to come back."

"You'll be waiting a while, then," said Tanya. "She's lying down with a headache. She sent Warwick to Tickey End for some groceries."

"Oh, good," said Fabian, rubbing his hands together. "About the food, I mean. Not the headache. Warwick always gets nicer food than Florence."

"Does he?" said Tanya, unwilling to acknowledge that Warwick had any favorable attributes at all. "I don't think so."

"Well, he must've bought nicer tea last time," Fabian said. "It usually tastes of stewed socks. I reckon Florence buys those cheap teabags and thinks no one notices."

Tanya rolled her eyes but said nothing. Instead she got up, lifted the lid of the tea caddy, and raked its contents over lightly with her fingers. What Fabian had described had nothing to do with the tea—of that she was certain. It had more to do with the old brownie that lived there.

Her fingers found the bottom of the caddy, yet no teeth bit her, and no cane rapped her knuckles. All it contained was teabags. The brownie was gone. She replaced the lid and frowned. She couldn't remember the last time she had seen it. Maybe it had moved on . . . or even died.

"Are they the decent sort or not?" Fabian asked. "The teabags?"

Tanya sat back down at the table. "I can't tell the difference."

Fabian grabbed the tea caddy and removed the lid, inhaling deeply. "You can smell it." He stuck it under her nose. "Go on, have a whiff."

Tanya took a couple of halfhearted sniffs. "If you say so."

He moved across to the window and gazed out toward Hangman's Wood. "Warwick's going hunting tomorrow," he said quietly. "He probably won't be back till the following afternoon."

Tanya stared at the table. Already, she knew where the conversation was heading, and it was one she wanted to avoid.

"I was thinking that we should take the opportunity to go back into the forest, like we planned." He cleared his throat pointedly. "Unless you've changed your mind."

"I didn't say that."

"You didn't need to. It's written all over your face."

"I haven't changed my mind. It's just...I don't see what we can achieve by it, that's all. Amos is old. Whatever he did or didn't do, he's surely paid for it. Maybe it should be forgotten."

"How can I forget? It's all I can think about! You know as well as I do that there's something strange about all this—I want to find out the truth. I thought you did too."

"I did...I mean, I *do*—"

Fabian was already walking to the door. "I can't believe this. I can't *believe* you're backing out."

"I'm not!" Tanya insisted.

"I thought we were friends," he said.

"We *are*," said Tanya. 'Which is why we should think about this some more—we were nearly caught last time. Your father doesn't need any more reasons to hate me."

"Well, you don't have to worry," Fabian said coldly. "I'll go alone. I'll probably have less chance of getting caught without you anyway. I shouldn't have even asked you to come."

Tanya froze at his words, unable to speak. All she could do was listen as his footsteps faded. When the hallway was silent and empty, she too made her way miserably to her room. As she passed the grandfather clock on the landing, its slow, steady ticking was all she needed to realize that, like the tea caddy, the clock was empty.

She climbed the rest of the stairs and went to her room, perturbed. The absence of the fairies was troubling her; something odd was afoot. It was only after she sank down on her bed that she noticed the envelope on her pillow. There was nothing written on it, not even a name. Tanya snatched it up, her heart thudding. It had to be from Red. Hurriedly, she broke the wax seal and removed a single sheet of paper, folded once.

It was a poem, written in black ink in a neat hand. Fleetingly, Tanya wondered if the poem was some kind of clever code—Red's way of covering her tracks— but the notion was over before it had ever really begun. Red was blunt and direct, with an urgency about her. She simply wasn't the type to write poems.

Tanya began to read.

IN A WOOD OF SECRETS WHISPERED ONLY BY THE TREES,

THE TALE OF A MISSING GIRL BEGAN ONE MIDSUMMER'S EVE.

HER EYES WERE THE COLOR OF MIDNIGHT; HER SKIN WAS PALE AS THE MOON,

HER HAIR WAS BLACK AS A RAVEN'S WING; HER NAME WAS MORWENNA BLOOM.

THOUGH WARNED, SHE PLAYED A DANGEROUS GAME AND WALKED THE WOODS ALONE,

SO CAME THE EVE SHE DISAPPEARED, NEVER TO COME HOME.

THE FOREST HELD FEW ANSWERS, FOR ALL THAT WAS FOUND THERE

WAS A SINGLE BRAIDED LOCK OF MORWENNA'S LONG, BLACK HAIR.

TEN YEARS AND FOUR WAS SHE THE DAY SHE VANISHED WITH NO TRACE;

AS WEEKS STRETCHED INTO MONTHS, THE TOWNSFOLK SOON FORGOT HER FACE.

SOME SAID THE GIRL HAD PERISHED, HAVING FALLEN TO HER DOOM,

LIKE OTHERS WHO HAD DIED BELOW IN THE WINDING, MURKY GLOOM.

SOME SAID THAT SHE HAD RUN AWAY TO SEEK A BETTER
LIFE,

SOME THOUGHT SHE HAD BEEN KILLED BY HE WHO
SOUGHT HER AS HIS WIFE.

AS TRUTH GOT LOST IN LEGEND, IT WAS CLEAR FOR ALL
TO SEE

MORWENNA THE REVEREND'S DAUGHTER WAS A FADING
MEMORY.

NOW MOST DO NOT REMEMBER—THOUGH THOSE WHO
HAVE THE SIGHT

AVOID THE PATH THE DOOMED GIRL WALKED THAT WARM
MIDSUMMER NIGHT.

FOR IN THE WOODS WHERE FOXGLOVES SWAY AND
SHADOWS SOFTLY LOOM

IT'S SAID MORWENNA ROAMS STILL, DANCING TO THE
FAËRIES' TUNE.

The poem was unsigned. Gut instinct told Tanya that
there was truth in it. She hastily stuffed the piece of
paper back into the envelope, and then tucked it into
the red scarf beneath the loose floorboard, her head
spinning with the sickening revelation.

Morwenna had been taken by the fairies.

For fifty years she had been trapped in their realm, unable to escape, or to tell anyone what had really happened to her.

*That's what she was trying to tell us,* Tanya thought helplessly. *And if Warwick hadn't found us in the woods that day she would have succeeded.*

For half a century Amos had lived under suspicion for a crime he had not committed, descending into madness.

*Amos was innocent.*

There were now two questions in Tanya's mind that needed answers. Firstly, who had left the envelope in her room? And secondly, whom could she confide in? She gripped the edge of the bedclothes and twisted them in frustration. If only Red were still there. If only she had told her about Morwenna Bloom. Red would have known what to do. But "If only" was no use, and Tanya knew it.

As she went to replace the floorboard, the glint of the compass caught her eye. And that was when the thought came to her.

❖❖

The forest was silent, but for the whispering of the breeze in the trees and the bubbling of the brook. Tanya stood on the edge of the woods, the compass in her hand, the iron nail in her pocket, and every item of clothing turned inside out. This time, she was taking no chances. Oberon stood beside her, looking up at her in a puzzled way as if he didn't understand what they were waiting for.

She exhaled shakily. Less than an hour earlier she had felt certain that she never wanted to set foot in these woods again, but the poem had changed everything. She knew that it had come to her for one reason; she was the only person who could help Morwenna now. Gathering her courage, she stepped over the brook and into the trees and began to walk, with no idea where she was going. The only thing that was keeping her calm was the knowledge that the compass would lead her safely home.

"I won't get lost," she told herself, aware of how small her voice sounded. "*I won't get lost.*"

She continued to walk farther into the woods. The twigs and moss crunched and rustled lightly under her feet, and once she had to sidestep to avoid treading on a decomposing mouse. A couple of times she stopped and looked around, unable to shake the eerie sensation that she was being followed. The second time she even called Fabian's name, suspicious that he might be spying on her again, but no one answered. She continued, ears straining for any telltale sound, but there was nothing. She had just started to relax when the first catacomb came into view.

Tanya eyed the missing part of the railing, recalling the desperation she had experienced the day Oberon had disappeared. She averted her eyes and hurried past.

Soon they came to a small clearing, where there was a thick fallen tree trunk in the middle. Oberon snuffled in the long grass, sneezing repeatedly as he disturbed a dandelion clock. She decided to sit for a while, to try to get her bearings and take a mouthful of water from the bottle she had brought with her. When she checked the compass, it was a shock to see that the house was in a totally different direction to what she had thought it would be.

Eventually she got up. She knew that she did not have much time if she was going to get back before anyone missed her, but she had no idea which way to go. It was hopeless, and she knew it.

"Come on, boy," she said to Oberon. "We'd better get back."

She had barely taken a step when she saw a small movement ahead of her within the trees. A glimpse of a hand.

"Morwenna," she called. "Morwenna Bloom... is that you?"

A grubby, rugged face peered out from behind a nearby tree. Its expression was one of terrible fear. Oberon crouched behind her, whimpering. Tanya took a slow step forward.

"Brunswick?"

The goblin edged out from his hiding place, his eyes wide. One finger was pressed to his lips, motioning for her to be silent.

"You mustn't, you *mustn't!*" he whispered, shaking his head fervently.

"Mustn't what?'

Brunswick scurried up to her and took her hand in his, then began tugging her through the trees, his eyes darting nervously over his shoulder.

"You shouldn't be here. You shouldn't have come!"

"Why not?" Tanya asked. "Brunswick, you're scaring me. Tell me what you mean!"

But the goblin would not tell. Instead he continued to pull her farther and farther into the woods at a maddening pace. The trees around them grew closer together now, their bark gnarled and ancient. It felt wrong to be there, as though they were intruding on a place undisturbed by time. Still Brunswick tugged her onward, even deeper into the woods. Between the greenery, Tanya caught a sudden glimpse of yellow. The goblin stopped and finally released her hand.

A beautiful old Romany caravan was almost completely consumed by the foliage. Brunswick had led her straight to the old gypsy woman.

"How did you know?" she whispered.

"You'll be safe with her," he said. "But I can help you no more."

Tanya stared at him, as several realizations hit her at once. She searched Brunswick's face for answers. Instead she found only more questions.

"Where are the other two goblins? And why... why aren't you speaking in rhyme?"

Brunswick shook his head again sadly and began

to back away, motioning for her to approach the caravan. She paused in front of the door, her hand raised to knock. Then she hesitated and looked back for Brunswick. He was gone.

Before she had the chance to hesitate any further, the door opened.

"Come in," said the old gypsy woman, her bird-like eyes drinking Tanya in. "I've been expecting you."

18

Inside, the caravan smelled of burning candles and herbs. There was a comfortable-looking armchair by the window, and next to a table sat a small dresser displaying all manner of curious bottles made of brightly colored glass, all with labels tied to their stoppers. A thick velvet curtain obscured the rear portion of the caravan, which, Tanya supposed, must be where the old woman slept. Curled up at the foot of a traditional broom was a smoke-gray cat. It eyed both her and Oberon suspiciously.

The strangest thing in the caravan by far was a thick book of puzzles that was propped open to reveal a partially completed crossword. Tanya gaped at it, momentarily thrown. Something so completely normal seemed out of place in the home of a so-called witch.

"What were you expecting?" the old woman snapped, making Tanya jump. "Toads and spell books? A collection of pointy hats? Eye of newt and wing of bat?"

"No," Tanya began, embarrassed. "It's just—" She broke off, unable to finish the sentence.

"I happen to *like* puzzle books," said Morag, crossly. "I don't know why everyone finds that so amusing. And for your information, I don't keep spell books." She lifted a bony finger and tapped the side of her head. "They're all up here."

Morag motioned to a seat at the table, and then set a bowl of water in front of Oberon. He lapped at it gratefully.

The old woman sat down, her wizened hands clasped together.

"I thought you would come sooner."

Tanya removed the compass from her pocket. It was a moment before she found her voice.

"I...I'd like to know why you gave me this," she said, finding it hard to meet the old woman's unfaltering gaze. "And how you knew I'd need it."

"Of course." Morag seemed unfazed. "I expect you know its use by now?"

Tanya nodded.

"I saw you in a vision recently. And I saw your... ability."

Tanya gaped, and Morag smiled.

"Do not be surprised. I too have abilities, although not quite like your own. Some call me a fortune-teller. Some call me a witch. Most know me as 'Mad Morag.'" She paused and gave Tanya a hard look. "Yes, I know what people say about me, and a little of it is true. I have a gift, and sometimes I can use it to help people—people like you."

"People like me?"

"Those who believe they have nobody else to turn to. And those who are not too afraid to accept my help."

"What else did you see?" Tanya asked, her fear slowly giving way to curiosity.

The old woman seemed to be considering her answer. "I saw a child stolen from its crib, long ago. And later, I saw a boy of about your own age . . . with a grievance of a different kind. Somehow, it is connected to your ability, the fact that you have the second sight. Am I correct?"

Tanya nodded, thinking of the poem's revelation of the true manner of Morwenna's disappearance. "It is now."

"This boy wants your help," Morag continued. "But there will come a time when you will need his help more. Much more."

Tanya frowned. The old woman seemed to be speaking in riddles.

Morag seemed to sense what she was thinking.

"I know you have many questions, but I'm afraid I am able to answer very few of them. I have a feeling that you mean to save somebody . . . and you will. But not in the way you would expect."

*Two people,* Tanya thought grimly. *Amos needs saving as well as Morwenna.*

"May I ask what it is you are doing?" the old woman continued.

"I need to...to bring someone out of the fairy realm," Tanya said. "But I don't know how to do it."

"I would advise against it," said the old woman immediately. "To attempt it is not an easy task. You will be placing yourself—and the boy—in grave danger. You may even become trapped in the fairy realm yourself."

"I've no choice."

Morag studied her, and Tanya thought she saw fear in the old woman's eyes.

"I thought you would say that." She got up from the table and hobbled over to the dresser. "I can be of some assistance," she said, reaching into the cabinet amongst the many objects inside. She began to remove several jars and bottles, mixing ingredients in a small bowl with a stone pestle.

Tanya felt her eyes drawn to the puzzle book once more. She simply couldn't help herself. Its normality made it seem alien.

"It's prejudice," she murmured unthinkingly.

"Pardon?" said Morag.

"Nine down. 'Preconceived opinion or judgment formed without facts.' The answer is prejudice."

Morag nodded toward a pencil on the table. Tanya hastily scribbled the answer into the grid. Afterward she stared at the compass in her hands.

"Where . . . where did you get this?"

Morag did not turn around.

"It was passed down to me by my mother. Many things are passed down through families that cannot be explained. It has helped a number of others before you find their way in times of need, and will continue to help others after you, so I would appreciate it if you could return it when you feel it is no longer of any use."

"How will I know when I don't need it anymore?"

"You will know," Morag replied. "It will simply cease to work." She closed the cabinet of the dresser, then sat back down and placed two objects on the table. One was a tiny pair of silver scissors. The other was a bottle, small enough to fit into the palm of her hand. Morag lifted the bowl of liquid she had been mixing and carefully emptied the murky, gray-green fluid into the clear glass.

"You know of certain ways to protect yourself. They will not be enough." She lifted the scissors and presented them to her. Tanya took them, and noticed a small red jewel cast in the cover sheathing the point.

"These are for you," said Morag. "They may look unexceptional, but they will cut through almost any material, apart from metal, wood, or stone." Then she picked up the bottle of green liquid. "This is for the boy—it will help him to see things . . . in the same way you do."

Tanya handed the items back regretfully.

"I can't take these. I've no way of paying you for them."

Morag's eyes narrowed. "I did not ask for payment."

Tanya felt her cheeks flush with embarrassment.

"But next time you visit, perhaps you might bring me a puzzle book."

Tanya nodded, biting her lips to stop herself from smiling.

"To bring a person out of the fairy realm, you must act when it is most accessible," Morag continued briskly. "An in-between time is what you need."

"In-between?"

"A magical time that is neither here nor there; neither one nor the other."

"I don't understand."

"The shift between seasons, for example. May Day, Midsummer, Halloween, and Midwinter are all very powerful times. Or the plane between sleep and waking. These are in-between places."

"But Midsummer has gone," said Tanya. "And it's months until Halloween!"

"You're quite right," said the old woman. "We are not near to any of those times. But there is one that occurs far more frequently, and is just as powerful." She paused and looked at Tanya expectantly. "Some know it as the witching hour."

"Midnight," Tanya whispered. "In between night and day."

"Once you have access to the person you wish to lead out from the fairy realm you must call their name, for many will have trouble remembering who they are after a time there. After that you must offer them an item of clothing to put on—if you have something that belonged to them before they were taken, then so much the better.

"Sew salt pouches into the lining of whatever garment you give them, and into your own. Do not accept anything they might try to give you. This is especially important of food or drink, no matter how tempting it may appear. To eat fairy food can render you powerless to them.

"Finally, there is a very important precaution you must take. The fairy realm does not run on the same time frame as our world. Time can be sped up or slowed down, and the consequences of this can be disastrous. To keep yourself protected you must cut a lock of your own hair off and keep it somewhere secure, where it cannot be meddled with. This will ensure that if the worst should befall you, then at least you will not lose any years of your life. You will remain the age you are now."

"But what if I were to get pulled into the fairy realm, then escape and find years had passed in this world? I would still be young, while everyone I had known would be old, or even dead!"

"That is a possibility," Morag agreed. "But the other possibility is far worse. Would you rather that you aged and lost years of your life, whilst those you loved had remained the same? If the world had remained the same and the fairy realm had sped up? No one would recognize you. No one would believe you. And your life would be close to its end."

Tanya shook her head in confusion.

"No...I mean, I don't know..."

"Think carefully while you still can," Morag said. "There is still time to change your mind."

Tanya stared solemnly at the compass, and at the tiny bottle Morag had given her. "Why are you helping me?" she asked hesitantly. The question had been burning on her lips since she had entered the caravan.

"Because I can," the gypsy woman replied. "And because I want to. Our pasts are connected through our ancestry. Together, maybe we can make right some of the wrongs of the past." Her eyes came to rest on the charm bracelet on Tanya's wrist. They narrowed, then her gaze shifted, moving over each charm in turn before finally settling on the empty space where the cauldron had been.

"Thirteen," she murmured. "Unlucky...for some." She met Tanya's gaze with her own, old and wise. Tanya searched the craggy face for any clue that she might know something of the bracelet's tragic first owner, but there was nothing to suggest that the comment had any hidden meaning.

Instinctively, Tanya knew that it was time for her to leave. Morag shuffled past her and opened the caravan door. Tanya stepped outside into the fresh air, gripping Oberon's leash tightly. A gentle breeze lifted her hair and wrapped itself around her. A hedgehog shuffled across the gypsy's path, oblivious to its audience. The woodland seemed so at peace and so beautiful that it was almost impossible to believe that it was home to such danger.

Despite the warmth of the day, Tanya shivered.

"Go, and be safe," said Morag, looking around suspiciously. "Stay close to the brook."

"Thank you—" Tanya began, but the old woman shook her head.

"There will be another time for thanks. We will meet again, I hope."

Tanya pulled the compass out of her pocket. The time had come to put it to good use.

# 19

Later that evening, feeling sick with nerves, Tanya left the house and made for the garden in search of Fabian. She stood beneath the oak tree and squinted up through the branches, but there was no sign of Fabian's gangling frame, nor was there any answer when she called his name. Knowing that he could not have gone far, she ambled through the garden, kicking at a few fallen leaves on the ground. The gate was open, propped in place by a heavy stone from the rock garden, and through it, Tanya could see a small figure in the distance sitting by the edge of the brook. It was Fabian.

She walked toward him slowly, trying to delay the inevitable. Fabian was sitting cross-legged at the side of the stream, flinging pebbles into the water. He did not look up as she approached, or even move at all when she sat down next to him. She realized he must have seen her coming. She tugged at a tuft of grass awkwardly. Fabian remained stiff and silent, refusing to be the first to speak.

"I . . . I'm sorry," she said eventually. "I still want to go ahead with the plan. If you want me to, that is."

Fabian threw another stone into the stream.

"I'm sorry too."

"So, when are we going back into the woods?" Tanya asked.

"I don't know." He threw a big rock, which made an even bigger splash. "What's the point? Perhaps some things should just be left well enough alone."

"The point is to prove that Amos is innocent," said Tanya.

Fabian fiddled with his shoelaces. "And if he's not?" he answered in a choked voice.

"He is," said Tanya, gathering her courage. "Listen, Fabian—"

But Fabian was only half paying attention. "What made you change your mind? You seemed so set against it before."

"I just . . . want to help," she mumbled, losing her nerve at the last moment. "We're friends, aren't we?"

Fabian gave a wry smile, and raked a hand through his bushy hair. "Yeah, I suppose. You really think he's innocent?"

"I know he is," she said. "There's something I have to show you." She reached into her pocket and pulled out the poem, then placed it in his hand hesitantly.

Fabian unfolded the piece of paper. Tanya watched, noting how his brow was becoming more deeply furrowed with every sentence. The time he took to read it seemed an eternity. When he had finished, his eyes were wide and his skin was very pale. When he finally spoke, his voice was shaking.

"Is this some kind of joke?" Fabian looked up at her, his eyes blazing. "Did you come and apologize just so you could make fun of me? Where did you get this?"

"It was left on my pillow," said Tanya. "It's not a joke. You have to believe me."

*"Believe you?"* Fabian snarled. He leapt to his feet in fury, screwing the poem into a tiny ball. He threw it at the ground with all his might.

Tanya hurriedly got up after grabbing the balled-up piece of paper.

"Fabian, *please*! Just listen to me—"

But Fabian was in too terrible a temper to listen. He turned on her, his face pink with rage, and she saw that his fists were clenched tightly at his sides.

"I don't know how you saw it. But I can assure you I don't find this funny."

He began to stalk back to the house.

"How I saw what?" She raced after him. "Fabian! *Wait!* What are you talking about?"

*"My book!"* Fabian yelled, brandishing the

battered brown journal. "You *saw* it! You *read* it! Now you can have a good laugh at my expense!"

Tanya stopped walking. "Fabian, I don't know what you're talking about."

The angry boy continued to storm away.

"I've never read your book! I swear!"

Fabian halted, and Tanya rushed over to him.

"Who wrote that poem?" he demanded.

"I don't know," said Tanya. "I told you, I just found it."

"This isn't funny. Did you write it?"

"Of course not!"

"Then who did?"

"I don't *know*," Tanya repeated. She eyed the journal. "What's in the book?"

"You already know."

"I don't know what's in the stupid book! I haven't got the faintest idea! All I know is that it obviously means a lot to you, and I would never snoop in it behind your back." She gazed at him, her eyes full of hurt. "You know I wouldn't. Or at least, I thought you knew."

Fabian did not answer.

"What's the use," Tanya muttered, pushing past him. "I should've known you'd never believe in fairies."

"No," Fabian hissed. "I *don't* believe in fairies, like every other intelligent person on the planet. Fairies are for children, for *babies*. What you saw—what you read—was a mere thought in a diary. And it was written when I was upset."

Tanya pressed her hand over her heart.

"I swear to you—on my *life*—that I didn't read your diary!"

"I don't believe you!"

"No," Tanya shouted, as her own temper flared up. "You don't believe me. And you don't believe in fairies, but you believe in ghosts, according to what you said after we saw Morwenna Bloom in the woods. And you believe in witches, don't you? You believe that the old gypsy woman in the woods has the power to curse and bewitch."

Fabian stared at her, his mouth open to retort, but no words came out.

"Strange that you should find it so easy to believe in some kinds of magic, yet not in others," Tanya continued. "Stranger still that you refuse to believe my word. I'm not lying to you, Fabian. Why do you find it so difficult to believe me? Is this how little my friendship is worth to you?"

"It's not a question of friendship," Fabian said, but the anger in his voice had subsided. "It's a question of what's real."

"The hair you had to cut off with Warwick's knife was real enough, wasn't it?"

"That was the gypsy woman, you even said so yourself—"

"No, I didn't. *You* were the one who suggested she was responsible. I just let you believe that because it was easier. The gypsy woman has been trying to help us." Tanya reached into her pocket and retrieved the tiny bottle Morag had given her. "This is for you. So you'll be able to see them."

Fabian let out an incredulous snort of laughter.

"*She* gave you that? And you expect me to drink it?"

"Why not? Then you'll have proof."

"Proof of what? The fact that the batty old crone has knowledge of herbs and plants?" Fabian sneered. "Ever heard of hallucinogens? If I drank that I'd be seeing all sorts! Mermaids, fairies, dragons and just about everything else!"

"Why are you so set on believing she's out to harm us?" said Tanya.

"Why are you so set on believing she's out to help us?" Fabian shot back.

"Because she already has. She gave me the compass, remember? Why would she go to the trouble of pretending to help us? If she really wanted to harm us then she would have by now."

"If you're so convinced of that, then drink some," said Fabian—but something in his voice betrayed him. He was faltering.

"What?"

Fabian nodded at the bottle in Tanya's hand, but the action was jerky and nervous rather than defiant.

"Try it. Let's see if it works." His voice was quavering.

"You don't understand," Tanya said slowly. "It's not for me...it's for you. She didn't give it to me because I don't need it. Fabian, don't you see what

I've been trying to tell you? What all the strange things about me add up to?

"The poem didn't convince me of the fairies' existence. Nor did Mad Morag. I was able to see them already. I've been able to see them for as long as I can remember. Now you can laugh at me, or call me a liar, but before you do at least listen to what I have to say, because if you don't, Amos will die being known as the man who murdered Morwenna Bloom and got away with it. Look at this, the part where it says 'he who sought her as his wife.' Don't you see? It's referring to Amos. He was in love with her! He's innocent!"

Fabian didn't walk off. He didn't shout, or laugh, or mock her. A mixture of expressions crossed his face in a few short seconds: confusion, fear, hope, dread. Finally, when he opened his mouth to speak, his clear blue eyes met Tanya's.

"I'll listen to what you have to say. But it'd better be good."

## 20

Fabian stared at the tiny bottle in his palm, slowly rotating it. Inside, the murky fluid tipped back and forth. Tanya sat beside him, watching the swirling water of the stream and breathing in its fresh smell. She had told him everything—omitting only Red and the changeling—and he had listened without interruption. Finally, it seemed that he believed her.

"The day after my mother died," he said eventually. "I was sitting in this very place." He stopped, and with a trembling finger, pointed toward a tree at the edge of the brook. "It was over there when I saw it. Warwick brought me here because it was one of my mother's favorite places. He didn't need to explain—I was old enough to know she was never coming back.

"We threw white roses and a bunch of rosemary into the water: the rosemary for remembrance and the roses because they were her favorite. I had just thrown the last flower when I noticed a creature sitting on the lowest branch of the tree. She was wearing a green dress and a hat made of woven grass. She...she looked straight at me, and then took off her hat and threw it into the water with the roses. I blinked, and she was gone. I would have put it down to my imagination if it hadn't been for the hat, still floating down the stream. I watched until it got pulled under the water."

"Did you tell anyone?" Tanya asked.

Fabian shook his head. "No, never. But I always remembered. A couple of months ago I wrote about it in here." He tapped the cover of his brown leather book. "I never saw anything like it again. I always put it down to the shock of losing my mum."

"Maybe it was," said Tanya. "Maybe grief opened up some kind of window in your mind. Or maybe it just appeared to comfort you. They can be seen by us when they choose, I think. Not all of them are bad."

Fabian ran his thumb over the tiny bottle, then removed the lid and sniffed its contents. "It smells even worse than it looks," he said, offering it to Tanya. "Which is bad considering that it looks like a liquidized frog."

"It stinks," she agreed. "I wouldn't want to drink it."

"Me neither," said Fabian. "So it's just as well I don't have to." He held up the lid of the bottle. On the underside was a thin wand that, due to the density of the liquid, Tanya had not noticed. Fabian pushed the wand into the bottle and then retracted it slowly. A murky droplet glistened at the end.

"Eyedrops," said Fabian. He tilted his head back and lifted the wand. "Let's see if they work."

Tanya placed a hand on his arm. "Don't waste it."

"I'm not wasting it. I'm testing it."

"We already know it will work," said Tanya. "Because the compass does."

"I don't care," Fabian said sulkily. "I want to try it now."

"Try it later," said Tanya. "Tonight, when everyone's gone to bed. That way, if anything happens nobody will be around to see it."

Fabian hesitated, then pushed the stopper back on.

"What about the goblin tooth? Can I at least see that?"

Tanya nodded. "It's in my room, hidden. I can show you."

"Let's go," said Fabian, springing to his feet. "Oh, but wait—Warwick's probably hanging around—we should go separately. You go ahead and I'll join you in a few minutes so he doesn't suspect we've been together."

"Good idea," said Tanya. "Come to my room when it's all clear."

❧❦

Warwick was sitting reading a newspaper when Tanya arrived back at the house. He barely looked up when she came through the kitchen door.

"Have you seen Fabian?"

"No," she muttered. "Sorry."

Warwick grunted dismissively, removing the sports section of the paper and discarding the rest. Tanya went to move past him but found herself jerking to a halt when she saw the headline on the front page of the newspaper. It was accompanied by a grainy photograph of a face she recognized: Red.

**MISSING CHILD: NEW LEADS.** Tanya snatched up the paper, ignoring Warwick's curious glance.

THE MOTHER OF A NEWBORN CHILD SNATCHED FROM AN ESSEX MATERNITY WARD SEVEN DAYS AGO FINALLY CAME FORWARD YESTERDAY AFTERNOON. THE WOMAN, WHO CANNOT BE NAMED FOR LEGAL REASONS, HAD ABANDONED THE BOY ONLY HOURS AFTER GIVING BIRTH. AT PRESENT, HER REASONS FOR THE ABANDONMENT ARE UNKNOWN.

THE PRIME SUSPECT IN THE ABDUCTION IS A TEENAGE GIRL SEEN ACTING SUSPICIOUSLY AT THE TIME THE CHILD VANISHED. THIS MORNING, DETECTIVES REVEALED THAT THEY BELIEVE THE GIRL TO BE FOURTEEN-YEAR-OLD ROWAN FOX, PICTURED AT LEFT, WHO HAS BEEN ON THE MISSING PERSON'S LIST SINCE RUNNING AWAY FROM A CHILDREN'S HOME ALMOST EIGHTEEN MONTHS AGO. MUCH OF THE GIRL'S BACKGROUND CANNOT BE

EXPOSED DUE TO HER AGE. INVESTIGATORS REFUSED TO COMMENT ON SPECULATION THAT FOX IS RELATED TO ANOTHER CHILD THAT DISAPPEARED WHILE AT THE HOME.

POLICE WOULD ALSO LIKE TO SPEAK TO THE GIRL IN CONNECTION WITH TWO OTHER ABDUCTIONS, BOTH OF WHICH OCCURRED IN THE PAST TWELVE MONTHS AND BEAR CHILLING RESEMBLANCES TO THIS ONE. IN AUGUST LAST YEAR, ONE-YEAR-OLD SEBASTIAN CONNOR VANISHED FROM HIS GARDEN IN KENT WHILE HIS FOSTER FATHER'S BACK WAS TURNED. TEN DAYS LATER HE WAS FOUND UNHARMED IN A DISUSED WAREHOUSE FOLLOWING AN ANONYMOUS PHONE CALL. TWO MONTHS LATER, TODDLER LAUREN MARSH DISAPPEARED FROM A SWEET SHOP IN SUFFOLK WHILE IN THE CARE OF HER OLDER SISTER. SHE HAS NOT BEEN SEEN SINCE. POLICE ARE APPEALING FOR ANYONE WITH INFORMATION TO COME FORWARD.

Underneath was a contact number. Tanya swallowed hard and put the paper back on the table. She felt sick with worry and confusion, no longer knowing what to believe.

"Something wrong?" Warwick asked.

"No," Tanya answered abruptly, annoyed at his attention. She left the kitchen and made her way upstairs. The door was ajar when Tanya reached her room. Frowning slightly, she pushed it open. The first thing she saw was the mess.

Every item she owned had been wrenched from the drawers and thrown across the room in a frenzied manner. The wardrobe doors were open and the contents emptied—there was now a pile of clothes, shoes, and coat hangers lying haphazardly on the floor. The bed had been stripped, and even the pillows had been ripped from their cases.

The second thing Tanya saw was the drain-dweller.

It was over by the fireplace, and, having rolled back the carpet, had lifted out the loose floorboard and was standing in the space where the shoebox was hidden with only its head visible. When it saw her it gave a small yelp of surprise and leapt out from between the floorboards. Tanya edged closer to the gap where the shoebox was. It lay untouched, still wrapped in the red scarf. The drain-dweller stood with its back pressed flat to the wall, not daring to move.

Tanya knelt and lifted the shoebox, grasping it to her chest. She stared at the fairy's crestfallen face.

"You're looking for something. What?"

The drain-dweller's eyes shifted craftily to Tanya's wrist, where the charms on the silver bracelet danced with her movements, glittering alluringly. The creature's pupils dilated at the sight of them. It seemed to be in some kind of trance. It had found what it was looking for. The awful stench of the drains filled Tanya's nostrils. She began to back away.

A loud rap on the door startled them both, and then Fabian pushed his way into the room.

"I saw one," he said, breathless with excitement. "In the garden! It was one of the goblins, the one with the bruises—" He broke off as he surveyed the mess. "What happened? And what the hell is *that*?"

He pointed in horror at the fairy, which was still gazing at the bracelet with a look of adoration that was tinged with madness.

Tanya stared at him, furious. "*It's the drain-dweller!* I don't believe you! You just couldn't resist, could you?"

"Sorry," said Fabian, looking anything but apologetic. In fact, he looked as if he had just won the Nobel Prize. "It's revolting!" he exclaimed, looking delirious and appalled all at once. He knelt and reached toward the suspicious drain-dweller. It lunged forward and snapped at his fingers, missing only by a fraction of an inch. Fabian jumped and retracted his hand quickly.

"This is incredible! *Amazing!* This is going to revolutionize the world of science!"

"Shut up, Fabian—" Tanya began, but her momentary distraction was all the drain-dweller needed. It threw itself upon Tanya's wrist with incredible force and began wrenching at the bracelet frenziedly.

"What's it doing?" Fabian yelled in alarm.

"Get it off me!" Tanya shrieked, batting at the creature with her free hand.

"Grab it by the neck!"

Tanya reached for the scrawny neck, but every time she made contact the creature wriggled and slid out of her grasp. Finally she managed to catch its head, though her grip was weak upon the slimy frog-like skin beneath her hand. As she tried to pry it away from her wrist her hand slid in front of the fairy's face. She felt a sharp pain, as if twenty little needles had pierced her all at once. It had sunk its teeth into her forefinger. She felt, rather than saw, the blood running down her arm and dripping from her elbow. In her shock she allowed the drain-dweller's head to slip free from her hand.

"You're bleeding!" said Fabian, horrified.

"Guard the bathroom," Tanya cried. "Put the plugs in the sink and the bath. We can't let it escape!"

With a final wrench the bracelet broke at the clasp. Now satisfied, the fairy slithered from Tanya's grip, its fist clenched around the object of its desire, and bolted for the open door.

Tanya flew past Fabian out onto the landing. "Don't let it get away!"

The drain-dweller was halfway down the first flight of stairs. Immediately, Tanya could see that it was struggling. In a split second she registered that the dry, dusty carpet was hampering its escape. The creature was used to slithering and sliding through moist pipes and water. It was not equipped for life on dry ground.

Tanya thundered down the stairs, fearing that any moment her legs were going to get tangled up in each other. She was gaining on it.

As the creature neared the grandfather clock on the landing, it stopped suddenly and froze. For a moment Tanya thought it was about to take refuge inside the clock—but then she saw what it was staring at.

The tip of a matted ginger tail was just visible from the side of the grandfather clock. It flicked once in agitation.

What followed would replay itself in Tanya's head in sickening clarity for years to come. Often she would ask herself whether Spitfire had had one last good pounce in him, whether she had vastly underestimated him, or if he had simply been lucky. In the scheme of things none of it really made a difference. The result was the same.

The drain-dweller's eyes widened as Spitfire sprang toward it. It did not try to run. It made no attempt to fight. Maybe it was too afraid to do either. Or maybe it just realized its fate and was accepting of it.

The creature did not scream when the cat's claws found their target, or even whimper as the broken, aged teeth clamped down on its windpipe for the kill. Spitfire, for his part, seemed to sense his good fortune, knowing enough not to push his luck by toying with his prey longer than necessary. There was a crisp, sharp snap, and then the drain-dweller's body twitched before going limp.

Tanya heard her own cry get lodged in her throat. The sound of it startled her, and urged Spitfire to make off with his rare catch. She could only watch as he loped down the stairs and into the hallway, eager to find a darkened corner to feast in.

She became aware of Fabian standing close behind her, and turned. His expression mirrored her own. Like her, he had no words to describe what they had just witnessed. In silence he stooped and picked something up from the threadbare carpet, then gently pushed it into Tanya's hand.

She looked down at the silver bracelet in her palm. Several of the charms were coated in blood, but whether it was the blood of the drain-dweller or her own she was unable to tell. Slowly, she turned and headed back up the stairs, the bracelet slippery beneath her fingers. She paused outside her room when she heard a door open in the hallway below. Then followed a low whistle.

"Looks like Spitfire's been earning his keep," Warwick said. "Did you see what he caught?"

Tanya stiffened.

"I think it was a mouse," she heard Fabian say in a dull voice.

"That's a lot of blood," Warwick remarked. "More likely a rat than a mouse. Didn't think he still had it in him. I'll get the mop."

Tanya did not stay to hear any more. Choking back a sob, she locked her bedroom door and shut herself in the tiny bathroom. She stood in front of the washbasin and held the bracelet under the hot tap, watching through blurred eyes as the water changed from red to pink to clear, disappearing down the plughole that had been the creature's home.

Silver glinted within its depths, and she was reminded of the lost cauldron charm. Something like regret stirred inside her at the thought of it being down there, alone, separated from the rest of the charms. Even if she was able to retrieve it and make the bracelet whole and complete once more, she knew she would never wear it again. Yet still she held it beneath the hot water, trying to wash the death from it. There she stayed, rinsing it until the water ran cold and her fingers were red and shriveled, crying until she had no tears left.

# 21

Tanya tossed and turned between the damp sheets of her bed. The humidity of the night ensured that sleep would not come. The bedroom window was ajar, allowing the scent of the fragrant summer flowers to waft through, something she usually welcomed. Tonight it seemed to be choking her. She could not get the death of the drain-dweller out of her mind.

Gradually the air turned cooler and drowsiness settled over her at last. Just as she started to doze off, a familiar noise called her back from the fuzzy depths of sleep: the unmistakable sound of wings in the air. Too late she became aware of the dull twitching in her eyelids, which, had she not been so preoccupied, she would no doubt have taken heed of several minutes ago.

Claws were scrabbling over the window ledge.

The curtains twitched and parted, and then the famil-iar black bird was gliding slowly toward her. Three other tiny figures followed. The bird shape-shifted in midair and then drew closer, eventually alight-ing on Tanya's pillow. There was an overpowering smell of woodland, then Raven was looking down at her. She seized a strand of Tanya's hair and gave it a spiteful tug before joining her companions at the foot of the bed.

Tanya stared at three sets of accusing eyes, fight-ing all urges to look away. Only the Mizhog seemed to be behaving normally—or as normally as could be expected. The moonlight streaming in caught some-thing wet and glistening that was partially hanging out of its mouth. A slug, Tanya realized, still half alive. The doomed creature wriggled feebly before the Mizhog sucked in the remainder and licked its chops. Repulsed, Tanya tore her eyes away and forced herself to concentrate on the others.

"What's wrong?" she asked, unable to mask the fear in her voice.

"I think you know," said Gredin. He reached out and flung a cushion across the room. It connected with the stool at the dressing table. The stool toppled over and hit the floor with a clatter.

Tanya grimaced at the noise. Feathercap fixed her with an icy stare.

"Your meddling brought about the death of one of our kind tonight," he said.

"I didn't meddle with anything. It stole something of mine and I chased it."

"Yes, you chased it!" Feathercap snarled, in front of her nose within a split second, so close that Tanya could see crumbs in his moustache. "To its death!"

"If it hadn't taken my things I wouldn't have chased it!" Tanya whispered.

Feathercap scoffed.

"Drain-dwellers aren't renowned for honesty or intelligence. The lure of the Thirteen Treasures would prove irresistible to such a dim-witted creature. You should have taken more care."

"The Thirteen Treasures?" Tanya shook her head in bewilderment. "I don't understand."

"Say no more, Feathercap," Raven warned.

Tanya glanced at her in astonishment, then looked to Gredin. Both were wearing twin expressions of anger mixed with anxiety.

Feathercap rounded on them. "It was only a matter of time before she worked it out for herself!" He turned back to Tanya. "You *taunted* it. You *tempted* it."

"How?" Tanya cried, forgetting to keep quiet.

*"You gave it one of the charms!"*

"She was not aware," said Raven.

"And then there was the girl," Feathercap spat, working himself further into his rage. "Oh, yes, your little talks with her haven't gone unnoticed."

Tanya clenched her fists beneath the bedclothes.

"I was trying to help her return that child. The *fairy* child. I don't see why you would object to that, unless you enjoy the chaos and disruption of the two worlds mixing. But maybe that's exactly what you want. I *know* about the Unseelie Court. Red told me."

"You know nothing about what we want," said Gredin. "And nothing of who we are. As for the other girl, she may have told you what she knows, but I can assure you that what she *does* know is far from enough. Not even close."

An interruption came as the Mizhog burst into a rapid succession of hiccups. Tanya watched with a sinking feeling. The Mizhog, being of a somewhat nervous disposition, had never reacted well to moments of tension such as these. It began retching violently. Moments later, as she feared, what was left of the slug reappeared on her bedspread. A final hiccup later the Mizhog recovered, picking at a flea on its belly.

Feathercap's face darkened as he stared across the room. He was gazing at the old painting above the fireplace.

"Echo and Narcissus," he murmured. "Interesting." He snapped out of his daze and turned back to Tanya. "You are familiar with the story?"

Tanya nodded warily.

"Refresh my memory," Feathercap said, but his tone was mocking.

"Echo was cursed by an enchantress," said

Tanya. "She could only speak the last words of other peoples' sentences. Narcissus was a vain young man who fell in love with his own reflection in a pool and wasted away. Echo pined for him until all that was left of her was her voice."

"Imagine," said Feathercap. "To only be able to speak the last words of other peoples' sentences."

Tanya felt her insides give an awful lurch. "You're threatening me."

Feathercap smiled. Lifting his hand, he mimed a knocking action in the air. The sharp sound of knuckles on wood resonated from the wardrobe—even though Feathercap hadn't touched it, was nowhere *near* it.

"Knock, knock," he said softly. "Who's there?"

In the quiet that followed a small sound caught her attention, almost like a whine. It was coming from the wardrobe.

"What's that?" said Tanya, drawing the sheets up around herself. "What have you done?"

The whining continued and was joined by a scratching noise, soft but insistent, gradually building into a frenzy. The wardrobe door began to shake and rattle as whatever was inside threw itself about, howling. It sounded like a demon.

Tanya leapt out of bed, the sheets gathered around her. She was halfway across the room when the wardrobe door burst open and Oberon shot out with a yelp, confused and plainly terrified. In a flash she understood: Oberon was simply a catalyst. The real trouble would start once he had inevitably woken the household.

"Here, boy," she said desperately, hands outstretched toward him. "Quiet now—it's all right!"

The bewildered animal would not be coaxed. He chased madly about the room, knocking over the table and chair in the corner. A pile of books flew into the air before crashing to the floor. Moments later the dog seemed to gather his wits, and set about the fairies, growling and barking. Raven and Gredin evaded him easily, gliding up to the safety of the ceiling. The Mizhog let out a high-pitched squeak and followed.

Feathercap leapt onto the windowsill, narrowly escaping a gnash of Oberon's jaws. He pointed a fat finger at Tanya. "This is for the drain-dweller."

A shower of sparks erupted from his finger, and the lower half of Tanya's face froze. She brought her hands up to her mouth. Her jaw was slack and open, her lips horribly numb.

Footsteps hurried across the landing.

"What's going on?" her grandmother called out.

"...*Going on*..." said Tanya, her mouth moving through no control of her own.

The bedroom door flew open, and the room flooded with light. Her eyes slowly adjusted to the new brightness. Florence swept into the room, her face a grim mask of white. Warwick followed shortly after. Tanya noticed his hand resting on the hunting knife he carried in his belt—an observation she made at precisely the same moment as her grandmother. Florence and Warwick exchanged glances, and he quickly dropped his hand.

Florence glanced at the ceiling with a peculiar look on her face. Tanya's head snapped up. It seemed her grandmother had been gazing straight at the fairies, but then she saw that the lightbulb was swaying frenziedly. One of them—most likely the Mizhog—must have knocked against it.

Above them, Amos stirred in his room. There were numerous shouted obscenities followed by a loud, constant banging, like a door being repeatedly opened and slammed. Florence's mouth was pressed into a thin line as she took in the scene: the overturned chair and table, the books scattered about haphazardly, and Oberon jumping up at the windowsill, still barking frantically.

"STOP THAT CONFOUNDED RACKET!" Warwick bellowed at him.

Oberon fled and cowered behind Tanya with a whimper.

"...*Confounded racket*..." she repeated, looking over to the window. Feathercap gave a last, satisfied smirk and then the fairies were gone.

"What exactly," Florence said coldly, "is that dog doing in here?"

"...*In here*..." Tanya echoed.

"What have you been up to?"

"...*Up to*..."

"Is this your idea of a joke?" said Warwick.

"...*A joke*..."

Tanya covered her mouth with her hands.

"Warwick," Florence snapped. "Take the dog downstairs and shut him in the kitchen."

"...*In the kitchen*..." Tanya mumbled from behind her hands.

Warwick pursed his lips and left, followed by a meek Oberon. Florence remained, standing stiffly, her slate-gray eyes hard.

"There will be no more of this nonsense. No more of this sneaking around in the night. If I find Oberon up here again I'll have him sent back home before you can blink. Do you understand?"

Tanya nodded, but the words spilled from her mouth nonetheless. "...*Do you understand*..." She looked down, unable to meet her grandmother's face any longer.

"Stop repeating everything I say!"

"...*Everything I say*..."

"I didn't expect this kind of insolence from you. Obviously you've been spending too much time in Fabian's company," said Florence. "I'm not amused."

"...*Not amused*..."

"Into bed—now." Her grandmother's lips were tight. "I don't want to hear another peep out of you." Without another word she left, closing the door abruptly.

"...*Out of you*..." Tanya whispered to the empty room. She stared at the painting hanging above the fireplace. A hot tear of anger and frustration slid down her cheek. The maiden's expression seemed to be mocking her.

Slowly, quietly, she walked into the bathroom, where the charm bracelet lay on the edge of the washbasin in a puddle of cold water. She picked it up, shivering as a bead of water trickled all the way down to her elbow like an icy tear. In the darkness she ran her thumb over each charm in turn. Some of them she could not decipher, but she was not willing to turn the light on and risk angering her grandmother further. Among those she could make out there were a dagger, a goblet, and a key.

*The Thirteen Treasures.*

Why hadn't she seen it sooner?

A family heirloom, passed down through generations by Elizabeth Elvesden, the first lady of the manor. A woman who had died in a mental institution, leaving her secrets stashed in diaries around the manor: secrets the family was desperate to keep hidden in order to preserve their good name. Secrets easy to label as madness.

*Secrets that Tanya now had a very strong feeling about.*

Elizabeth Elvesden may have seemed mad— but she hadn't been. Elizabeth Elvesden had been a changeling.

22

Wednesday dawned crisp and clear, with just a hint of a chill in the air. As usual, Tanya was up early. That morning, Amos's yells had served a useful purpose. When listening to him from her room below, Tanya had not repeated a word of it and was able to gauge that the fairies' spell had worn off.

After the previous night's events she wasn't hungry, but had decided to force some breakfast down. For the first time, Florence had not bothered to make breakfast, and was nowhere to be seen. Now, Tanya was standing at the kitchen door munching mechanically on a crumpet while watching Oberon sniffing about in the back garden.

Warwick came into the kitchen. Now that she was no longer alone, Tanya became aware of the sound of her own mouth chewing noisily. She stopped and swallowed, resisting the urge to cough as a stodgy lump got lodged in her throat.

"Didn't know anyone else was up yet," said Warwick, in his usual sullen manner. He flicked the switch on the kettle, then spooned instant coffee into a mug.

"I didn't sleep very well," said Tanya. As soon as the words were out of her mouth she realized how stupid she sounded.

Warwick gave his usual grunt and turned his back on her.

"I don't think any of us slept well," he muttered. The strong smell of cheap coffee filled the kitchen as he poured boiling water into the mug. He left without another word.

Less than a minute later Fabian came into the kitchen and sat down at the table. He looked at her expectantly.

"What are you looking at?" said Tanya, annoyed by his staring.

"*What are you looking at?*" Fabian mimicked immediately.

Tanya scowled. "So you've heard."

Fabian grinned. "Of course. Warwick told me. I can't believe I slept right through it. Sounds like it was a hoot."

"It wasn't me, Fabian," Tanya said tiredly. "It was *them*. The fairies. They came to punish me for... for what happened to the drain-dweller."

The smirk on Fabian's face died instantly. "You mean they... did that? Made you repeat everything?"

Tanya nodded. "And that's not all. I found out why the drain-dweller was so obsessed with getting the charm bracelet. It wasn't just because it was shiny. It's because the charms on the bracelet symbolize the Thirteen Treasures."

"From the Seelie and Unseelie Courts?" Fabian asked.

"Yes. Whoever commissioned the bracelet would have wanted something personal, something of significance to them. The legend of the Thirteen Treasures is an obscure one, which means that the original owner of the bracelet must have had a strong connection to the fairies."

"What kind of connection?"

"The kind that gave some of the descendants in this family—including me—the second sight."

"A changeling," Fabian finished. "So we have to trace it back to its original owner, then you'll have your answer."

"I think I already know who the original owner was. She's wearing the bracelet in the portrait in her room. It was Elizabeth Elvesden." Tanya got up and closed the kitchen door, after taking a quick peek into the hallway to ensure they were alone. She took a seat at the table opposite Fabian.

"I'll help you go through with this plan to save

Morwenna Bloom so we can clear Amos's name," she said quietly. "But after that, I'm done with the fairies."

"What do you mean?" asked Fabian. "It's not like you'll just stop seeing them, is it?"

"I know I won't stop seeing them," said Tanya. "I don't have any choice in the matter. But what I do have a choice in is how I react to them. Everything that they've ever done to me has been as a result of something I've done. Someone I've tried to tell about them, or something that's affected them. All they've ever wanted is my silence. So maybe if I give them what they want, they'll leave me alone. And maybe I can start to live a normal sort of life."

"That's a lot of 'maybes,'" Fabian said quietly.

"I know," said Tanya. "But 'maybe' is all I have."

Fabian stood up and opened the back door. He hovered in the doorway, and was knocked off balance as Oberon barged past him in his eagerness to get out into the garden.

"He's violent, you know," Fabian said. "Amos, I mean. It's no surprise people thought he was capable of...of what he was accused of." He paused and brought his hand to his temple. "Remember... remember that bruise I had? I told you I fell. But I lied."

Tanya said nothing. She had suspected as much all along.

"When we found out who the girl we'd seen

in the woods that day really was, I got desperate," Fabian continued. "After I told you about Morwenna that night, I stayed on the second floor and waited until Amos left his room to use the bathroom—I knew that it would give me a couple of minutes to look around—he takes ages moving around these days. I waited in the alcove—it seemed like I'd been there for hours by the time he finally emerged. As soon as he was out of sight I crept into his room."

"What were you looking for?" Tanya asked.

"Anything," said Fabian. "Anything...that might suggest his innocence...or his guilt."

"If the police cleared him, do you honestly think you'd be able to find anything after all this time?"

"I don't know." Fabian closed his eyes. "It was awful. There was junk everywhere...stacks of old newspapers...clothes he hasn't worn for years, and probably never will again. Gifts he's never opened... still in the wrapping paper. I've heard my father telling Florence about how he won't have anything thrown away, but I didn't realize to what extent. I found some really creepy stuff..." he broke off and shuddered.

"Like what?"

"A lock of hair." Seeing the alarmed look on Tanya's face he quickly added, "Don't worry, it's not yours. It's too dark. It was in a box with his wedding ring and some photos of my grandmother, and other stuff that belonged to her. It must have been hers— she was dark.

"It was so cluttered in there it was hard to think straight. I was just about to give up and leave when I found something. A scrapbook of newspaper clippings, all about Morwenna—dozens of them. There was even one dating back to before she disappeared."

"Why would she be in the paper before she'd disappeared?"

"She'd won a local talent competition—apparently she had a gift for poetry."

"She must have written the poem I found," Tanya said slowly. "But that doesn't explain how it came to be in my room." She frowned. "So then what happened?"

"I started reading through the clippings," said Fabian. "But I must have been in there longer than I thought because Amos came back...and found me."

"He hit you?"

"He started screaming at me to get out," said Fabian. "I froze at first. And then when I tried to get past him to get out of the room, well...I think it must have scared him. He struck out at me. And... and the worst of it is...I don't think he even recognized me anymore."

Neither of them said much for a while after that. There were no words that would bring any comfort to Fabian, and they both knew it.

From the hallway, the grandfather clock chimed the hour, breaking the silence.

"Warwick will be leaving soon," Fabian said in a low voice.

"Are you prepared?" Tanya asked.

"I've got the map, flashlight, and all that kind of stuff."

"I've got the compass, and an old iron nail to carry in my pocket. And I've also sewn a couple of salt pouches to carry in our pockets as extra protection. If any fairies attack you, break the pouches open and throw it at them. I'll need a lock of your hair too, in case...you know."

"In case we get trapped in the fairy realm," Fabian finished grimly.

Tanya nodded and hurriedly continued. "Try to wear something red if you can."

"I don't have anything red."

"Then turn your clothes inside out. And whatever you do, don't forget the tonic that Morag gave you." She quickly moved on as Fabian gave her a scornful look.

"We need to leave earlier than we did last time if we're going to make use of the in-between. We have to find Morwenna before then, so we can lead her out of the fairy realm at the stroke of midnight—that's when it's most easily accessible."

Fabian nodded thoughtfully. "I'll make sure my watch is absolutely accurate before we leave. I'll set the alarm to go off at midnight."

Tanya felt a prickle of fear at what was to come. It seemed they had thought of everything. Yet still she failed to trust that it would be enough.

The morning dragged on. Warwick left while it

was still early. After loading a stack of hunting supplies into the Land Rover, he drove noisily through the gates and onto the dirt road, away from Elvesden Manor.

At midday, Tanya looked at the clock on the landing.

*Twelve hours to go.*

Throughout the day Oberon was restless, sensing her unease. He seemed unable to keep still for more than a few minutes at a time and wandered from room to room, only adding to Tanya's trepidation. Finally, the sun slipped down in the sky until it disappeared altogether, leaving darkness to wrap around the manor like a heavy blanket. The grandfather clock ticked on.

◆◆

The house was still and quiet. Tanya edged down the stairs. On the landing Spitfire was fast asleep at the foot of the grandfather clock, splayed out like a matted ginger rug. She sidestepped him and proceeded toward the darkened kitchen, where a low rumbling noise caused her to pause before she realized that the noise was Oberon snoring. She was just about to step into the kitchen when the sound of smashing glass came from a nearby room.

Her eyes darted across the hallway. A sliver of light was visible from below the living room door. She caught Florence's exclamation of annoyance.

Tanya slipped into the kitchen and hid in the first place she could think of: under the large oak table. Oberon looked up at her lazily from his basket, and for one awful moment it looked as if he was going to come over and give her away.

"Stay!" Tanya hissed.

Oberon stayed.

The door opened and Florence came into the hallway, grumbling in a low voice. She fumbled about, banging and clattering in one of the cupboards, then plodded back to the living room. Tanya listened as shards of broken glass were swept up, and then Florence came into the kitchen, her dowdy slippers just visible from where Tanya sat crouched under the tablecloth. Her grandmother threw the broken glass into the trash, then left, turning the hallway light off. The slap of her slippers was audible on the carpet as she shuffled upstairs.

Tanya closed her eyes in relief. She climbed out from under the table, her legs shaky beneath her, and went over to Oberon, who was now looking very puzzled as to her odd behavior. From her pocket she pulled out the red beaded scarf and wrapped it around his neck, tucking the loose ends into his collar. The two of them slipped out into the cool night air, through the garden, and onward toward the gate.

Fabian was waiting on the other side, silent and paler in the face than usual. He jumped when Oberon stuck his wet nose into the palm of his hand in greeting, then regarded the dog strangely.

"Isn't that your scarf he's wearing?"

"He needs protecting too," Tanya said stiffly.

"Well, I don't think red is his color," Fabian cracked.

Tanya was too anxious to force a laugh. "Just keep quiet," she said. "We don't want to draw attention to ourselves."

Fabian shut up immediately, his hand straying subconsciously to the top of his head as if remembering the raven's attack on their last attempt to enter the woods.

They began to walk to the forest, Oberon bounding off ahead. He was getting rather accustomed to these late night walks by now.

It was a clear night. A crescent moon hung in the inky sky above them, and the stars glittered like a gauzy silver veil. Tanya folded her arms tightly around herself, glad she had dressed warmly. Over jeans and her only red T-shirt she had chosen to wear the old raincoat, the same one she had worn on the night of the storm. In the right pocket of the coat she had the compass and the iron nail; in her left, the scissors that Morag had given her, and a small cloth bag of salt.

As they approached the brook Fabian paused to squint around in the darkness.

"What's the matter?" Tanya asked.

"Nothing," Fabian muttered.

"*Tell* me."

"I've just...just got a feeling we're being followed. Don't look. Let's just get into the forest."

"Have you seen someone?"

"No, I haven't seen anything," said Fabian. "It's just a feeling. Keep moving."

They walked briskly, neither of them attempting to make conversation. Too soon they were at the brook, the forest sprawling before them.

"Where's the flashlight?" Tanya asked.

"It's in the knapsack," said Fabian. "I'll get it out once we're in the forest—the light could be seen from here." He crossed the brook and Tanya followed, the water rushing past her feet as she struggled to see the slippery stepping stones. Within minutes they stood on the border of the forest.

Fabian took off his rucksack and knelt on the ground. He pulled out the flashlight and the map, then Morag's tonic. Quickly, he removed the stopper and anointed both eyes.

"What time is it?" Tanya asked.

Fabian hoisted the bag up on his back. "Thirty-one minutes to midnight. We have to hurry."

Wordlessly they walked into the trees. Within the forest, the only sound was the dry rustle of dead leaves underfoot as they shuffled through. Tanya followed Fabian several yards into the woods, and almost went tumbling to the ground after tripping on a fallen branch. Finally Fabian flicked the flashlight on.

"Do you still think we're being followed?" Tanya asked in a low voice. "If we are the light will give us away."

Fabian's eyes flickered from side to side.

"I don't know. But we have to use the flashlight now. We won't get far without it."

He unfolded the map and squinted at it. "We should head to the second catacomb—that's where we saw her before, so it makes sense that we might see her there again." He tapped the map. "It's not far; we should see the first catacomb coming up fairly soon."

They headed off, the forest eerily quiet. Occasionally the yellow eyes of nocturnal creatures stared at them out of the darkness. After a short distance, Tanya exclaimed as something heavy hit her leg.

"What is it?" said Fabian.

"It's the compass," said Tanya. "It's fallen through a hole in my pocket into the lining of my coat. The nail must have pierced it and made a hole—it's gone through too."

"Give it here," said Fabian. "I'll put it in my bag—it'll be safe there."

With some difficulty, Tanya squeezed her hand through the hole into the coat lining and retrieved the compass, but she was unable to locate the iron nail. It would have to stay there. "Make sure you put it somewhere secure," she said, handing the compass to Fabian. "If we lose it we'll only have the map to rely on."

They carried on walking farther into the trees, until they were so far in that Tanya was beginning to get the horrible feeling that they were going the

wrong way. Seemingly out of nowhere the first catacomb came into sight.

Fabian broke into a jog, heading past the
railings.

"This way!" he called over his shoulder. "It can't
be far now!"

Tanya ran after him, straining to keep sight of
the flickering flashlight as he sprinted ahead. "Slow
down! I can't see!"

Very soon they came into a small clearing.

"This is where we saw her," said Fabian. He
aimed his flashlight at the dense trees surrounding
them, his hand shaking with adrenaline.

"Are you sure?" said Tanya. "I don't see the
railings—perhaps this is a different clearing."

Fabian consulted the map. "But I'm sure this is
it—it must be."

"Look," said Tanya suddenly, pointing past a
thick tree. "Shine the flashlight over there."

Fabian held the flashlight up, and a flash of silver
glinted through the trees.

"There it is."

As they edged closer to the railings, a chilling
sound cut through the air.

"What's that noise?" said Fabian, his eyes darting about fearfully.

"It sounds like somebody...*crying*," Tanya
murmured.

Fabian crept forward and Tanya followed,
her heart hammering hard in her chest. Past the

railings, sitting at the foot of a tree, a dark figure was hunched over and hugging her knees. Her long, black hair spilled to the ground where foxgloves were growing in abundance, swaying softly in the night air.

"It's her," said Fabian. "It's Morwenna Bloom."

Tanya stepped forward and a twig snapped under her foot, but the girl did not look up. Instead she continued to sob into her hands.

"Morwenna," Fabian called, finding his voice at last. "Morwenna Bloom!"

At the sound of her name the girl looked up, and Tanya was startled to see that she wasn't crying after all—she was laughing.

"You found me," she said, standing up and brushing the leaves from her dress. She looked exactly the same, barely a day older than in the photograph.

"We know what happened to you all those years ago," said Tanya. "And...and we've come to help you." She couldn't believe how easy it had been to find the girl...almost *too* easy.

"You've come to help me? How?"

"We want to help you find a way out of here," said Tanya. Suddenly, and for reasons she could not fathom, she became frightened. In the eerie moonlight, Morwenna looked almost wraithlike. Tanya took the scissors out of the raincoat and stuck them in the back pocket of her jeans, then offered her coat to the girl. "Take this. It'll protect you."

Morwenna took a step toward them, a strange

little smile playing on her lips as she took the rain-coat. "And what do you have to protect yourself, I wonder?"

A low, rumbling growl had begun in Oberon's throat. Tanya looked down and saw that the dog's hackles were raised, and his body was completely rigid. He had placed himself directly between Tanya and Morwenna.

It was then that Tanya knew there was something horribly, terribly wrong.

"Protect me from what?"

Morwenna stared at her with glassy, coal-black eyes.

"Protect you from me, of course."

For a moment Tanya thought she had misheard.

"Do you know why I'm here?" Morwenna's voice was high, singsong. It chilled Tanya's blood.

"I'm here because of something that happened fifty years ago. And now, the only thing that can set me free is the debt that is owed me."

"What debt?" said Fabian. "What are you talking about?"

Morwenna smiled then. A cold, twisted smile. "The debt is from a friend of long ago." She looked Tanya directly in the eye. "Your grandmother."

"What?" said Tanya, backing away. "I don't understand!"

"Of course you don't. How could you? You see, Florence and I had...an understanding, many years ago, a *pact*, if you like. I kept my part of the promise, but Florence did not. Now she has to pay the price."

"And what is the price?" said Tanya, dreading what she was about to hear next.

Morwenna took another step toward her. "You are."

23

Tanya wanted to run, but was prevented from doing so by a combination of sheer, gut-wrenching fear and a morbid desire to hear more. Out of the corner of her eye she saw Fabian, frozen to the spot.

"I...I still don't understand."

"Then let me explain," Morwenna hissed. "A long time ago you and I were not so different. Lonely...misunderstood...as you know, friendship does not come easily to those like us."

"Those with the second sight," said Tanya.

Morwenna smiled. "Yes. Those with the second sight. But then I *did* find a friend—someone who understood me, and whom I understood in turn because we were the same. That person was your grandmother."

"My grandmother doesn't have the second sight. You're lying."

"Am I?" said Morwenna. "The look on your face tells me you might not be quite so sure. I *know* Florence. She would have hidden it well. She would have wanted to protect you from the truth, from this. She pushed you away to do that. My guess is that the two of you aren't exactly *close*."

Tanya stared, dumbfounded, then lowered her eyes.

Morwenna laughed. "Just as I thought. Ever wonder why you weren't welcome? Why she didn't want you around? Well, you're about to find out."

"Why are you saying all this?" Tanya whispered. "What does any of this have to do with me?"

"It has everything to do with you. You've got your grandmother to thank for that." Morwenna twisted a strand of black hair around her finger. "Florence and I were best friends. Inseparable. We did everything together. However, her parents allowed her more freedom than mine allowed me." Her face darkened. "My father could be very...*difficult*. The honorable Reverend Bloom...or at least, that's what it looked like from the outside.

"The reality was somewhat different. He was a dominating, controlling man. I had to beg to be let out of the house on some occasions. One day, we were walking in the forest, Florence and I," Morwenna scowled. "I was upset. My father had revealed his plans to have me sent away to a new boarding school in London when the summer ended. Florence begged me not to go; it would mean her losing the only friend she'd ever known. I didn't want to go either, and so we began to talk of running away.

"We had been talking for a while when we realized we were not alone. We were being watched... and listened to."

"The fairies," Tanya said slowly.

"They made an offer to us both, a way out of our problems. A place where nobody would find us, nothing could harm us, and we would never grow old. The fairy realm."

"But they took you..." said Tanya. "They led you astray...they *trapped* you..."

Morwenna continued to speak as if she had not heard.

"It was my chance of escape—but Florence was not so sure. She was torn between coming with me and staying with her family, but we did not have much time. The fairies had given us until Midsummer's eve to make our choice. I pleaded with Florence for days, but still she could not decide. Then, the day before Midsummer's eve, she had an argument with her parents in which terrible things were said. After that she made her decision—we vowed to leave and never return.

"But Florence had always been the weaker of us. I knew that doubts would start to creep into her mind.

Her word was not strong enough for me to trust, and so I made her swear to keep her promise. We pricked thumbs, sealing the pact in blood.

"Midsummer's eve arrived, and I waited in the woods. Florence never came. I went to the manor, where the groundskeeper told me that she was feeling unwell. In other words, she had lost her nerve. But it was too late for me. I had to go on."

"The groundskeeper was Amos, wasn't it?" said Fabian. "It was my grandfather."

"The lovesick fool," said Morwenna. "He begged me not to go when I told him I was running away. I gave him a lock of my hair to remember me by, and told him to keep it secret and safe. Little did he know his little 'love token' was part of a bigger plan. Into it I had also woven a few strands of Florence's hair, stolen from her comb, to strengthen the promise she had made."

"A lock of hair?" Fabian's voice was strained.

"The key to my immortality," Morwenna said slyly. "Something of myself as I was. Its preservation in the human world would allow me to be seen by the mortal eye when I chose and keep me forever fourteen. And so I shall be still, when I return.

"At midnight, I passed into the fairy realm. To begin with I was happy, although I knew I would never forgive Florence's cowardice. But as the years passed, I found that an immortal existence is a lonely one. I came to regret my decision. However, when you give yourself willingly to the fairy realm, there is no way out, save one."

"And what is that?" Tanya asked, her voice hoarse.

"That another mortal of second sight and linked by blood should exchange places with me," said Morwenna. "I knew of no blood relatives with the second sight. But by making our promises in blood Florence had linked herself to me. Thus she was the only one who could have taken my place, but she was far too clever to venture into the woods. So I waited.

"Years passed. Florence married, and was expecting a child. Finally, I saw the opportunity I had been waiting for. Never underestimate the power of a mother's love."

"You stole the baby to take your place." Fabian's voice was thick with disgust.

"No," said Morwenna, with a cruel laugh. "The child shared Florence's blood, of course, but it did not have the second sight; therefore it could not have taken my place in the fairy realm. The child was merely a bargaining chip…I stole the baby to lure Florence into the woods. I had the child brought to me. I knew Florence would guess who was behind it, and face up to her past. When she found us she begged for her child, as I knew she would. I told her I would return the child if Florence would exchange places with me then and there. If she refused, I would take the baby into the fairy realm and she would never see it again.

"Florence knew there was no escape. She agreed to exchange places, but begged me to take pity on her and allow her a few years to raise her child. She promised that if I would give her seven years she would willingly take my place. She swore that on the child's seventh birthday, she would come back and pay her debt. Stupidly, I agreed. For after so many years, what did a few more matter? I had lost nothing of my life. I could afford to show a little mercy. Little did I know then that she'd tricked me." She stared hatefully at Tanya. "The child I'm speaking of was your mother."

Tanya remembered the hidden nursery.

"But my mother was born on the twenty-ninth of February—the extra day of a leap year."

Fabian gasped. "So her true seventh birthday wouldn't be until twenty-eight years later!"

"Indeed," said Morwenna. "Nature had allowed Florence another escape. After that I knew I had no chance of getting anywhere near the child again— Florence would have taken steps to ensure that the child was well protected. All I could do was wait for the years to pass until she would have to fulfill her promise. But as the time neared, something unexpected took place. Another child with the second sight linked by blood to Florence was born. And with it, the perfect opportunity for revenge." She smiled at Tanya, completely demented-looking. "*You.*"

"No...," Tanya protested.

"I must say you took some finding—you were

protected well," said Morwenna. "But not well enough."

"Who was protecting me?"

Morwenna did not answer. "At midnight our places shall be exchanged."

"*No!*" Tanya shouted. She turned to Fabian, but he was motionless, with an absolutely petrified look on his face.

"The trees...look at the trees!"

Fairies were emerging from their hiding places, and some of them were unlike any she had ever seen before: broken, twisted beings that looked as if they knew nothing of goodness. They had skin like bark, and limbs of twigs and branches. They *were* the woodland. And then, within the depths of the trees a tiny movement in a moonlit clearing caught her eye. Fabian was right. They *had* been followed.

A face was visible from within the trees for a split second before vanishing—a familiar face. One that Tanya had thought she would never see again. For a moment she wondered if she had simply made the whole thing up in her mind, but then the face appeared again, a finger pressed tightly to its lips, warning her to keep silent.

The face belonged to Red.

Quickly, Tanya averted her eyes, her mind racing. What was going on?

"Bind her!" said Morwenna.

Oberon snarled and snapped as the fairies approached.

"You're outnumbered," said Morwenna. "And if you do not call the dog off, I promise you they will kill him."

Tanya glanced at Oberon. It was a risk she couldn't afford to take. She called him off, despite his whines of protest. He nuzzled her in confusion, but she pushed him away.

"*Run!*" she yelled to Fabian, but the fairies were swooping already, forcing her backward until she hit a tree. She felt herself being bound tightly to the trunk with something she could not see or fight against; something cold, thin, and sticky. The fairies trussed her up until she was unable to move an inch then slithered back into the shadows, all except for an ugly old fairy crone who held her arm with a surprisingly strong grip.

"Staying with us?" she wheezed. "You'll make a fine playmate for my children. Let's hope you last longer than the others..."

Fabian's eyes were wide with dread.

"She's protected! Leave her alone! *You can't touch her!*"

Morwenna's lip curled in contempt as she looked at Tanya's T-shirt. "The color red merely acts as a concealment from the fairies...which you surrendered the moment you called my name."

"Then how about this?" yelled Fabian. He reached into his pockets and pulled out one of the small cloth pouches Tanya had sewn. Fumbling with a penknife, he made a small incision in the cloth and allowed some salt to spill into his hands. He hurled it into the face of the fairy crone and dashed to Tanya's side. The hag backed away, screaming hideously and clawing at her eyes. Tanya watched in horror as her skin blistered and bubbled, and she crawled away, out of sight. More fairies advanced.

"Watch out!" Tanya shrieked.

Fabian turned, throwing salt in every direction. Howls of pain and fury filled the night as some of the salt made contact—but all too quickly it was gone, and new fairies were already replacing those that had been injured and were scuttling away.

"There are too many of them!" Fabian whispered. "And I don't have any more salt!"

"They don't know that," Tanya gasped urgently.

"Not yet," he said. "But it won't be long before they realize." He began wrenching at Tanya's bonds, but it was useless. He succeeded only in cutting his hands.

"Spidertwine," said Morwenna, savoring the word as if it were delicious to her. "It is enchanted, and therefore unbreakable by mortal hands. They say it fetches a fine price at the fairy markets. Mainly it's used for weaving nets used in the changeling trade, magical nets that can't be broken easily. It was used to capture your mother all those years ago. Ironic that it should play a part in your fate also."

The bonds seemed only to grow tighter as Tanya struggled, cutting into her and drawing blood. Then suddenly she remembered the scissors.

"Fabian! The scissors...they're in my pocket. Morag said they'd cut through almost anything!"

Fabian grappled with the spidertwine despite his wounds, but to no avail. Morwenna watched with obvious gratification. Tanya knew then, with absolute conviction, that whatever the girl had once been she was beyond mercy now. Half a century in the fairy realm had accomplished that. All that remained was a shell capable of revenge and hatred, unrecognizable as something that used to be human.

"I can't get at them," Fabian said. "I can't reach the scissors!" He finally gave up his fight with her bonds, and slowly stepped back. The resignation on his face was unmistakable.

"I'm sorry," he whispered, backing away farther. He hesitated, and then ran without another word.

"What are you doing?" Tanya screamed. "You can't leave me! Fabian, you *coward*!"

But Fabian was already gone.

## 24

Fabian sprinted blindly, stumbling through the darkness. He knew from the look on Tanya's face that she thought he had abandoned her—just as he'd intended. It had been necessary for her to believe it in order for his plan to work, for if Morwenna had guessed what he had in mind she would never allow him to leave the woods alive.

A low scurrying noise behind him told him he was being chased, and in that instant his fear turned to panic.

"*Leave him!*" Morwenna shrieked from within the depths of the trees. "*The boy is not important!*"

The scurrying fell back and then stopped altogether, until all Fabian could hear was his own ragged breathing. Without warning the ground inclined, and he went sprawling to the earth. There was a horrible splintering sound, and the flashlight suddenly went out.

"No," said Fabian, feeling around in the darkness. "*Please, no*..."

Already he knew that the flashlight was useless. He clambered to his feet shakily. The forest was pitch-black.

"*Think!*" he told himself. "Calm down and think!" He pressed a button on his watch and the tiny screen lit up. It was seventeen minutes to midnight.

He knelt down and patted the earth blindly until he found his knapsack. It had flown off his back in the fall. It was a moment before he remembered what was inside it.

"The compass!"

Almost crying with joy, he ripped the bag open and rummaged inside until his hand closed around the smooth, cold brass. He pulled it out, and using the light from his watch, read the needle. It was pointing straight ahead.

Without further ado Fabian battled on. He ran for what seemed like forever, until his limbs ached and his lungs were burning, but he did not stop once. Every second was precious.

Twice more he fell, tearing both his clothes and his flesh, but he held on to the compass with a vise-like grip and plowed onward. When the edge of the forest appeared he felt an elation he had never known before, and a renewed sense of strength surged through him.

Then he was out of the forest and hurtling toward the manor.

※

Back in the woods Tanya slumped against the tree, her energy spent. In her attempt to reach the scissors she had become even more entangled in the spidertwine, and now her right hand was caught at a painful angle behind her back.

"Why didn't you try and take me before?" she said, her anger finally overwhelming her fear. "You had the chance weeks ago, the day Fabian and I were lost in the forest."

Morwenna brushed a black tangle away from her face. "I was leading you away that day," she said, with a mad grin. "My plan was to take you so far into the woods that you would never find your way out—at least not before midnight. But then help arrived."

Tanya remembered how she had kicked Warwick that day, and wished with all her heart that he would somehow magically appear now.

Morwenna laughed, reading her mind. "There's no one to save you this time. Even your little friend has deserted you. He didn't wait around once he knew his precious grandfather was innocent, did he?

"If it's any consolation, he'll never make it out of the forest. Hangman's Wood has a strange way of eluding mortals. He'll be wandering around, lost for days. Half-dead by the time he's found—if he ever is found."

"How did you know it was me that day?" said Tanya. "You'd never even seen me before!"

There was a short silence before Morwenna replied.

"I have an informant."

Tanya began to struggle again, her eyes scanning the woods desperately for any sign of rescue. If Red was still there, she was staying well hidden.

·◆·

Fabian reached the house, his lungs ready to explode, then flew through the kitchen, not even stopping to shut the back door behind him. He ran swiftly up the stairs to the first floor, then to the second. He paused outside his grandfather's room.

The old man was mumbling to himself over the low murmur of the television. Thinking quickly, Fabian rapped on the door, then darted along the corridor and into the alcove.

Amos stepped out into the hallway unsteadily. "Warwick? Is that you?"

Quick as a flash, Fabian pulled the tapestry aside and slipped into the servants' passage. There, in the darkness, he felt his way along the wall, counting the doors until he came to his grandfather's room.

With bated breath he turned the handle. Luck was on his side.

The door opened and Fabian peered into the disordered room. The main door was ajar, and there was no sign of Amos anywhere. He stepped inside, and a wave of desperation washed over him. His eyes scanned the room, darting from one pile of junk to another. He crawled on the floor to peer beneath the bed. He pulled out several cardboard boxes, stuffed with clothes and yet more newspapers, and over-turned them. His grandmother's belongings were still there; the abandoned wedding ring rattling about loose. The lock of hair was nowhere to be seen.

He saw the newspaper scrapbook lying on the bedside table. He grabbed it, thumbing through the pages. Several clippings fell to the floor. He snapped it shut and threw it on the bed. Quickly, he went to the chest of drawers and began rummaging through his grandfather's clothes.

"Where would he keep it, *where*?"

He could not believe he had seen it and not made the connection—the most obvious connection of all. The destruction of the hair would break the spell of Morwenna's youth. It was this, Fabian knew, that she valued above all. And it was all he had to bargain with.

The chest of drawers yielded no answers. Fabian closed the last drawer clumsily, clothes spilling out. In frustration he kicked at one of the boxes which he had not bothered to push back under the bed. It landed with a thud, and he flinched as footsteps came thundering back down the hallway.

"*Warwick!*"

Amos appeared in the doorway. His sunken eyes were pits of madness.

"I didn't do it!" he spat. "I keep telling them it wasn't me. She ran away!"

"I...I know," Fabian whispered. He began to back away, toward the servants' door.

Amos walked jerkily to the unmade bed and sat down.

"I loved her, I loved her," he repeated, rocking softly. His withered hand moved across the bed-clothes and slipped beneath the pillow. It was all Fabian needed.

With a speed that surprised himself he sprang forward and flung the pillow aside. There, beneath the space where his grandfather laid his head every night, a lock of hair was looped like a thin black noose. Guilt eroded him like acid rain as he tore the lock of hair from the old man's frail fingers.

Amos cried out like a wounded animal.

Fabian made his escape through the servants' door, his grandfather's cries ringing in his ears. He emerged from behind the tapestry, waiting a moment to make sure the coast was definitely clear. Hearing nothing but Amos's tortured wailing, he slid out of the alcove—and collided with a hard body that was standing just around the corner.

Fabian gasped as he looked up.

"W-what are you doing here? I thought y-you'd gone hunting!"

"Change of plans," Warwick hissed, taking in his son's ripped and bloody clothes. "I decided to come back early—and a good thing too, by the look of it!"

He grabbed Fabian's shoulder roughly. "Now you better tell me what *you're* up to this time of night!"

Fabian opened his mouth to speak, but no words would come out.

"*Explain yourself!*"

"Warwick!" Amos called out.

Warwick glared at his son. Then, still holding on to his shoulder, he marched him along the hallway to Amos's room.

"What is it, father?" His usually gruff voice was surprisingly gentle.

Amos shuffled to the door, his shoulders shaking wretchedly as he began to sob.

"He took it...he *took* it."

Warwick caught sight of the hair in Fabian's hand, and a flicker of recognition crossed his face. "What are you doing with that? What do you want with your grandmother's hair?"

Fabian instinctively held the hair behind his back.

"It's not...it's not my grandmother's hair."

"Give it to me!" Amos sobbed. "I promised her I'd keep it forever!"

Warwick's eyes widened. "Where's the girl?"

Fabian froze.

"*Where's Tanya?*"

"She's...she's in the woods!" Fabian croaked, unable to contain it any longer.

Warwick's face went completely white. Without a word, he grabbed Fabian's arm and wrenched the lock of hair out of his grasp.

"What are you doing?" Fabian cried. "Give it back!" He raced after his father, who was already halfway down the stairs, leaving Amos sobbing behind. He caught up with him on the first-floor landing, and tried to snatch Morwenna's hair from his father's hand.

Warwick lashed out angrily.

"Give it back!" said Fabian. "You don't understand!"

His father turned and shook him like a dog shaking a rat. "You little fool! It's *you* who doesn't understand! Do you realize what you've done? All these years we've been working to protect her—and now you've led her straight into danger!" Warwick turned and continued down the stairs, slowing only to step over Spitfire at the foot of the grandfather clock.

Fabian felt his knees give way beneath him as the truth finally dawned. Warwick knew everything. "We didn't know," he said feebly. "We were just trying to help!"

"*Help?* Who did you think could be helped?"

"Both of them! Amos and Morwenna!"

"They're beyond saving! Amos's life was over the day the rumors started! And as for Morwenna Bloom, did you even consider the consequences if she should come strolling out of the forest, fresh-faced and fourteen years old after fifty *years*? They can't be saved, either of them! *They could never be saved!*"

Fabian could not answer. His father's words

pounded heavily in his skull. A door creaked from the first floor, then Florence's face appeared over the banister. She looked haggard and half-asleep, and was in her nightgown. "Warwick? What's going on? Is everything all right?"

"Everything's fine," Warwick said, his tone flat. He gave Fabian a look that warned him to keep quiet. "Just this one, getting up to mischief as usual."

"Oh," said Florence, giving Fabian a sour glance. "Well, I'll see you in the morning, then."

Fabian stared at his father as Florence's bedroom door closed. "You're not going to tell her?"

Warwick pulled on his boots. "No. I'm not."

"She has a right to know!"

"She'll know soon enough," said Warwick, grimly. "And when she does—if Morwenna succeeds, it'll destroy her."

Fabian blinked back tears of shame and checked his watch. It was seven minutes to twelve. "We're running out of time!"

"You think I don't know that?"

Warwick left the house through the front. Fabian followed him and watched in confusion as his father stalked around the side of the house toward his den.

"What are you doing?" said Fabian. "We need to go back to the woods, now!"

Warwick threw open the door to the den. "Get in there!"

Fabian stepped forward hesitantly. Never before

had his father allowed him anywhere near his work-room, let alone inside it, but as Warwick shoved him between the shoulder blades he fell through the door and all became clear.

The far wall was stacked with cages from top to bottom, one on top of the other. Inside the cages were fairies. In the largest cage at the bottom of the stack were two of the ugliest creatures he had ever seen. The taller of the pair, who had a somewhat toadlike quality about him, grasped the bars and grinned.

"Don't just stare," he said. "The key's over there!"

"Where's the other goblin?" Fabian asked, feeling dazed. "Tanya said there were three of them."

"Brunswick poses no threat. He's part human. A changeling. He simply mimics the other two because it's all he knows."

Fabian surveyed the rest of the cages. There were easily a dozen, each containing one or more fairies. In one a wizened little creature with a cane sat clutching a teabag as if its life depended on it. The hearthfay was in another—a tiny, ugly girl in a dish-rag dress peering out from behind a curtain of long hair. Her face brightened as he looked at her, and she gave him a shy, pleading look before huddling into herself once more.

Warwick grabbed his air rifle from the opposite wall and began loading it.

"Why are they in cages?" Fabian whispered.

"Because that's what I'm paid for!" said his father. "And one of them has betrayed us!" He grabbed a bunch of keys from the mantel—next to which was a large vat of a familiar looking gray-green liquid.

"But how . . . ?" said Fabian, suddenly starting to feel very sick. "How come they haven't escaped?"

"The cages are iron. They can't escape until I release them."

"All this time," said Fabian. "You knew what really happened to Morwenna Bloom."

Warwick slipped his hunting knife into his belt.

"And all this time the hair was there, right under my very nose. Florence always suspected that Morwenna might have been clever enough to leave something behind to preserve the pact—and herself." He examined the lock of hair carefully, then folded it and put it in his pocket. "The pact was created in the woods where the magic is strongest. Only there can it be destroyed."

"But it's nearly midnight!" Fabian cried, almost beside himself with panic.

"There is still time," said a voice that Fabian did not recognize.

"Raven," Warwick exclaimed.

Fabian spun around and saw three small figures standing on the ledge of the open window: one male, one female, and the other a mangy creature with moth-eaten wings. It was the female who had spoken. He took in her feathered gown and her chiseled features. *The raven.*

"She's in the forest," said Warwick. "We've got to leave now."

Raven nodded. "There's no time to waste. But there's something you need to know—Feathercap is gone."

"We have not seen or heard from him since yesterday," said Gredin.

Warwick's lips were pressed into a thin line.

"How do you know you can trust them?" Fabian asked. "Why aren't *they* in cages?"

Warwick had already left the den. "They're on our side."

Fabian ran outside. He was starting to feel strangely detached from reality, as if he had stumbled into an alternate universe where nothing was what it seemed. His father was not a groundskeeper, he thought numbly. His father was not a caretaker. His father was a fairy hunter.

Warwick sprinted to the mud-spattered Land Rover. "Get in!"

Fabian fell into the passenger seat with barely enough time to shut the door before Warwick released the hand brake and sped toward the open gates of the manor, spraying grit into the air behind them.

"I just hope we make it in time."

❦❦

In her room at the back of the house, Florence's eyes fluttered open at the screech of the Land Rover speeding urgently through the night. It sounded like Warwick, she thought drowsily; but her eyes closed again as sleep pulled at her. Muttering softly, she shifted position. It couldn't be, she reasoned. Warwick watched the woods and guarded the house most nights—but he always went by foot. Always.

She drifted further away; to a place free of thought and worry. She was tired, dog-tired. Sleep had never come easily when her granddaughter was in the house. Until tonight.

Ironically, this was to be the best night's sleep she'd had in a long time.

## 25

Tanya's limbs were aching. Every inch of her was tired from fighting, but her bonds had not given in the slightest. Finally her body sagged against the tree in despair. Red wasn't coming. No one was coming.

"The poem was a clever touch. You knew we'd try and solve the mystery, didn't you?"

Morwenna stepped toward her, the motion reminiscent of a snake slithering toward its prey. "Yes, I did. Though I would never have thought of it if it were not for my guardian."

"What guardian?" said Tanya, fear creeping back into her. "What are you talking about?"

Morwenna laughed. "All born with the second sight are appointed a guardian from the fairy realm—whether they are aware of it or not. I suspect that you were not?"

Tanya shook her head.

"The guardians I speak of serve the purpose of protecting our best interest. My best interest was finding you."

"Then who is my guardian?" said Tanya. "Why weren't my best interests protected?"

"Oh, they were," said a familiar voice. "You were protected. Or at least, for as long as I allowed you to be."

"*You!*" Tanya whispered.

Feathercap emerged from the shadows.

"It took a long time for me to get you here. *I* delivered the poem. *I* took the newspaper clipping from Amos's room and put it into the book for you to find. And I gave you a reason to hold on to the witch's compass. Without my interest, you would have discarded it."

"It was you," Tanya realized. "On the bus that day. You wanted to buy the compass from us."

"No, I *pretended* to want to," said Feathercap. "Because I knew then that you would keep it. It was easy. All of it, so very easy. I knew you wouldn't be able to resist following the clues, trying to solve the mystery of the missing girl. You and your silly little friend."

"So this is what you've all wanted, all these years? To lure me here, for this? For *her*?"

"No, not all of us," said Feathercap. "Just me. The others were working to protect you—but I fooled them. With the division of the realm I managed to convince them I was loyal to the Seelie Court, and to them. Gredin never fully trusted me. But I was too clever for him...too clever by far. You see, when Morwenna left the mortal world, nobody dreamed that her guardian would remain behind. It was my most closely guarded secret." He gave a triumphant smile.

"So who is my guardian?" Tanya demanded.

"Gredin is your guardian," said Feathercap. "Raven is your grandmother's. Both agreed that it was in your best interest—and Florence's—to protect you from the truth."

"And the Mizhog?"

Feathercap sneered. "Let's just say the Mizhog was saved by your grandmother many years ago from an unpleasant fate similar to the drain-dweller's. It's been loyal to her ever since."

"If they're protecting me, then why don't they come?"

"Because they are outnumbered. And because it's too late," Morwenna told her. "In just over a minute, I will be free and you will take my place. Feathercap will remain here to ensure that you do not escape. I'll finally have the freedom that's rightfully mine."

A white-hot rage took hold of Tanya then, possessing her in a way she had never before experienced. "You don't deserve to be free."

"What did you just say?" Morwenna's voice was dangerously quiet—but Tanya no longer cared.

"You're selfish, and cruel, and you don't *deserve* to be free!" she shouted. Her whole body was trembling.

"All these years, you've festered with hatred. Blaming my grandmother, when the only person to blame for all this is *you*. You had a choice—and you chose this. My grandmother chose her family. She stayed. Her freedom is her own. She's suffered for it."

"*I don't care!*" Morwenna shrieked. "We had an agreement! Florence betrayed me—she deserves to be here now, the coward! Not me! *Not me!*"

"You don't care!" Tanya cried in disgust. "Of course you don't! Why should you when other people have paid dearly for *your* mistake? Not just my grandmother but Amos too. His reputation was ruined because of what you did. *But you don't care!*"

Morwenna started to walk away, weaving between the trees like a ghost. "The exchange has already begun."

Tanya thrashed violently in the bonds. She could only watch as Morwenna's form glided from sight... and listen as Feathercap jeered at her attempts to escape. Terror engulfed her. She heard herself sobbing before she even realized she was, before she felt the hot tears cascading down her cheeks. Oberon jumped up at her, whining in terror and confusion. An image flashed in her mind—the image of her own face on futile posters with one empty, awful word: MISSING.

*I don't want to be the girl who vanished in the woods. I don't want to be another of Tickey End's missing.*

Something was moving through the darkness,

coming toward her in a dark blur. Feathercap noticed it a split second after Tanya.

*Red.*

The momentary distraction was the opportunity Oberon had long been awaiting. With a perfectly timed lunge, Feathercap was silenced forever.

❦❦

The Land Rover screamed to a halt just short of the edge of the brook, and then Warwick and Fabian jumped out and went dashing through the water toward the opening in the forest. A shrill sound pierced the night.

Fabian ran even harder.

"What is that?" Warwick panted, as they reached the edge of the woods.

"It's the alarm on my watch! I set it to go off at midnight!"

Warwick fumbled in his pocket and pulled out the lock of hair, his hands shaking. "Take it! I've got some matches—we have to burn it!"

Fabian held out his hand, but the hair slipped through his fingers and fell to the ground.

"Where is it?" Warwick yelled, striking a match in an attempt to light up the area. "Fabian, *you idiot*!"

Fabian dropped to the ground and began hunting desperately.

His watch continued to scream like a banshee foretelling certain death.

❧❧

Red hacked violently at the bonds. Slowly but surely they began to loosen, until eventually the strands fell away and disintegrated. Her hands were dark and wet with blood. The spidertwine had sliced her fingers as she had extracted the scissors from Tanya's back pocket.

"What are you doing here... how did you know?" Tanya sobbed. "Where's the baby?"

"He's safe." Red continued to hack, speaking breathlessly. "I made the exchange, but the circus folk wouldn't allow me to travel with them. Said the police had been sniffing around, asking questions. So I decided the best thing would be to come back here and hide out for a bit longer. I was just about to go into the tunnel over by the church when I saw you and the boy coming out of the garden gate. So I watched and followed... luckily for you."

Finally, the last thread was broken. Tanya was free.

"We need to get out before midnight... she's trying to switch places with me—"

Red silenced her with a nod of her head. "I heard everything. We need to move."

She grabbed Tanya's arm, pulling her through the woods. Things rippled in the darkness. The fairies lurked just out of sight, waiting for the moment that

Tanya would be surrendered to them. Oberon circled them protectively, and Red pulled her knife out and held it aloft. Then she began to run. Tanya sprinted after her, running for her life, zigzagging through the trees.

"We've got to get you out of the woods," Red panted. "Before Morwenna leaves. We're nearly out of time—"

Her words echoed meaninglessly in Tanya's head. Something was wrong.

"Stop," she moaned. A strange humming had begun in her ears, like a swarm of insects.

"We can't stop!" Red hissed. "Move. I said MOVE!"

"I can't," Tanya whispered, staggering to a halt despite Red's attempts to support her. Gradually the humming evolved into a whisper of voices all around her. Faces within the trees awoke. Gnarled finger-like branches reached out to her. Vines disentangled themselves from tree barks and snaked toward her. The forest stirred with life.

Tanya understood what was happening. The switch was taking place.

Her strength left her. She sank to the ground, her eyes clenched shut and her hands clamped tightly over her ears. A strand of ivy was beginning to work its way up her leg. Red sliced it away with her blade, only for it to be replaced with another. She heard Red telling her to get up—Red pleading with her to move—but Tanya could not.

She thought of her parents and wished she could see

them one last time. She thought of her grandmother, and wished that things could have been different between them. She thought of Fabian and Warwick, and what would become of Amos. She wondered if Red would ever find her brother. She even pictured Spitfire, curled up at the foot of the grandfather clock with his bones jutting out of his mangy fur.

The last thing she thought of was Oberon, her beloved, faithful dog. He had stayed by her side until the end. Then all thought fell away, leaving nothing, only darkness. Oberon began to howl.

A sharp pain in her thumb brought her back. Tanya struggled into consciousness and looked down. Fresh blood ran from a new wound.

"How did I . . . ?" she began drowsily, seeing Morag's scissors in Red's hand, but not understanding. She felt herself slipping away again, being tugged and pulled by the foliage wrapping itself around her—but not before she saw Red's hand.

Red's poor, bloodied hand.

Red's poor, sliced fingers. Red, whose blood was mingling with her own as she gripped her hand tightly. And Red was holding her, cradling her head. Willing her not to go.

"Take me," Red was whispering. "Take me instead. She has a life to go back to. I don't. You took it from me. Take me instead."

Take me instead.

*Take me instead.*

And the vines and branches crawling toward

Tanya—and those that already ensnared her—paused for the briefest of moments before slowly withdrawing, releasing her from their clutches and continuing on their way—to Red. Inch by inch they crept over her like leafy tentacles, pulling her away from Tanya...away from the mortal world.

Red did not resist.

In moments, she was surrendered completely; swallowed by the forest.

❦❦

Fabian's hand closed around the hair, along with a fistful of earth.

"I've got it!"

Warwick struck another match, the yellow flame hissing to life. He seized the hair and held the match to it. It flared up instantly and he dropped it to the ground.

They watched in silence as it burned away to nothing, until all that remained was the charred remnants of fallen twigs and leaves where Morwenna's hair had been.

Fabian's watch finally went silent.

"I never realized," Warwick said softly. "All this time...I thought the hair was my mother's. She was dark too...I never saw the significance until tonight. All the time he was trying to find a replacement for Morwenna. He never got over her."

"How long have you known?"

Even in the darkness, Fabian could read the regret in his father's eyes.

"Ever since Tanya was born."

"What will happen to Morwenna now that the pact is broken?" Fabian whispered.

"She'll feel it, instantly," said Warwick. "It should be enough to deter her from wanting to go ahead with the exchange." He began to run deeper into the woods, calling over his shoulder.

"We have to find Tanya!"

Fabian followed his father, neither of them aware that an alternative exchange had already taken place.

◆◆

The edge of the forest was in sight, the moon just visible through the trees. Barely lucid, Tanya staggered toward it. Only Oberon, tugging at the other end of his leash, was supporting her. Her eyes were swollen and sticky with tears, and her head felt woolen.

Red was gone; vanished into the fairy realm like a footprint in sand. In trading herself instead of Tanya, she had saved them both.

Tanya was almost at the woods' edge when she realized she was not alone.

Just paces in front of her, on the path ahead, Morwenna Bloom was moving toward the opening in the trees. And as Tanya watched, an initial surge of anger dispersed as it became apparent that something was very wrong.

Morwenna pushed herself onward, but her movements were slowing. Tanya heard her breathing change, becoming ragged and labored. Her back hunched, feet moving slowly now, hobbling and shuffling. She looked like she was in pain. Aching... or very, very tired.

"What's happening to me?" she murmured.

The voice that emerged from her lips was not that of a fourteen-year-old girl.

*Not tired... but old.*

With mounting horror, Tanya now knew what had happened. Fabian had not left her in an act of cowardice. Fabian had gone to destroy the lock of hair—the link to Morwenna's youth. And he had succeeded.

The horrified whimper that reached Tanya's ears then was her own. At the sound of it, Morwenna turned to face her.

"You?" she rasped, in an old woman's voice. A strange new voice that Tanya could see was even more terrifying to Morwenna than it was to her. "How...? It's not possible that you're here..."

The confusion and malice on her face shriveled with her flesh. It wrinkled, withered, and puckered, sagging and hanging loosely over the contours of her skull as every one of the fifty years Morwenna had cheated caught up with her—all of them at once. The effect of it was like poison, and truly terrible to witness.

Tanya was powerless to do anything except scream. And scream.

Morwenna looked down at her hands and cried out. No longer were they smooth and soft; they were growing withered and twisted before her eyes.

*"No!"*

She grabbed a strand of her long hair, but it was now coarse and white like wool. Slowly, she lifted her hands to her face, and felt the hollows of her cheeks and the lines of her skin. She reached her twisted hands toward Tanya. Her lips were drawn back in a hideous grimace over teeth that were blackening and loosening, then crumbling and dropping out.

Tanya turned on her heel and fled. Back into the woods, back the way she had come, sobbing and desperate and more willing to face whatever the woods held rather than stand before the grotesque figure of Morwenna Bloom.

She never saw Morwenna trying to follow her along the path. For in the time it took the old woman to take but a few steps, Tanya was long gone. And so Morwenna was utterly alone when the combination of the aging process and the subsequent shock of it took their final toll on her body.

❦❦

Tanya was huddled on the ground, cowering into Oberon, when they found her.

A calloused hand brushed her hair back from her face, and then came a voice, familiar... and yet not.

"She's in shock." Warwick's voice. Still gruff and clipped, but now edged with concern.

"Will she be all right?" This from Fabian.

Tanya stirred, comforted by his voice. Fabian's face came into focus, his eyes clamped shut. His expression was carved with guilt and misery.

"I left her," he said in a small voice. "I left her, Dad. But I had to . . ."

"Fabian?" Tanya croaked.

Fabian's eyes flew open. He took her hand and gripped it tightly. "I'm sorry," he whispered. "I'm so sorry—I had to let you think . . ." he gulped. "The lock of hair. Amos had it all the time."

"I know," she told him, managing a weak smile. "You were brave to do what you did."

She gazed at Warwick. "You were protecting me. You and my grandmother. That's why you didn't want me at the manor—because of what could happen."

"Florence wanted to tell you," Warwick said softly. "But she was too afraid. And ashamed. When she made that pact with Morwenna she was young and naive. She's been paying for it ever since."

"Not anymore," Tanya whispered. For she alone knew that Morwenna had paid the ultimate price. But for now, she would not—could not—speak of what she had seen.

There were no more words after that. Just Tanya's own thoughts inside her head as Warwick wrapped his coat around her shoulders and lifted her exhausted body into his arms, ready to go back to the manor.

❧❧

It was still early the following morning when Morag locked up the caravan and shooed the protesting cat outside. It was not often she ventured into Tickey End midweek, and she wanted to go about her business and get back before it got busy. She was almost at the edge of the forest when she saw what lay ahead, just awry of the path and partially hidden in the undergrowth.

The woman was dead, and had been for several hours. Morag could tell that much before she had even knelt down by her side. Her puckered mouth was open in a silent scream, her claw of a hand clasped around her upper left arm.

"Heart failure," Morag murmured, reaching out to close the woman's lifeless eyes. But as she looked into those dead black pits, her hand froze and she withdrew it sharply before making contact. For even in death, there was something altogether malevolent about her.

Without further ado she set off along the path to Tickey End, her pace a little quicker than usual now that she knew she would be making a detour to report the grisly find. She did hope it wouldn't hold her up too long.

# Epilogue

Like most of the graves in the little churchyard, Elizabeth Elvesden's had been neglected. And like the nearby manor that had been her home for a brief time in her short life, it was now covered in ivy, with just a hint of gray stone visible between the evergreen leaves. Yet despite its forlorn appearance, the grave had never been forgotten.

Tanya watched as her grandmother knelt to pull out another handful of weeds, then gazed across the fields, past the forest toward where the manor stood in the dappled sunlight. Her mother was due to arrive shortly to take her home. This time Tanya knew, with a gladdened heart, things would be different. The fairies, *her* fairies, would come again, but in their own time. She no longer feared them.

Almost a week earlier she had awoken in her bed, fully clothed and groggy, as though she had slept for a hundred years. As she came out of her slumber she became aware that someone was holding her hand, and looked up into the gray eyes of her grandmother. It had taken Tanya a moment to recognize her, for the hardness about her had gone, as though a great weight had been lifted. For a long time, her grandmother had talked. And Tanya had listened, learned, and forgiven.

The newspaper articles concerning the whereabouts of Rowan Fox continued for a short while after the night of the exchange, though they were given less and less precedence as it became clear that the trail on her had gone cold. But when she scoured the papers, another story caught Tanya's attention: the discovery of a body in Hangman's Wood.

The dead woman, estimated to be in her mid- to late-sixties, had suffered a fatal heart attack. Her identity, though, and how she came to be in the forest at the time of her death were to remain a mystery— except to those involved. For it was then that Tanya finally spoke of Red to Fabian, Warwick, and her grandmother, revealing the true horror of what had happened that night in the woods—and the intervention of the girl who had saved her, with the hope of saving her brother too.

❧

They cleared the last of the weeds from the grave and replaced them with fresh flowers.

As they passed by the forest on the way back to the manor, Tanya stared into the trees, a question on her lips that she feared the answer to.

"What will become of Amos?"

Florence shook her head unhappily. "There's

nothing that can be done. We may know the truth about Morwenna Bloom, but few would believe us. They'll carry on thinking what they want to think. All we can do for him now is make his last days comfortable, but with his state of mind even that won't be easy. He's constantly tormented by her memory. She's the root of his madness."

A soft breeze stirred in the trees above, carrying with it a scent of wild herbs. One of the scents seemed to overpower the rest, sharp and distinctive. A sudden memory was evoked in Tanya's mind; the memory of words spoken by Gredin one night. At the time, those words had instilled fear into her. Today, they filled her with hope. The forest had been listening.

"We can't change what happened," Tanya said slowly. "And we can't change what the people think. But maybe there *is* something we can do for Amos."

❦

*There is a place where rosemary grows freely by a stream that flows uphill. The domain of the piskies. Heathen creatures. Unpredictable, dangerous, some say. The rosemary, renowned for its aid to memory, grows tainted. The properties are reversed.*

*Yet even piskie-tainted rosemary has its uses. In the correct quantities it has the power to extract a memory from a mortal head forever.*

*Such as the memory of an old sweetheart.*

# Acknowledgments

Thanks to my family, friends, and loved ones—my first readers especially: Darren, Mum, Theresa, Janet, Tanya, Rachel, and Lucy. Also to Lauren for all the fairy dust.

A big thank you to Madeleine Buston at the Darley Anderson Agency, and to Nancy Conescu and the entire children's team at Little, Brown and Company.

# ★★ TAYLOR SWIFT ★★

# Get the SCOOP

★ ★ ★ ★

**unauthorized biography
by Ronny Bloom**

Adapted from *Taylor Swift:
Country's Sweetheart*
by Lexi Ryals

*PSS!*
Price Stern Sloan
An Imprint of Penguin Group (USA) Inc.

PRICE STERN SLOAN
Published by the Penguin Group
Penguin Group (USA) Inc., 375 Hudson Street, New York, New York 10014, USA
Penguin Group (Canada), 90 Eglinton Avenue East, Suite 700,
Toronto, Ontario M4P 2Y3, Canada
(a division of Pearson Penguin Canada Inc.)
Penguin Books Ltd., 80 Strand, London WC2R 0RL, England
Penguin Group Ireland, 25 St. Stephen's Green, Dublin 2, Ireland
(a division of Penguin Books Ltd.)
Penguin Group (Australia), 250 Camberwell Road, Camberwell, Victoria 3124, Australia
(a division of Pearson Australia Group Pty. Ltd.)
Penguin Books India Pvt. Ltd., 11 Community Centre, Panchsheel Park,
New Delhi—110 017, India
Penguin Group (NZ), 67 Apollo Drive, Rosedale, North Shore 0632, New Zealand
(a division of Pearson New Zealand Ltd.)
Penguin Books (South Africa) (Pty.) Ltd., 24 Sturdee Avenue,
Rosebank, Johannesburg 2196, South Africa

Penguin Books Ltd., Registered Offices: 80 Strand, London WC2R 0RL, England

Photo credits: Cover: Larry Busacca/Getty Images; Insert photos: first page
courtesy of Jon Kopaloff/FilmMagic; second page courtesy of Noah Graham/
National Hockey League; Michael Buckner/Getty Images; third page courtesy of
Mike Flokis/Getty Images; Pool/Getty Images; Kevin Mazur/WireImage; fourth page
courtesy of Marcel Thomas/FilmMagic; Frazer Harrison/Getty Images; CBS Photo
Archive/CBS; fifth page courtesy of Lester Cohen/WireImage; Eric Charbonneau/
WireImage; sixth page courtesy of Andrew Walker/Getty Images; Maury Phillips/
WireImage; seventh page courtesy of Frank Micelotta/Getty Images; Ethan Miller/
Getty Images; Eric Charbonneau/WireImage; eight page courtesy of Jon Kopaloff/
FilmMagic; Don Arnold/WireImage.

Library of Congress Control Number: 2009021955

ISBN 978-0-8431-9968-0          10 9 8 7 6 5 4 3 2 1